LUANN K. EDWARDS

All Things Possible
Love in Pleasant Springs

LuAnn K. Edwards

Dedication

To Gerry Wakeland.
Thank you for encouraging me to write.
I am grateful for your friendship.

A story of surrendering the past, present,
and future to the Lord.

Jesus looked at them and said,
"With man this is impossible,
but with God all things are possible."
Matthew 19:26

One

Mid-May
Pleasant Springs, Tennessee

Mom skittered through the kitchen, banging pots and pans and muttering to herself.

I pressed my lips together and took a calming breath. I stopped mixing the brownies for my weekly donation to Creekside Children's Home. "Mama. Stop." I scooted closer to her and grasped her shoulders from behind. Sensing the tension in her muscles, I held her steady and soothed her with a gentle massage. "What's gotten you riled up today?"

She coughed, brought a shaky hand to her forehead, and whined. "This house requires a lot of work. Why didn't your aunt teach you more about running a bed-and-breakfast when you lived with her in Texas after high school?"

"I'll clean everything as soon as I finish my baking." With a tender touch, I turned her toward me. "Why don't you take a break and sit out on the covered back porch with my pup or take him for a walk down by the creek?"

"I don't want to." Mom pouted and propped herself against the counter, near three glass loaf pans of rising bread dough.

I smiled and motioned to the screen door. "Snowbunny loves the creek. His tail goes crazy when he hears croaking frogs or when he sees birds splashing in the water. You'll enjoy it too. So peaceful and calming there." I peeked out the window. "Have you seen this blue sky? Such a beautiful sunny morning."

"Beautiful? Huh." She hung her head and moaned. "Noisy frogs at the creek. And Snowbunny wants to sniff everything when he's there. He'll get filthy." She looked up. "Now, if there were a few cows gently mooing and wading in the water, then it might be beautiful and peaceful."

I kept my voice calm, despite my frustration, and gazed into her eyes. "You miss Dad, don't you? On certain days, you appear more restless than usual." I sighed and placed my hand on her upper arm. Am I doing enough to show her how much I care? I gave her a brief hug. "Remind me what happened on this day."

Tears puddled in her eyes. "A year ago today, the doctor told your dad that he didn't have long to live."

I gave her another hug and held her close. How can I ease her pain? The anniversary of Dad's death drew nearer.

I stepped back, pulled a tissue from my apron pocket, and wiped tears from her face. "How can I make this easier for you?"

She shook her head and blinked away a tear. "Nothing, my precious Pearl." She enjoyed calling me by the nickname she'd given me as a young child.

"If something comes to mind, tell me."

"I'll go sit outside for a while, to rest, and pray." She trudged to the screen door and turned to face me. "There's one tiny thing that will help."

I dashed to her side and touched her cheek. "Anything, Mama."

Her voice filled with longing. "You can't bring your dad back, but I really miss the cows." She swiped her fingers across her face. "Your dad loved them so much."

I snapped my eyes open wide. "But you sold them with the farm. They're gone."

She bit her lip. "Not our old cows. Any cow. To remind me of special times with him." She fingered the locket hanging from her neck, a precious gift from Dad many years ago, and hurried out the door. With her voice raised an octave, she said, "Thank you, dear."

One tiny thing? Impossible. How do I get her a cow? I can't keep one here at Maggie's Place. But I told her that I'd do anything to help her. A warm glow of sunlight filled the room and warmed my skin. I nodded. Somehow, I'd find a way.

I returned to my brownie batter and poured it into a baking pan. After I placed the brownies in the oven and set the timer, I sat at our square kitchen table decorated with a vibrant bouquet of freshly picked wildflowers. I crossed my legs and prepared my list of farmers in the area to contact. But would any of them care enough to help?

With the rich, sweet aroma of chocolate filling the air, I glanced over my short list. I'll call the first four of them if I must, to find someone who will allow me to keep a cow for Mom at their farm. But what if they won't? What will I do if they all say no? I can't let that happen. Someone must say yes. I don't want to contact number five.

I snatched my phone off the table and called the first two farmers. After they mentioned my blog posts, they hung up on me. If the others reject my request too, then what?

A personal meeting might work better. I planned to visit farmers three and four on my way to deliver the goodies to Creekside.

The timer buzzed, and I removed the mouthwatering brownies from the oven.

While I washed my baking dishes and focused on all I needed to do, Mom returned to the kitchen.

"You appear deep in thought. Everything okay?"

"Wonderful." I grinned, hoping to brighten her mood, despite the heaviness in my heart from the sorrow she carried and the overwhelming task before me. "Planning my day."

"How many guests do we have scheduled to arrive this afternoon?"

"One couple for two nights." I grabbed a dishcloth and wiped down the countertops. "They want to hike in South Cumberland State Park."

"I'll get the blue room ready."

I hung the dishcloth to dry and pointed to the pan cooling on a rack. "And after these brownies have cooled, I'll take them to the children's home and run errands while I'm out." I asked her if she needed anything in town before she rushed upstairs.

Since Dad passed away and Mom moved in, I had little to do around here. She made sure everything was ready for each guest. I'm glad she's here, but I'm bored with nothing to do but hang out at The Hair Haven, where I get most of my blog material.

After I removed my apron and hung it on a hook in the pantry, I made my way to my room to check my appearance and to relax awhile. Perhaps I needed a new purpose.

Thirty minutes later, after savoring a mouthful of brownie, I darted out the door to visit farmers three and four on my list.

Farmer number three yelled at me as soon as I got out of my car and asked me if I could read. He pointed to a "No Trespassing" sign on his front fence. When I opened my mouth to speak, he pointed to the sign again and stared me down. I'd never seen him so inhospitable in the past. What had I ever done to him?

Back in my car, I tapped my fingers on the steering wheel. That's it. I wrote something about his oldest son caught shoplifting in a blog post—three years ago. Why couldn't he let it go?

Farmer number four used words to express his dislike for me. After two choice ones, he said, "I don't have time for you, Maggie Stone. Don't need the whole town knowing my business."

What did I do to deserve his hostility? I reported news, not as an official journalist for the weekly newspaper, but through my weekly blog posts every Wednesday. People sought the truth, and I made it my mission to deliver it. Not my fault that sometimes the truth hurts. And today's blog post was every bit as true as the one about the boy shoplifting.

With my morning slipping away from me, I needed a quick lunch. When I returned home, the comforting scent of warm, homemade bread greeted me, reminding me of a worry-free childhood. I closed my eyes and allowed the captivating aroma to surround me.

"Oh, Mama, thank you. I imagine this is how heaven smells." She'd prepared her scrumptious chicken salad featuring two of my favorite ingredients—crunchy pecans and juicy grapes—and piled it onto the soft, warm, fluffy bread.

When Mom left the kitchen to fold our guest towels after lunch, I remained at the table and pondered the daunting task that loomed before me. Now, there was only one farmer who remained on my list. Number five. Reed Ruby.

I'd never written about him or his family, so perhaps he'd help me out. I crinkled my nose and twisted my mouth to the left. But what if I encounter his son, Wade? Am I ready to face my past? My stomach churned at the thought. But if it helps Mom, that's a good thing.

I'd avoided Wade for the past two months since he'd returned home from Texas to help his dad on the farm. Wade had gone through a divorce two years ago, but I hadn't yet learned his story except that he had a stepson in Texas. One day, I hoped to learn more.

But today, besides taking homemade brownies to Creekside Children's Home this afternoon, I had one crucial task on my agenda—visit Reed Ruby.

Mom wanted a cow, and I'd do anything for her.

Even if I had to stumble upon my old boyfriend.

Two

I drove north on Main Street, passed Chicken Coop Road, and turned right onto Tater Peel Road. The fifth house on the left, the one with a dingy picket fence and peeling paint, belonged to the Rubys. I pulled into their driveway and stopped to take it all in, while my heart and mind flooded with conflicting emotions. Memories from long ago.

On the left was a graveled area for parking two cars and a sidewalk leading to a wooden porch that spanned the entire front of their white, two-story home. Two rocking chairs and six hanging flower baskets overflowing with a vibrant mix of what looked like petunias adorned the porch. To my right and across from the house, a wrought-iron bench sat beneath a large oak tree, along with containers filled with more blooming flowers. Wade and I had shared many conversations and stole a few sweet kisses beneath that tree, serenaded by the soothing sound of cows mooing in the pasture behind us.

And straight ahead, the long driveway followed a picket fence on the right that led to a barn, and across the driveway a stable sat on the left. I couldn't see their detached garage from this angle, but if they hadn't torn it down, it stood behind the house.

I parked in the gravel area at the front of their house, turned off the ignition, and massaged my throbbing temples.

Would Mr. Ruby remember me and my relationship with his son? I cringed and placed my hand on the door handle. What's the absolute worst-case scenario? Like the others, he might say no. But that wasn't the worst. Dread washed over me at the prospect of seeing Wade again.

When I climbed out of my car, the scent of freshly cut grass filled the air. I took a deep breath to calm myself. But it didn't help. I lumbered to the front door with my purse strap over my shoulder wearing a just-above the knee black pencil skirt, light gray blouse, and three-inch strappy sandals.

Reed opened the front door and welcomed me on the porch with a toothy grin. "I'm surprised to see you. What brings you to our neck of the woods?"

When I told him that I had a farming matter to discuss, he referred me to his manager, who was in the barn or stable. He would have told me if Wade was his manager. At least, I hoped he would.

Time to charm this manager guy. Easy, if he doesn't already know me. I tip-toed down the gravel driveway in my heels. Was I about to regret coming here? Perhaps I should have tried to talk Mama out of a cow. I removed my purse from my shoulder and clutched it in front of me.

~

Wade snagged a brush and ran it down the horse's back. "Good boy. Feels soothing, doesn't it?" After a thorough grooming, he rubbed Copper's forehead. "We'll take another ride tomorrow." He led the light chestnut-colored horse through the back of the stable and into a fenced field with his solid black horse, Champ.

Back inside the stable, Wade strode to the main entrance, crossed the driveway, and entered the barn.

When a vehicle's door slammed shut, Wade stuck his head out the barn door and glanced down the driveway. He watched a woman exit a red sedan and make her way to the front of the house.

He stood too far away to get a clear glimpse of her face, but he recognized her gait, even though he hadn't seen her in twenty years.

Maggie on a mission. What did she want from his dad?

Wade slipped into the shadows of the barn and peeked through a crack in the boards. Maggie strutted down the sidewalk with her head held high until she reached the gravel. He smirked when she seemed to falter and lift her heels to make the somewhat long trek toward him on the toes of her fancy shoes.

He stepped out of the barn, narrowed his eyes, and glared at his first love.

The first woman who'd rejected him.

~

A man wearing a black cowboy hat emerged from the dark barn into the sunlight. My pulse quickened and my palms grew sweaty. I stopped and moved backward. Wade? Why didn't Reed tell me the manager was his son?

The only man I'd ever loved gazed at me with lifeless blue eyes. Where was the sparkle? Or the cute dimples that melted my heart every moment we spent together? I pushed back my shoulders and took a step forward. And another.

Wade stroked his throat and sneered. "What do you want?"

I tucked a strand of hair behind my ear and squinted. "After twenty years, that's how you greet me?"

"How did you expect me to greet you? A warm embrace?"

I watched the cows grazing in the pasture to my right. Should I turn on my irresistible charm to win him over? Worked years ago. But we've both grown up since then. "Not an embrace, but perhaps a welcoming smile for someone you once cared about."

He jutted out his chin and tightened his jaw. "Nope. Hard to smile at the woman I followed to Texas, only to have her tell me to get lost."

I fingered the top button of my blouse. "I never told you to get lost."

"Oh, no? Then what did you tell me?"

My voice trembled, and I spoke just above a whisper. "I said you didn't need to marry me."

"And to leave and never return. Remember?"

I stared at the coarse gravel beneath my shoes. "You gave up quick enough. I expected you to fight for me."

"When I returned to your aunt's bed-and-breakfast, as you say, to fight for you, she informed me that you moved back here. I'd already secured a job and a place for us to live in a neighboring county there."

"Aunt Tilly never mentioned your second visit." I swallowed hard and furrowed my brow. "I lived with her until I finished college."

He widened his stance, and, with sternness, he said,

"Makes no difference now. Why are you here?"

The gentle mooing of cows reminded me of my mission and the desire of my mom's heart. "Do you have any calves?"

"Maybe." He crossed his arms over his wide, muscular chest. "Why do you care?"

I tilted my head to the right. "My father died last year, and Mama sold their farm. She loved her cows and misses them. She thinks a cow of her own will help her get over her loneliness with missing Dad."

"What's that got to do with me or my dad?"

"I'd like to buy one of your cows for my mom but keep it here on your farm for her to visit."

He chuckled and shook his head. "You're kidding, right?"

"Not at all. You liked my mom, and she adored you." I inched closer, hoping to bridge the physical and emotional distance between us. "This would mean so much to her."

He relaxed his stance. "Let me get this straight. You want to buy a cow for your mom to visit?"

"Yes. I want to tell her the cow is hers."

"And what about the cost of keeping the cow here for you? Feeding, caring for, medical needs, etcetera? You plan to pay those expenses too?"

"Yes. I want her to own it, but have you take care of it for her. I don't have room at my bed-and-breakfast to keep a cow."

"You understand, don't you, that we often sell the calves before their first birthday?"

"Not a problem."

"Do you expect me to pull one out for her and treat it differently?"

"Mama understands she can't keep a cow forever."

He turned his back on me, and his broad shoulders bounced up and down.

"Are you laughing at me?" I placed my hands on my hips. "Why doesn't anyone care about my mom and how important this is to her?"

He turned around and shook his head again. "Look, I think it's awesome what you're trying to do for your mom, but I can't help you. Your idea is ridiculous."

He had to say yes. I took a step forward and folded my hands. "What will convince you to change your mind? This is important to me." I brought my folded hands under my chin. "Please." My voice quivered. "Just consider it. My mom's only request is for me to get her a cow."

"Not my problem." He pointed down the driveway. "Leave. Get off our property." Again, he turned his back on me and crossed over to the stable.

A wave of disappointment hit me hard. Like a punch in the gut. I stomped my foot and peered at the stable door where Wade had disappeared moments before. No. I wouldn't give up that easily. I couldn't. Not when it concerned my mama.

I muttered to myself. "You haven't seen the last of me."

~

Wade didn't need Maggie hanging around the farm with her mom. He sauntered into his makeshift office. "But she won't give up until she gets her own way." He tossed his hat on the desk. And he'd wanted to marry her? Life with her would've been pure torture. A cow? No way.

He slid his Bible across the desk and turned to his

bookmark where he'd place it at chapter one of James. He read verses two and three aloud. "Consider it pure joy, my brothers and sisters, whenever you face trials of many kinds, because you know that the testing of your faith produces perseverance."

"Pure joy? Dealing with Maggie would be anything but pure joy. A trial—for sure." He raked his hand through his hair. "Testing my faith, Lord?"

He pulled out his desk chair, lifted the Bible, and focused on verse five. "If any of you lacks wisdom, you should ask God, who gives generously to all without finding fault, and it will be given to you."

When he plopped into the chair, he bowed his head. *Lord, I'm here to take over the family farm for my dad so he can retire. I want a smooth transition, and Maggie can't help me with that. I say Maggie needs to mind her own business and stay out of my way. But if You're asking me to deal with Maggie, I'm going to need a ton of Your wisdom.*

He continued reading but stopped, dumbfounded at verses sixteen and seventeen. "Don't be deceived, my dear brothers and sisters. Every good and perfect gift is from above, coming down from the Father of the heavenly lights, who does not change like shifting shadows."

No way, God. Maggie will never be 'a good and perfect gift' from You.

Three

Before I backed out of my parking space at the Ruby farm, I searched my purse for my lipstick. Wade is impossible. Cold-hearted and stubborn. Like an unrelenting ice storm. A shiver coursed down my spine. How did I ever find him appealing?

Who am I kidding? What we had meant everything to me. I moaned and continued to rummage through my purse. My lipstick. I tugged down my visor mirror and reapplied my favorite color, plum aglow.

Pleased with my appearance, I pressed the ignition button and twisted around before I backed out. A white Ford Fiesta hatchback pulled down the driveway and turned left toward the back of the house and the detached garage. Lou Sterling from the café? A little late for a lunch delivery and too early for dinner.

What business did Lou have with Reed or Wade? A blog post in the making? This could be a worthwhile visit, after all. Reed and Lou? But I'll need more information to move forward. After I drop off the brownies at the children's home, I'll take a trip to Mama Lou's Café.

I headed back into town, arrived at Creekside Children's Home at 3:05, checked my makeup and hair in the rearview mirror, and climbed out of my car. A minute later, I rang the buzzer and admired the colorful flower beds on each side of the front porch. The cheerful call of a cardinal perched on an oak tree to my right entertained me and lifted my spirits while I waited.

I smiled my most charming smile when the door swung open, expecting to see Todd Butler, the director of the home. But Lanie Meadows greeted me with a scowl that created deep lines on her forehead. I backed away from her intense demeanor. "Is Todd here?"

Lanie stiffened. Her words struck me like a whip. "Oh? I assumed you were here to make up more lies about me."

What was her problem? I widened my eyes and gawked at her. "Aren't you going to invite me in? I brought brownies."

"Yes, invite her inside." Todd greeted me with a warm welcome. "We enjoy Maggie's visits."

Two of the five children staying at the home ran up to me and greeted me with hugs. The younger child, a boy who'd turned six two weeks before, said, "Thank you, Miss Maggie. Can you make me another football cake?"

I tousled his curly blond hair. "Perhaps for your next birthday."

The older child, a girl around ten, snatched the plate from my hands. "I love brownies." With the little boy following behind, she ran with them to the kitchen and called for the house mom.

I faced Lanie and bristled. "Some people appreciate me."

"I'd appreciate you, too, if you told the truth in your blog posts." Her scowl deepened. "You portrayed me as being incompetent."

"Now, now, ladies." Todd pulled Lanie off to the side and spoke in a whisper. I tried to eavesdrop, but his hushed tones made it impossible to overhear.

He turned to me and pointed behind him to the main part of the house. "Why don't the two of you go into the visitation room and chat? I'm sure you can resolve this matter."

Lanie pulled her phone from her pocket. "I need to take this call first." She slipped into a room off the foyer.

I glanced at Todd, seeking his input. "Besides bringing you baked goods, I'd like to do more. What are other ways I could help here?"

"That's great. I think we still need a volunteer in the clothing closet on Monday and Friday mornings."

"What's involved with that?"

"Sort through the donated clothing and prepare it for display so foster parents and children can shop."

I lifted my eyebrows. "Sounds perfect. When can I start?"

Lanie returned to the foyer before Todd answered. "The visitation room is this way." She led the way through the living room and kitchen to a cozy room with orange walls, where we sat across from one another at a square table for four.

I crossed my legs underneath the table and grinned at Lanie. "What did I get wrong with my post today?" I chuckled and rested back in my chair. "You lost three jobs in the past two months. What are you doing here? Winning Todd's favor so he'll hire you?"

She narrowed her eyes and bent forward. "I already have the job. I'm his codirector."

"Oh?" I straightened and clasped my hands in my lap. "Since when?"

"Monday." She pressed back in her chair and pursed her lips. "For your information, I lost two jobs in three months. Not the other way around." She scratched at what resembled a mosquito bite on her forearm. "After agency cutbacks in Chattanooga, I stayed in the city and searched for a job there until my apartment lease ended. That's when I moved back to Pleasant Springs and started my job with Clancy County Children's Services."

"But you got fired within three weeks."

"Yes, my manager ended my employment. But did you know or care that she offered me my job back?" Lanie shot me a fierce glare. "Or I worked at Mama Lou's Café as a temporary placement to help her out with her new coffee menu? She didn't fire me. In fact, I'm helping her out with new coffee recipes for the next couple of weeks."

"I didn't know those things. But I wasn't far off in what I reported."

Lanie stood and shoved her chair under the table with force. "Doesn't matter that you were only off a little. You never tell it straight in your blog posts. Why didn't you come to me and ask for details?"

My mouth dropped open. Her hostility was impossible to ignore. "I never tell it straight?" I lifted my chin. "Would you have shared the details?"

"Not with you." When she turned, something glittered on her left hand.

I jumped up. "Why wasn't I aware of your engagement? Luke Gibson, right?"

She spun to face me and raised her voice. "Not a

word. The local newspaper will announce it on Friday." She pointed her finger at my face. "Stay out of it."

"But the townsfolk expect me to tell positive news and negative. They'll love this."

Lanie crossed her arms and huffed. "Under one condition."

"Which is?"

"You first retract what you wrote today and set the record straight. Then, you may share about our engagement. But I want to read everything you plan to print first."

"I don't work that way."

"Fine. But if you write anything I disagree with, Luke might become your worst enemy. You are not one of his favorite people."

"What did I ever do to him?"

Lanie shrugged and walked away.

I couldn't think of anything I'd written about Luke.

Todd met me in the foyer on my way out. "Lanie oversees the clothing closet. Just talk to her about volunteering. She'll get you all set up."

"Lanie?" I wrinkled my nose. "I'll get back to you."

~

Wade wandered into the kitchen where Reed and his lady-friend Lou chatted at the oval table between sips of sweet tea. Wade slumped into a seat to the right of his dad and across from Lou.

She jumped up, grabbed a glass from the cabinet, added ice, and filled it with tea. "Here. You seem like you could use a drink." She placed the icy cold glass down on the table in front of him.

After he thanked her, he removed his cowboy hat

and laid it on the table to his right. "Dad is one lucky man to have you in his life." He looked at his dad and frowned. "Did Maggie tell you what she wanted?"

"Nope. Didn't give her the chance. Told her that she needed to talk to my manager."

Wade shook his head and told Reed and Lou about Maggie's need for a cow. "Can you believe it? She wants to buy one of our young cows and pay for us to take care of it for her."

"Would that be difficult to do?" Lou's eyes darted between Wade and Reed.

Reed thought for a second and tapped his chin. "Not impossible, Son."

"And let her and her mom visit their cow whenever they please?" His voice grew louder. "Am I supposed to keep it in the enclosure near the barn, away from the other cattle?" With a sudden jolt, he jumped up and knocked his chair over with a loud thud. "All the time? And what about the bull? I'd have to keep her cow away from him since he sired her."

Wade took a deep breath, picked up his chair, and softened his tone. "Sorry about that."

Reed relaxed back in his chair. "Weren't you considerin' a new bull'?"

"I'm not sure yet."

Lou peered at Wade and arched her brow. "Would it be impossible to show Maggie kindness and do this favor for her and her mom?"

Wade plopped down into his chair. "I can't believe you'd want her to hang around here while visiting her mom's cow." He snickered and leaned toward Lou. "We're talking about the town gossip. Do you want her to tell her blog readers you and Dad are an item?"

Lou gazed at Reed, who said they'd talked about going public with their relationship. "Won't be terrible if Maggie beats us to it."

Wade stared at Lou. Her face glowed brighter than he had seen in the past two months. "Anything I should know first?"

Lou reached over and touched Reed's arm. "Tell him, honey."

Reed wiped his hand across his forehead. "I asked her to be my bride, and she accepted."

Wade jumped up and patted his dad on the back. "Congratulations old man." He stepped over to Lou's chair. "I think this would please Mom. She thought the world of you." He planted a kiss on top of Lou's head.

She beamed and thanked him. "We were thinkin' of just tellin' Maggie and lettin' her announce our engagement, so it's no problem with her hangin' around here."

"No problem for you. But a Texas-size one for me." Wade stepped behind the empty kitchen chair.

"Son. Instead of her buyin' one of our cows and havin' to pay for its upkeep, why not negotiate a deal and have her help you here on the farm? You could use another pair of hands."

Wade laughed so hard his sides ached. "That's a good one, Dad. Ask her to work it off."

Reed rose, moseyed to Wade's side, and placed his hand on his son's shoulder. "Not a joke. Spendin' time together will help both of you. Sounds like you have relationship troubles to work through."

Wade jerked away from Reed, eyed Lou, and turned back to his dad. "Relationship troubles?"

Reed returned to his chair. "I'm just sayin'—"

"You've already said too much." Wade narrowed his eyes at Lou. "How much of this do you know?"

"Don't you worry about me. All I remember is the two of you were an item a long time ago." She stood and pushed her chair beneath the table. "Reed hasn't said a word about why you broke up. But I sense a need to resolve somethin' there as well. This can help you both."

Wade yanked his hat off the table, stormed out the back door, and jogged to the stable.

An arrangement with Maggie could never be beneficial.

Four

Instead of turning into Mama Lou's Café, I drove past the restaurant and stopped at the Hair Haven located across the street and kitty-corner from the café. If anyone could provide the inside scoop about Lou and Reed, it would be Eileen Noble, my favorite stylist. The bell over the door jingled when I entered, and a mixture of hair dye and nail polish assaulted my nose.

Eileen sat in a hair dryer chair and called me over. "My next appointment is running late, so I have time to share a surprising story with you."

"About Lou Sterling?"

She yanked her head backward. "Nothing to tell about Lou. She leads a quiet and respectable life."

"You know nothing?"

She scrunched her nose and stood. "Do you?"

"Have you noticed her leaving the café at odd hours?"

Eileen stared out the front window. "Well. Now that you mention it, I've noticed she leaves earlier than she used to. Debbie Sue closes most evenings."

I raised my eyebrows and stepped closer. "How long has this been going on?"

She ran her finger across her lower lip. "A few months, I guess."

"And you didn't think it was newsworthy?"

"Should I have?"

I smirked and dropped my purse to the floor. "Do you have any idea where she goes?"

"I know where I'd go if I left here early every day." She returned to the dryer chair, sat, and lifted her feet off the floor. "Home to prop up my aching feet."

"You deserve it." I thanked Eileen and dashed out the door. Whatever she wanted to tell me could wait.

I hurried across the street and into the café. Perhaps Lou's head server, Debbie Sue, had helpful information to share.

She prepared a coffee drink at the counter for a customer I didn't recognize. Based on his clothing of khaki shorts, a green T-shirt, and ball cap, I assumed he was a tourist visiting the state park. I waited in line behind him. The aromatic blend of chai, vanilla, and espresso filled the air, creating a cozy and inviting atmosphere.

He accepted his drink, turned to me, and beamed. "This is my lucky day. Stop to buy a coffee and meet the woman of my dreams."

Debbie Sue chuckled behind the counter. "The usual?"

I nodded and peered at the young man, who had to be around twenty-five—over ten years my junior. "Thank you for your kind words, but I'm afraid I'm far too much for you to handle." I didn't want to hurt his puffed-up feelings for himself, so I added, "You're a real cutie, but my heart belongs to my puppy, Snowbunny."

He dipped his head and bolted out the door. I've been told I'm a beautiful woman by more than one man. My looks are my best quality. But I lack in other areas.

Debbie Sue rang up my sale. "You sure got his attention. He wasn't as pleasant with me."

Seeing an opportunity to get information, I said, "You're a lovely young woman. Any sensible man would be delighted to have you for his girl."

She blushed and wiped the counter with a towel. "Anything else I can get you?"

"Some information will be helpful."

Debbie Sue took a step back and squinted. "What information?"

"Does Lou have a man friend?"

Debbie Sue paled and stuttered. "I. Uh. How would I know that?"

I leaned closer and softened my voice. "Is she having an affair?"

"No." Debbie Sue gawked at me. "She's involved with someone, but neither she nor he are married or spoken for."

I smiled and touched Debbie Sue's hand where it rested on the counter. "You're telling me that she's not seeing Harry from the hardware store?"

"Of course not." Debbie Sue smacked the counter with her hand and grimaced. "She's dating old Reed Ruby. Has for six months. I don't know who told you . . ." She covered her mouth. "You tricked me. You made up that story about Harry." Her eyes glistened with unshed tears. "I could lose my job for this."

"Don't worry, sweetie. I never reveal my sources."

"You mean your snitches?" Debbie Sue moved away from the counter and turned her back on me. "Go away."

~

Wade despised feeling trapped. His dad and Lou thought he should let Maggie and her mom keep a cow at the farm. But if he agreed, he'd have to interact with Maggie a lot. And if he told her that she couldn't buy one, but she'd need to work it off, he'd see her even more often. That would remind him of the past and stir up old feelings he had tried so hard to forget. He clenched his hands into tight fists, causing his knuckles to turn white. He couldn't allow her charm to get the best of him. No other choice but to refuse her request.

The stable walls seemed to press in on him. He needed fresh air. He clutched his hat and escaped to his pickup. Time for a brief drive to his favorite spot on the family farm to clear his head before supper.

The driveway led to a gate where he stopped, opened it, and then closed it again after he passed through. To his left lay a small pond situated just beyond the gate and behind the stable. He headed to the backside of the property, where a hill overlooked a larger pond, and today, several cattle grazing nearby. He loved to park on top of the hill to admire the majestic great blue herons and listen to the cheerful quacking of the ducks that frequented the area.

In this peaceful setting, he often prayed and asked for God's guidance. Today, he needed the Lord to soften his heart if God wanted Maggie on the farm.

Wade completed his time of prayer with an "Amen." Disappointed by the absence of ducks or herons, the only sound that broke the silence was the annoying croaking of frogs.

He climbed inside his truck and drove back to the front gate near the stable. When he pulled through the gate and parked between the stable and the barn, another annoyance awaited him near the house.

Maggie had returned.

~

After my visit to Mama Lou's Café, I stopped by my bed-and-breakfast and met my two guests, Carl and Jenny Monroe. I thanked them for their stay and gave them suggestions of places and restaurants to visit while in the area. I also gave them a trail map for the state park. "And tomorrow morning, I'll have a goodie bag filled with treats and water for your hike."

My bed-and-breakfast was a two-story house with two bedrooms downstairs and three upstairs. Most of the downstairs rooms were private for my personal use and closed off from the guest quarters. Three bedrooms upstairs, each with a private bath, along with a shared dining and living area downstairs, made up our guest area. The front door served as the exclusive entrance for guests.

After the Monroes thanked me and left for dinner, I told Mom that I had one additional errand to run and I'd be back for supper. I changed into jean capris, a sleeveless yellow top, and denim-colored sneakers. Loaded with all the ammunition I needed to get Wade to agree to my request for a cow, I made my way back to the Ruby farm.

While I climbed out of my car, Wade jogged up to me wearing a frown.

"No need to get out. Get back in your car."

I slammed my car door and stood beside it. "A rude way to welcome your guests."

"I didn't expect you back so soon."

"But you expected me to return?"

"I remember you being persistent."

I pushed back my shoulders. "Yes. I go after what I want and get it, if that's what you mean."

"Did you misunderstand what I told you earlier?"

"Not at all." I stepped closer to him and pointed to the house. "But I'm aware of what's happening here."

"What's that?"

"Let's take a walk behind the house and I'll show you."

Wade grabbed my arm. His hand, like my dad's, strong and calloused from years of farm work, gently squeezed my arm. "No need to go there. I can tell you to leave from here."

I grinned and tilted my head to the right. "You don't want me to confirm Lou Sterling is still here three hours after she arrived."

"None of your business."

"I'm making it my business. There's a story here my readers will love."

Wade lowered his chin. "You think you're pretty smart, don't you?"

"You could say that." I looked him in the eye. "And because they want to keep it private, I'll agree to not tell my readers if you agree to sell me a cow for my mom and keep it here."

He stiffened and pinched his lips together. "So now you're adding blackmail to your long list of tricks?"

"What tricks?"

He shook his head and motioned to my car behind us. "I have no need of you. Time for you to leave. Now."

I glanced over his head. Reed and Lou approached from the backyard.

Wade turned and waited for them to get closer. "You want her to share your story? Fine. But I want nothing to do with her."

Reed wrapped his arm across Wade's shoulder. "What's got you so upset?"

Wade spun out of Reed's grasp. "She offered a bribe. I let her have a cow, and she won't write about you and Lou's relationship." He glared at me and snapped. "What's your opinion of someone who will do anything to get their own way?" He pivoted on his heels and strode toward the barn, releasing a frustrated grunt. Reed followed behind and called out for Wade to stop.

Lou stepped closer and touched my elbow. "You already knew about us?"

"I figured it out today when you arrived here and didn't return to the café." I gazed at Reed and Wade where they stood in front of the barn. To protect Debbie Sue, I didn't want to admit too much.

"Reed and I would like you to announce our engagement in your blog post if you'd like to. We're ready to go public."

I widened my eyes and moved back a step. "Engagement?"

She wiggled her eyebrows and squealed. "We've dated since November."

"How didn't I know this?" I brought my hand to my mouth. Were my snooping abilities slipping?

Lou faced the wrought-iron bench beneath a large oak tree across from where I'd parked my car. "Can we sit for a moment?"

We took a seat next to one another, and Lou said, "The cow for your mom is important to you, isn't it?"

I crossed my legs. Mom's weariness played out in

my mind. "She misses Dad."

I eyed the red and white impatiens that grew in containers around the bench where we sat. One of my favorite memories of Wade. The bench where we shared our first kiss.

Lou placed her hand on top of mine. "You miss your dad, too, don't you?"

I raised my head and focused on the barn. "Not like I should. He ruined my future with Wade."

Five

While Wade ate his breakfast on Thursday morning, Reed interrupted him by giving unwanted advice. "Let her have a cow. Will give you and Maggie a chance to work through things. You owe yourself and her that much. And you'll get needed help around here."

Wade stuffed the last bite of his pancake, dripping with maple syrup, into his mouth. "I don't owe her anything. And even if I agree with this harebrained idea of yours, she has a bed-and-breakfast to run. She can't help me with ranch chores."

"Ranch chores?" Reed stood and pushed his chair toward the table. "Son, this here is a small family farm."

"A farm I intend to run like a big Texas ranch." He chugged down the last of his orange juice. "In fact, I ordered a sign to put up in the driveway as you come onto the property."

"A sign?"

"Yep. Wrought iron." He raised his arm, stretching it far above his head to form an arch. "Ruby Ranch. Should arrive soon."

"Ruby what?" Reed moseyed to the pantry, placed

the bottle of syrup inside, and returned to the table. "We'll be the laughin' stock of Clancy County."

"You worry too much." Wade rose and rinsed the sticky syrup off his plate before he put it in the dishwasher, relieved he'd gotten his dad off the subject of Maggie.

"Lou gave Maggie permission to announce our engagement in a special edition she's puttin' together for tomorrow." Reed picked up his dirty dishes and added them to the dishwasher. "Tell her that she must work off the cow by doin' *ranch* chores." He chuckled, slipped by Wade, and headed down the hallway near his bedroom.

Wade sneered and hollered after him. "I'm forty-one years old. Are you telling me that I must do this against my will?"

Reed raised his voice. "Nope. But I do hope you'll pray and ask God what He wants you to do and give Maggie a chance. She told Lou somethin' that made her doubt your understandin' of why things didn't work out with the two of you."

"Oh, yeah? And what was that?"

Reed peeked around the corner of the hallway and lowered his voice. "Don't know. Lou's tryin' hard to keep her mouth shut and not go repeatin' what she hears. But Maggie told her somethin' Lou thinks is important."

Wade stormed out and headed straight for the stable. "Okay, I'll pray." *Lord, keep Maggie away from me. She's a manipulator and a liar. She's a gossip and a blackmailer. I cautioned my stepson Logan to never hire someone of her questionable character. Why would I consider doing so? No. Even if she is the prettiest woman I've ever known.* He softened his voice. *Smells like fresh flowers and fit perfectly in my arms all those years ago.*

A few moments later, he led Champ from his stall into the field behind the stable. When he returned for Copper, he stopped, peered into the horse stalls, and grinned. But it might be fun to watch Maggie muck out manure-covered stalls and groom horses. This might work out after all. And he'd have her help with the cattle vaccinations and repairing fences. She wanted a cow. He'd give her a cow and so much more.

But when she learns she'll need to work ten hours a week to pay for the cow and its upkeep, she'll give up on this stupid idea of hers.

After all, she has a business to run.

~

With the Monroes fed and equipped with their goodie bag for hiking, I took a seat at the kitchen table and wrote my special edition blog post for Friday. I corrected my misinformation regarding Lanie's job situation and announced her and Luke's engagement. After their story, I penned a lovely announcement about Lou and Reed's engagement too.

While we sat on the Ruby's bench and chatted, I couldn't help but smile at the thought of Lou's kindness. She may be the closest person I had to a friend. Most of the townsfolk shied away from me. Those at church were kind. But even they vanished when I hunted them down for a story. I assumed they didn't like me. Dad would not have approved of their actions or mine.

Dad wanted me to work on the farm with him and Mom. He didn't like me sneaking around with Wade while I was still in high school. And he wasn't happy when I went off to Texas to stay with Aunt Tilly for the summer and ended up moving there to attend college.

Over the years, I couldn't escape his displeasure. He never thought my bed-and-breakfast was a worthwhile endeavor. And his death left me with a sense of emptiness. With him gone, I could never gain his approval.

Mom entered the kitchen after I completed my blog post and took a seat across from me. "I'm excited about my new cow. When can we visit her?"

I mustered up a momentary burst of perkiness. "I'm still working on the details. Give me another week."

She covered her mouth and coughed. "You're the best daughter a mama could have. My Pearl. A real gemstone."

I stared at my computer. Mom thinks I'm a good daughter, but I never lived up to my dad's expectations. If he had learned my secret before he passed away, it would have killed him.

"I heard a car door." Mom jumped up and darted to the window. "The Monroes are back from their hike."

"That's surprising. They told me they'd be gone until this evening." I stood and met them at the front entrance.

Carl shook his head and watched his wife dash up the stairs. "Jenny insists we hurry back home right away. Our three-year-old, Charlie, got stung by a bee early this morning, and he keeps crying for his mommy."

"Oh, my." I touched my chest. "Bee stings can be serious. I hope your little boy is okay."

"His papa said he's fine."

Jenny appeared at the top of the stairs. "Did Blake say where our daughter was when this happened? She should have watched Charlie more closely." Jenny placed her hands on her hips. "Or Mom. Where was she?"

Carl looked up at his wife. "You can ask her when we pick up the kids." He glanced at me. "I'd better help Jenny pack." He hurried up the stairs.

I called out to him. "Don't worry about your bill. I'll only charge you for one night."

"You don't have to do that." He made his way back down the steps. "We're past your check-out time. We reserved two nights, and that's what we owe you."

"I want to do this. Charlie needs his mama."

~

During Wade's mid-afternoon break, he sat at the kitchen table and looked up the phone number for Maggie's Place. He'd driven by once or twice when he was south of town in recent weeks, but he'd never stopped. From the outside, the house appeared pleasant and a comfortable place to stay, and the flower garden overflowed with color.

He clicked on the number, pressed speakerphone, and waited through three rings.

Maggie greeted him with a touch of professionalism, as he expected she would with any caller.

After he identified himself and paused, he said, "Are you available tomorrow afternoon to stop by? I'd like to discuss your request."

"Do you mean the cow for my mom?"

He confirmed and rested his elbow on the table and

his hand on his forehead.

"What time?"

Reed entered the kitchen and ambled to the refrigerator. "Invite her to dinner tomorrow evening at 6:00."

Wade cringed and glared at his dad.

Reed removed the sweet tea jug from the fridge, faced Wade, and mouthed, "Ask her."

"How about dinner here at 6:00? Don't know what we're having, but Lou will cook up something special, so it'll be good."

"Dinner?" She paused for a moment. "Okay."

"Dad's idea." He sighed and clenched his fist. "Not mine."

Reed narrowed his eyes at Wade and pressed his lips together.

"I heard." Was that regret in her voice? "Ask Lou if there's anything I can bring."

When they ended their call, Wade pocketed his cell. "Why did you do that?" He stood and strode to his dad, who gulped down his sweet tea. "I don't want her here at our dinner table. She's not welcome here."

"You have a responsibility to yourself and her to resolve this."

"And I told you that I don't owe her anything." He ran his fingers through his hair. "Well, maybe a bit of kindness."

Reed placed his hand on Wade's shoulder. "Son, you owe her a lot more than that."

Six

Reed poured himself a cup of coffee, added cream, and sat across the table from Wade. "Since you're on your mid-morning break, check out Maggie's special Friday post."

"Did she tell the truth or half-truths?"

Reed chuckled. "She did a fine job on our engagement announcement."

Wade stood, put his empty sweet tea glass in the dishwasher, and strode to the door.

"Aren't you goin' to read her post?" Reed's chair squeaked across the floor. "She corrected some false news she'd reported and apologized too."

With his eyes wide, and his voice filled with doubt, Wade turned back to his dad. "Maggie made an apology for something she wrote?"

Reed nodded and raised his brows.

"Whoa, that's bigger news than your engagement announcement. I'll check it out later." Wade stepped outside and headed to the barn. He needed to round up a six-month-old calf and her mama from the back pasture. The final calf to wean this spring. He'd arranged for Tim, the teenaged son of a farmer who lived nearby, to help him and expected him soon.

When Tim arrived, they piled into Wade's pickup along with Tim's Aussie, Nubbins. That herding dog knew her stuff. They located the mama cow and her calf, and Nubbins herded the two while the men followed along in the truck. Upon reaching the barn, Wade and Tim directed mama and her calf into the pasture closest to the house, to the right of the driveway, and secured the gate. Mama and her calf had plenty of fresh grass and water and would spend a day together there.

Wade encircled the calf and looked her over. Solid brown and in need of a refreshing rain shower to cleanse the caked mud from her back. But yeah, a pretty young thing.

A fine calf for Maggie's mom, *if* he gives in.

~

Mom and I tidied up the bed-and-breakfast on Friday afternoon. She worked inside, and I spent time outdoors. We used a landscaping company for lawn care, but I took care of planting and weeding the perennial flower garden and the annuals planted around the yard. I delighted in the sweet fragrance of lilacs in spring, the vivid red and yellow canna lilies in summer, and the captivating purple asters in the fall.

Snowbunny barked and whined inside. He wanted to follow me outdoors, but he would have gotten too dirty in the garden. I knelt on an old towel for padding and plucked out weeds and pieces of grass growing around my black-eyed Susans while enjoying the earthy smell of the soil. Why did Reed want me to come to dinner? Has Wade agreed to allow me to buy one of his cows?

Mom must have grown tired of Snowbunny's

yapping inside. She let the dog out the back door to join me. I couldn't get much weeding done with him running around me in circles. Twice, he stopped his running and covered me in slobbery kisses. That's enough. Time to get ready for dinner at the Rubys.

I entered through the back door and strolled past my mom, who'd pulled out leftovers for supper. "Did I forget to tell you that I have plans tonight for dinner?"

"Plans? If you told me, I forgot." She coughed and clutched her chest.

"Your cough hasn't gotten better. Do you need a doctor's appointment?"

"I'm doing okay. Just my allergies."

"Let me know if it gets worse." I kissed her on the cheek. "I plan to leave here at 5:45."

"Got a date tonight?"

"Sure, Mama. Still believe in miracles, huh?"

She held onto my shoulders and peered into my eyes. "You are beautiful, sweet, intelligent, and a gift from God. Don't you ever forget it."

"And you're my mom. Not surprising you would say those things about me."

"Because they're true." She grinned and touched my cheek. "So, where are you going tonight?"

She didn't realize the difficulty I'd had with finding a cow for her, and I didn't want to get her hopes up. "Going to town to meet some friends for supper."

I zipped into my bedroom to shower and change. I hated lying to my mom. But what was one more? I didn't have friends to meet for supper. Not real friends. Except for my snitches, and possibly Lou. And as much as I longed for genuine friendship, the opportunity had already passed me by.

~

Lou busied herself at the stove. She poured olive oil into a skillet, scrambled two eggs in a small bowl, and added more ingredients to the counter.

Wade noticed cut-up pieces of chicken, a bag of frozen peas and carrots, chopped fresh onion and garlic, and a heaping bowl of fluffy cooked rice. "What will this be when you're finished?"

"Chicken fried rice."

"Not sure I've had that before." He stuck up his nose in disgust.

"You'll like it. Trust me."

"How can I help?"

"Set the table and then check to see if your dad's ready for your guest."

"Maggie is not my guest. She's dad's guest." He scowled and shook his head. "I'm still uncertain about this idea."

Lou turned to Wade and smiled. "I apologize if I'm meddlin' in somethin' that's not my business, but the two of you should spend time together so you can both put the past behind you."

Wade detected a twinkle in Lou's eye and walked closer to her. "You're not playing matchmaker, are you?"

She returned to her hot skillet and added the chicken pieces, causing them to sizzle. "Not at all. I doubt either of you is interested in that. But you might become friends enough to not cringe at seeing each other."

His chest tightened. "Yeah, don't get your hopes up for that to happen." Wade believed her to be sincere, and he agreed in part. But neither Lou nor Reed knew the complete story. Maybe Maggie and he could come to some agreement to work together here on the ranch and permit her to keep a cow here for her mom, but nothing else.

He refused to let himself get hurt again.

~

A pleasant drive north on a mostly sunny day with a high of eighty degrees, and I hoped this evening would be as lovely with Wade, his dad, and Lou. What awaited me? The sun peeked through a cloud while five vultures circled the sky to the west. I released a heavy sigh. Had Wade softened to the idea? Or were those birds a sign Wade was waiting for my demise?

I didn't relish the idea of seeing him every time I took my mom to visit her cow. But I couldn't find anyone else who wanted to help me. If he agreed to let me buy a cow, we'd need to keep each visit short and have limited interaction. Get mom in and get her out. No questions asked, and no answers given.

When I arrived, I parked my car in front of the house and made my way to the front door. Reed welcomed me with the same warmth he had two days before and invited me inside.

The furniture looked newer, except for a comfy, well-worn recliner draped with a colorful crocheted afghan near the brick fireplace. I remembered the arched doorway leading into the kitchen from the living room and the wooden stairway to my right that led upstairs.

Lou greeted me from the kitchen and invited me to join her and Wade. Reed took the lead and gestured to a seat on the right, which gave me a clear view of the back door. Knowing I had a fast way out provided a sense of relief.

Lou placed the food in the center of the table and took a seat across from me. Reed sat to my left and Wade to my right. Great. Looks like one big happy family. Or not. Wade's tight expression held resentment and not happiness. He didn't want me here, and I understood his discomfort.

If he only knew the truth.

Seven

After our delicious chicken fried rice dinner and a lot of meaningless chitchat, I helped clear the table and offered to load the dishwasher while the guys finished their coffee. I hadn't broached the subject of a cow and neither had they. So why was I here?

While I emptied our glasses in the sink, Lou asked me about Memorial Day. "Are you helpin' with the parade or any of the festivities around the gazebo this year?"

"I offered to help with the bounce houses. There's something special about the sounds of kids playing and laughing." I put the glasses in the dishwasher.

"Sounds like fun." Lou shooed me away with the wave of her hand. "Reed's a tremendous helper. You go on outside. Wade has somethin' to show you."

I stared at Wade with my eyes opened wide.

He scooted back his chair and stood. "We might work something out." His smile seemed forced.

"I'm ready." I hurried to the back door and opened it.

Wade followed me out, and the door slammed shut behind him. "I brought her up here this morning. Her and her mama."

Thankful I'd worn my tennis shoes, I scrambled

across the gravel driveway and toward the barn. There, in a pen in front of the barn, lay a young calf. "What an adorable face. And those big brown eyes. Mama will love her." I turned back to Wade and noticed his furrowed brow. "How old is she?"

"Six months. We brought her up today to wean her. Tomorrow we'll take her mama away and move her just outside this fence. They'll see each other, but the calf won't be able to nurse."

"How long will you keep her before she's sold?" I returned my attention to the calf and refrained from clapping my hands in victory.

"No plans to sell. Getting a new bull instead."

"Fabulous." I extended my arm through the fence, hoping to interact with the young cow. "How much do I owe you?"

"About ten hours a week, through August, and she's yours."

I pulled back my hand and gawked at him. "What?"

"That will cover the cost of the cow and her upkeep for a year."

A surge of heat rose from deep within me. "But that wasn't the deal. I want to buy her and pay for her upkeep."

"We haven't made a deal. That's what we're doing now. You can have this cow if you work for her."

I placed my hands on my hips and quipped. "But I have a bed-and-breakfast to run."

Wade crossed his arms and shot back. "And I have cattle to care for and need extra help."

"Doesn't Reed help you?"

"Sometimes. But between his aching back and

tinkering in his workshop in the garage, he's cutting back on farm work." Wade smiled at the calf and her mama. "I realize this might not be a perfect fit for you, and that's all right. I'll hire someone to help if you're too busy to do this. But you won't be able to buy or keep a cow here." He turned away from the fence and headed back toward the house.

"Wait." I jogged up to him and walked the rest of the way by his side. "I'll do it."

He stopped and squinted at me. "You'll do it?"

"Mama wants this cow." I nodded and pursed my lips. "I'll do it for her."

He pinched the bridge of his nose. "But. But. You said you were too busy. With your bed-and-breakfast."

"That's not what I said." I stomped my foot on the gravel driveway. "I said I had a bed-and-breakfast to run. But Mama takes care of most of it, anyway. This will give me something new to do."

He sneered and looked down his nose at me. "Fantastic." His words oozed with sarcasm. "Let's have a piece of pie and work out the glorious details inside."

~

Wade opened the screen door, slipped inside, and let the door close before Maggie stepped in.

"Ouch." She followed him inside, rubbing her nose. "Is this how you treat your employees?"

Lou squealed and jumped up from her chair. "She agreed to help you?" She darted to Maggie and hugged her. "I'm so happy for your mom. You're an amazing daughter to do this for her. Shows how much you care about her and her needs."

"Yep. Amazing." Wade snickered, moved to the cabinet, and removed three pie plates. "I need pie."

"Sounds yummy to me." Reed stood, opened the freezer, and pulled out the vanilla ice cream.

"What kind of pie did you make, Lou?" Maggie eyed the latticed pastry on the table.

"Fresh strawberry." She beamed and removed a sharp knife from the knife block. "Have you picked any berries this season?"

"Not yet. I need to get Mom to the strawberry farm before they're gone. She loves picking her own berries."

"Reed and I picked ours earlier today. Their strawberries are plump, ripe, and juicy. The perfect treat."

Despite the company, Wade did his best to enjoy his pie and ice cream while they chatted about the cow. "Bring your mom over tomorrow to meet her calf." He swirled his melted ice cream into the strawberries and pie crust.

"I'm busy tomorrow, but I can bring her Sunday after church if that works for you."

"After 2:00 will work."

"Sounds good." She shoved a spoonful of pie and ice cream into her mouth. "And I'll get to pick my work hours, won't I?"

He held back a laugh. "I need you every Monday, Wednesday, and Friday. We'll start work at 6:00 a.m." He smirked and added, "Includes holidays."

Maggie sat up taller. "But I have plans for Memorial Day."

"Cancel them. Horses and cows don't celebrate holidays."

She squeezed her eyes shut and reopened them. "But I've been thinking about volunteering at the children's home on two of those days."

"The children's home?" He narrowed his eyes and shook his head. He found that hard to believe. "You are free to help there after you leave here."

"But they need me in the morning."

"So do I."

She huffed and gave him a piercing glare. "What chores will I be responsible for?"

"The normal stuff."

"Which means?"

"Your dad had a farm. You learned what needed to be done to care for horses and cows. Didn't you?"

"He bought it my senior year of high school, and I stayed busy with my studies and a certain young man. I didn't do any farm chores." She reached over and put her hand on Wade's arm. "Don't you remember?"

He pulled his arm away from Maggie's reach. "Then I guess I've got my work cut out for me and will need to train you."

Reed chuckled, and all eyes focused on him. "Wade's a outstandin' teacher. And I can't shake the feelin' that somethin' big is gonna happen this summer."

~

Did he say, 6:00? In the morning? I get up early most days, but I'm not ready to work at 6:00. We don't serve breakfast for our guests until 8:30.

On my drive home, Eileen from Hair Haven called me. After I answered, she said she had something to tell me about Jill Drake. Jill and I attend the same church, and she and Lanie Meadows are sisters.

"You said you saw Jill today?"

"Just now. At Mama Lou's Café. She and hunky

Doctor Stewart were chummy."

"Really?" I turned into Harry's Hardware's parking lot on South Main. "How chummy?"

"They sat next to each other in a booth. Like close. They laughed and elbowed one another. Sure seemed like love in bloom."

"Cozy, huh?"

"That's a superfine way to describe it." She giggled and sighed. "Cozy and affectionate, if you ask me."

I thanked her for the information and disconnected the call. Perhaps it's worth mulling over this story before publishing it. After messing up Lanie's job situation, I didn't want to get her sister upset with me too. I pulled back onto South Main Street.

But how did plain Jill catch Doctor Stewart's attention? I hadn't met him yet, but rumor had it that he was the newest heartthrob in Pleasant Springs and single.

When I arrived home, Snowbunny met me in the kitchen. I knelt next to him and raised the pitch of my voice. "Hello precious. Did you miss mommy?" I stroked his back for a few minutes and took him outside. When we returned inside, I brushed his long white fur while he relaxed in my lap. Jill and Doctor Stewart? I grinned and snuggled Snowbunny.

Mom needs to get her cough checked out, and I must make sure she gets an appointment soon with the good-looking doctor.

Eight

While we savored our lunch of gooey grilled cheese sandwiches and steamy tomato soup on Saturday, I suggested Mom visit Doctor Stewart.

"My cough isn't that bad."

"We'll see how you feel after the weekend."

She narrowed her eyes and scoffed. "Is it my health that concerns you, or are you hoping to meet the new physician?"

"I am only concerned about you and don't know what I would do without you." I cleared the dirty dishes from the table and carried them to the sink.

"And that twinkle in your eye means you need to keep me healthy, so I'll continue to help you here, and has nothing to do with the handsome doctor?"

Our laughter echoed through the kitchen. "You know me too well. But I'll be the judge of whether he's handsome."

Mom rinsed our dishes and placed them in the dishwasher. "His sister Becca is a pretty woman, so I expect he's good-looking too."

"I guess he is, and if your cough doesn't get better, I'll make an appointment for you, and we'll know for sure."

She stepped closer to me and rubbed my arm. "Honey, I appreciate you taking such good care of me. You didn't have to invite me here to live with you after your dad died, but I'm glad you did."

I wrapped my arms around her. "I asked you because I love you and enjoy our time together."

With a quick peck on my mom's cheek, I zipped outdoors to finish my gardening tasks. After I'd extracted weeds and dead-headed flowers for two hours on my knees, my cell vibrated in my pocket. I took off my work gloves, pulled out my phone, and accepted Eileen's call.

"You won't believe what I heard."

My heart rate peaked, and I stood. "Tell me."

"Jill Drake."

"Did you see her out with Doctor Stewart again today?"

"Not me, but one of my clients from Poplar Ridge saw her. Said she was at Pete's Barbeque, and this time with Doc Winston." She shrieked in my ear. "Can you believe it? Two dates, two men, back-to-back. This must be news."

"She works part time at his animal clinic. A business lunch?"

"Then why drive fourteen miles away to eat when we have fine dining here in Pleasant Springs?"

"You think they didn't want anyone to learn they had lunch together?"

"That's right. My friend said when she walked past their table, Doc said, 'We're beyond that, Jill. Please call me Jake.'" She raised the pitch of her voice. "Sounds like they're taking their relationship to the next level."

I thanked her for the information, asked her to keep me posted if she received any further news, and ended the call.

Wow. I can't believe Jill went on two dates in two days. She must be quite the catch. But I don't know why. Well, she can have Doc Winston. So not my type. But Doctor Stewart remains to be seen.

~

Wade saddled Copper, mounted, and rode to the back pasture to check on his cattle. While there, he assessed the fencing. The perfect task for Maggie. Although he didn't check the fencing often, if she became a nuisance, he could send her out back to do the job and create distance between them.

He located a slanted post and made a mental note to monitor it. On his way back to the stable, he stopped on top of his favorite hill, dismounted, and led Copper down to the pond for a cool drink. There, the low, repetitive drone of a bullfrog serenaded them.

How did he get into this situation? He'd see Maggie much too often. How long could he endure that? He blamed his dad and Lou. They urged him to release grudges, show kindness, and make amends. But how could he do that? Now that she had reappeared in his life?

Wade forgave Maggie years ago, and God wanted him to show her kindness, but he had no interest or intention of inviting her back into his life. He couldn't allow himself to be swayed by her cunning ways again.

While Wade waited for Copper to finish his drink, he gazed out over the pasture and reminisced. Not about Maggie, but about a young girl with long, wavy, dark hair from his church in Texas.

He opened his wallet and pulled out a crumpled ten-year-old newspaper article from the Abilene Herald. "Gemma R. Garrison and her horse, Pearl, won their third barrel racing competition."

Gemma, the girl who'd reminded him of Maggie.

~

Mom and I arrived at the Pizza Shack at 6:00 p.m., parked near the back door, and entered there. When we slipped inside, the host motioned us to the booth closest to us at the back of the restaurant and nearest to the kitchen. The aroma of freshly baked dough and spices welcomed us.

But our booth was not my favorite. This one had a tall back reserved for the owner and his staff for private meetings. Mom took the bench which faced the front entrance, and I slid into the one with the tall back. I couldn't observe anyone but Mom, the servers, and customers going to and from the restrooms.

"Keep an eye out for anyone we know, and tell me as soon as you see them." I snagged a menu and flipped it over to the pizzas. "We should have gone to the front entrance. A better chance to learn something new for my blog posts."

"Honey, can you take a break from working so hard on your blog? Relax and enjoy your evening." She covered her mouth, coughed, and apologized. "This isn't the best place for me with my cough. Everyone will fear I'm contagious." She reached across the table and touched my menu. "Order us a pizza for takeout instead. I'll wait in the car." She scooted off her bench and dashed out the back door before I could respond.

I leaned back in my seat and scowled. My plan to get her out of the house and gather information for future posts didn't work out as I'd expected.

The server arrived to take my order, and I told her our plans had changed. "I'd like it to go."

"No problem. We should have that for you in fifteen minutes."

I sighed and shook my head. What a waste of time. I can't see a thing. But I'll draw attention if I move to Mom's seat now. I peeked around the corner of my bench and twisted back again. Jill Drake and Luke Gibson's younger brother Eddie? They appeared rather comical together. She's taller than him. And a minimum of three years older. This couldn't be a date. Three different men, three dates, in two days?

"This booth is perfect." Jill's voice echoed nearby. The host sat them in the booth behind me. Could this get any better?

My pulse quickened. I grinned from ear to ear and scooted to the edge of my seat. I strained to hear every detail of their conversation.

"What's your favorite pizza?"

Eddie said nothing. At least, if he did, I couldn't hear him.

"Is pepperoni and sausage okay with you?"
Still nothing.

"Terrific." A slight pause followed. "What have you been up to since we saw each other at Becca's new home?"

I wrinkled my nose and shrugged. Why didn't I know Becca and Pastor Ben found a house? I strained to hear more.

A soft, "Not much," met my ear.

"What do you do when you're not working at PS Automotive?"

"Um. Church. Play with my puppy."

I tapped my foot and fiddled with a paper napkin. Boring. The two doctors, perhaps, but Eddie?

"Lanie mentioned you have a beagle. My Babs is a beagle too."

"Yeah."

"Maybe we can get them together for a play date at the dog park."

"Yeah."

The server took their order, and their electrifying conversation continued.

"Besides your dog, work, and church, what keeps you busy?"

"Friends and family."

"Do you get to spend much time with Luke and his foster son, Billy?"

"Some."

I rested my elbow on the table and massaged my forehead. Pizza, please hurry because I'm about to fall asleep. Poor Jill. This must be her worst date ever.

"What holds the greatest meaning in your life?"

Again, silence.

"Your reason to awake every morning and start a new day."

"Easy." He chuckled, and with a hint of glee in his voice, he said, "The Lord."

"Tell me more about your relationship with Him."

I squirmed on the hard wooden bench. No, please don't. I love God as much as the next person, but I wasn't in the mood for a sermon. And thankfully, I didn't have to listen. My server waved a box at me and met me at the back counter where I paid her and snuck out the back door.

After dinner, I would craft an engaging blog post about Jill's love life.

Nine

Wade finished his morning chores and headed to the house to get ready for church. He'd visited three churches since he'd returned home but hadn't found the right one for him.

He passed Lou's car parked behind the house in front of the garage. When he ventured inside, she and his dad stood in the kitchen, ready to step out the back door.

Wade asked them to wait a minute. "Are you two nervous this morning?"

They'd attended church in Chattanooga for the past six months to keep their relationship a secret from people in Pleasant Springs. But now that their engagement was public, they planned to attend their church in town for the first time as a couple.

"Not nervous, but I expect to be uncomfortable. People like to make a fuss over the craziest things." Reed took Lou by the hand. "You can join us, Son."

"Maybe another time. I'll check out Pleasant Springs Community Church today. They have a new pastor."

Lou opened the back door. "Tell Maggie hello for us. We look forward to seeing her and her mom this afternoon."

"Maggie? Does she attend there?"

"I thought you knew." Lou brought her hand to her mouth. "I should learn to keep my mouth shut."

"Thanks for the heads up. I'll try Joy Fellowship instead."

Wade hurried upstairs and got ready for church. He left home in time to arrive early, hoping to find a familiar face. But after two decades away, he didn't remember many people.

He passed a young man in the foyer who seemed familiar, but he couldn't place him. The guy dipped his head like he recognized him too.

Wade stopped and flashed a smile. "I'm Wade, first time here. Do you think you can give me a quick tour before the service starts?" The young man stuck out his hand. "I'm Eddie Gibson. I think I worked on your pickup at our automotive shop in town."

"Yes, three months ago, before I moved back to Pleasant Springs."

"I'll be happy to show you around and introduce you to a few people too." Eddie led Wade to the welcome center nearby, around the corner to the coffee counter, and pointed out the restrooms. Next, he guided him to a couple chatting near the entrance of the worship center.

Eddie introduced his brother, Luke, and Luke's fiancée, Lanie.

"So, you're the couple whose engagement Maggie mentioned with my dad and Lou Sterling's."

Lanie's face brightened, and her eyes grew wider. "Your dad is the man marrying Lou?"

"Yep."

"And you know Maggie?"

"Unfortunately." Heat rushed up his neck. "I'm sorry. I shouldn't have said that."

Lanie pulled her lips inward and didn't respond. She likely shared his feelings about Maggie.

Luke took Lanie by the elbow. "We'd better find a seat." He looked at Wade and invited him to join them.

"Sounds excellent."

After the service, Wade's new friends invited him to join them for lunch. They met at La Casa, where Lanie requested a table for five.

While an employee cleared and wiped off a table, Wade scanned the Mexican restaurant, taking in the vibrant earth tones of the furnishings. Laughter and chatter echoed around them, and the enticing aroma of fresh garlic and onions filled the room.

Lanie's attention shifted to Wade. "We're expecting my sister, Jill." Lanie followed the host to a table for six in the center of the restaurant where he, Luke, and Eddie joined her.

Jill arrived soon after and introduced herself. After Wade did the same, she pulled out the empty chair to his right, across from Lanie.

When Jill sat, her eyebrows shot up. "You're Reed's son? I heard you moved back two months ago to help your dad on the farm."

He noticed her eyes dart to Eddie, who sat at the end of the table on Wade's left. "Did you have a good morning?"

Eddie nodded and perused his menu.

Jill glanced around the table. "Where's Billy today?"

Luke chuckled and focused on Jill. "Mom can't get

enough of him. She insisted he stay at her house last night. And he loves being with her."

Wade creased his forehead and opened his menu. "Is Billy your son?"

"He's my foster son." Luke wrapped his arm around Lanie's shoulder. "Lanie was the caseworker who placed him in my home."

After they ordered tacos and enchiladas and received their drinks, Lanie explained to Jill that Wade visited Joy Fellowship that morning.

Jill leaned toward him. "How did you like the church?"

"I enjoyed it." He sipped his sweet tea. "But I'm used to a traditional service. I want to check out a couple more churches before I decide where to attend."

"When you make your way to Pleasant Springs Community Church, I'll be happy to show you around."

"I plan on it. People say the new pastor is outstanding."

"He's incredible. But I'm a bit partial. His wife, Becca, is my best friend." She relaxed back in her chair. "We're more traditional than Joy Fellowship. I think you'd like it."

Attending the same church as Maggie didn't appeal to him. She might get the wrong idea. And he couldn't allow that to happen.

~

Mom jabbered on our drive home from church. "Pastor Peterson delivered his best sermon today."

I smirked and rolled my eyes. "Only his second week here."

"But he's preached as a visiting preacher twice before."

I slowed when we neared Mama Lou's Café. "Do you want to go straight home or stop for coffee?"

"Home to check on Snowbunny. He gets lonely when we both leave the house."

"Well, if the church people hadn't made such a fuss when I took him with me, he wouldn't be stuck at home. I don't understand why it's an issue to have him at church. He's good and quiet."

"People aren't used to having dogs at church except for service dogs."

I turned into our driveway and parked my car. Snowbunny *is* my service dog. No one understands me or loves me as much as he does. Perhaps Mom. And Aunt Tilly, before she passed. But not Dad and never Wade.

I twisted to face Mom. "After lunch, I have a surprise for you. We're going to take a drive and make one stop."

"Oh, honey. I want to stay home and take a nap. This cough has me worn out. And besides, the weather app says rain is moving in. You go for your drive, and I'll stay here."

"Rest when we get back. We won't be gone long." When I stepped out of the car, the delightful chirping of birds greeted me.

Mom climbed out and muttered to herself.

I met her at the front of the car. "I think the weather app is incorrect. Such a beautiful sunny day. You'll be glad you went with me. I promise."

Mom pointed to a cloud darkening to the north and huffed. "You and your surprises. I'll give you one hour, including wherever we're traveling to. That's it. Then I want to return home and rest."

When we finished lunch, Mom and I dressed in casual clothing and climbed into my car. My dull life was about to get worse. With the trouble I'd have to endure, paying off this cow, seeing Wade often, and getting filthy, Mom better be thrilled.

I backed down our driveway.

"Stop. Can't we take Snowbunny with us?"

"He'll get too dirty."

Mom crinkled her nose and pouted. "If he's not going, I'm not going either." She crossed her arms.

"Okay. But he must stay in the car. I'm not giving him another bath this soon."

"Fine. Run inside and get him."

I pulled up to the back door, got the dog, and gave him to my mom. "You hold on to him."

"Why didn't you snatch his carrier?"

"We're late. Expected at 2:00 and it's already 1:55."

"Oh, my. We're visiting someone?"

"Yes." I curled my upper lip. "But no one important."

~

When Wade arrived home, he enjoyed listening to the stories about how the people at church showered attention on Lou and his dad. The attendees were glad to have the couple back and wondered where they'd been. A few in the congregation had figured it out but kept it to themselves. Would be nice if everyone kept their thoughts to themselves instead of writing blog posts filled with speculations.

"Are you still expecting Maggie and her mom?" Lou cleared dessert plates from the table.

"Any time. We agreed on 2:00."

"Do you mind if we join you?" Reed stood and joined Lou at the sink, where she rinsed the dishes.

"Great. I won't have to be alone with Maggie and her mom."

"You'll be alone startin' tomorrow when she's workin' with you." Reed put a plate in the dishwasher.

"Don't remind me."

Lou faced him and grinned. "This will be important for the two of you. There's a noticeable amount of goodness in you both. In time, I pray you'll also find it within each other."

Wade strode to the back door and glared at his dad's fiancée. "I still think you're trying to set us up, but it won't work. You don't know her as well as I do."

Lou flashed her widened eyes at him. "But you knew a teenaged girl. She's matured since then." She ambled closer to him and placed her hand on his upper arm. "I'm sure you're not the same young man she knew back then either."

Wade raised both palms facing her and took a step back. "This conversation is over." He opened the door and walked toward the stable. A rain cloud hovered overhead.

He'd always liked Lou and was glad his dad found a woman to share the rest of his years with. But she needed to back off.

He didn't need her unsolicited advice clouding up his life.

Ten

At the sound of thunder in the distance and gravel crunching along the driveway, Wade looked up from refilling the cattle trough. Maggie and her mom. Just in time for the rain. He dropped the hose, strode to the spigot, and turned off the water before he met them in front of the barn at their passenger side door. Why was Maggie's mom blindfolded?

Maggie jumped out of the driver's side before he could open Mrs. Stone's door. "Don't say a word. This is a surprise. Let me help her out of the car." She rushed around the front of her vehicle and stepped on his boot when she slid in between him and the passenger side door.

Wade flinched and moved a step back. When she opened the door, he said, "You—"

Maggie twisted and flung her hand over his mouth. "Not a word." She peeked back at her mom. "Be careful. We can't let Snowbunny out."

"Oh, my. I recognize that man's deep voice, but I can't place it." Maggie's mom turned to the right, and as Maggie helped her out of the car, the sound of a yappy mutt echoed from inside, causing Maggie to fuss.

"Careful, Mom."

"Do I smell manure?"

Maggie turned to the fancy-looking, long-haired, white dog. "Stay."

Lou joined Mrs. Stone and wrapped her arm around her elbow. "Yes. Manure."

"I recognize that voice too. Lou Sterling?" She brought her hands together and squealed. "We're at the Ruby farm, aren't we? I heard that you and Reed got engaged."

Maggie slammed the car door. "Take four steps forward." She and Lou led her mom to the area of the fence where her surprise awaited her.

Lou confirmed her engagement and giggled. "A dream come true."

Mrs. Stone yanked her arm away from Maggie's hold. "I'm taking this stupid blindfold off." She tore it from her eyes and gazed at the cow and calf. "Has my dream come true too?" Mrs. Stone folded her hands beneath her chin. "Is one of these beautiful cows mine?"

"Yes, Mama. The calf is yours." Maggie wrapped her mom in a sideways hug.

Wade cleared his throat. "After three months of—"

Maggie released her mom and approached him with her palm raised. She gritted her teeth and hissed. "Hush. She doesn't know about our arrangement."

Mrs. Stone charged toward Wade. "Been too long." She hugged him and tightened her squeeze. "I don't know if I'm happier to see my calf or you."

He grinned when she pulled back.

"Do I have you to thank for this precious young heifer?"

Maggie let out a soft snicker. "You have me to

thank. Not him. And you should be happier to meet your cow." She mumbled something he couldn't make out. "What shall we call her?"

"Easy. Let's name her after my favorite person. Maggie."

When Maggie shook her head, her long waves danced around her face. "Might get confusing."

"Well then." She pressed her fingers to her smiling lips. "What about my second favorite name to call you? Pearl."

Wade gripped his hands around the picket fence post.

Lou glanced in his direction and caught his eye. "What's wrong? You turned pale."

Reed joined them along the fence where Wade clutched the wooden post. "Son, you don't look all right. Let's get you inside."

Wade lifted his shoulders, released his hold, and backed away. He fixed his eyes on Maggie. "Pearl? Why Pearl?"

"What's the big deal?" She flicked her wrist, chuckled, and squinted her eyes at him. "Maggie means, pearl. That's all."

He needed to get away from her.

~

I watched while Wade, Lou, and Reed hurried to the house. What just happened? I turned to my mom, interjected lightheartedness into my voice, and pointed to Pearl. "She's a beauty, isn't she?"

Thunder rumbled nearby, and the rain cloud above released a gentle sprinkle.

Mom furrowed her brow and suggested we head home because of the rain and come back when Wade felt better. She dashed to the passenger door and opened it. Before I could remind her to watch out for Snowbunny, the dog jumped out and took off as fast as his mini legs would take him.

"Snowbunny, no. Come back here." I chased him until he crawled under the fence and into the pasture where Pearl and her mama grazed.

The back screen door slammed shut, and Lou jogged my way. She pointed at Reed, who made his way to the barn. "Reed's going through the barn and opening the gate to this pasture. He'll chase your dog back through the fence so you can catch him."

While I thanked her, the rain cloud above unleashed a downpour. And whenever Reed tried to guide Snowbunny through the fence, the dog ran in the opposite direction.

I rested my palm on my forehead and yelled. "Keep him out of the poop and mud."

Reed gave up and raised his hands. "He's all yours. Come and get him."

I darted through the barn and through the gate to the pasture. "Snowbunny, come to Mommy." I slipped onto my backside and pushed myself up again, while Snowbunny snuck under the fence, zoomed across the driveway, and halted in front of a gloating Wade.

By the time I arrived, drenched, exhausted, and filthy, a grimy Snowbunny had made a new friend.

Wade rose from a squatting position while my dog ran circles around his legs. "The brown spots on his fur give him character, don't you think?"

I recoiled and blocked the offensive smell with my hand. "What a mess. I don't dare put him in my car. He reeks."

With the rain easing up, Reed joined us. "Son, offer the lady the hose out at the barn. She and her dog could both use it before they drive home."

I thanked him and carried the dog an arm's length in front of me. On our trek to the hose, the sun reappeared.

I drenched Snowbunny and patted his fur with an old towel Lou gave me. With a second towel wrapped around him and another one around me, I made it back to my car, where Mom sat inside waiting for us.

While I drove home, Mom snuggled Snowbunny and offered to get his bath ready. She also suggested we pray for Wade.

"Why?"

"He wasn't well."

"He seemed fine when he returned outside and made a snide remark about Snowbunny."

"But he appeared awful prior to going indoors. Something's wrong, and we need to pray."

"You pray. I'll drive." I sighed and focused ahead. Everything changed when mom mentioned Pearl. Why?

"Amen."

I had heard none of Mom's prayer except for her last word.

We turned into our driveway and parked near the back door.

"After I give Snowbunny his bath, I'll finish my blog post for Wednesday."

"Are you going to tell everyone about my new calf?"

"No, Mama. Not this week." I climbed out of the car and closed the door. I had shocking news that would jolt the townsfolk.

News about Jill Drake and her three eligible bachelors.

~

Lou pulled a mug from the cupboard and offered to fix Wade a cup of hot herbal tea, but he refused.

"I'm fine. I don't know what happened out there. Too much sun."

Reed parked himself at the kitchen table and asked Wade to join him. "What's this about Pearl? That's what upset you, isn't it?"

Wade stood behind a chair but didn't pull it out to sit. "Forget it. I've got to get back to my chores." He turned toward the back door.

The sound of Reed's chair squeaking across the floor stopped Wade from heading outside. His heart racing, he turned to face his dad.

Reed placed his hand on Wade's shoulder. "Son, whatever has consumed you for the past two decades needs to be put to rest. Time to talk to someone about this." He hugged Wade and patted him on the back. "I'm here for you. Lou too. Or a local church pastor." He stepped back and locked eyes with Wade. "Please talk to someone soon."

"You already know what started it. I shared with you what happened when I proposed to Maggie."

Lou gasped and touched her neck.

Wade eyed her. "You didn't know I'd proposed?"

She arched her brow. "No, I didn't. I only knew that you were a couple for a while."

"She told me no. She didn't need me."

"That doesn't fit with what she told me last week." Lou closed the distance between them. "I'm sure that was hard for you."

"And it's bothered him ever since." Reed scowled and put his arm around Lou's waist. "He needs to forgive her and let this go."

"Lou just confirmed Maggie is still lying about our relationship." Wade's voice boomed. "And you don't know what's happened since we broke up. I learned something twelve years ago but thought it couldn't be true. I kept defending Maggie. But I can't do that any longer. The evidence I've ignored came to light with one name. Pearl."

Lou sat at the table and stared up at him. "Why is that a big deal?"

Wade removed his wallet from his back pocket, pulled out the newspaper article he'd carried with him for the past ten years, and tossed it onto the table.

"I'm not holding unforgiveness for her because she didn't want to marry me. I'm struggling because twenty years ago, Maggie Stone lied to me."

Eleven

This wasn't the first time I had to get up earlier than usual, but I hadn't planned my morning well. By the time I got out the door to make the drive to the Ruby farm, I was already late by ten minutes. And without breakfast. When I stopped in town at the four-way stop, I checked my glove box for something to eat. Anything. A melted protein bar? I peeked at the expiration date. January. The year before. Great. I guess no breakfast for me.

When I arrived at the farm and pulled down the driveway, Wade waited in front of the barn with his arms crossed. His face lacked expression. I parked my car next to his pickup and climbed out.

He approached, wearing a scowl. "You're late. Be punctual if you want that calf for your mom. Do you understand?"

"What's got you so uptight this early in the morning?"

"Let's just say I'm sorry."

"You don't sound sorry about anything."

"I'm sorry I let you talk me into this harebrained idea of yours to let you keep a cow here for your mom." He drew his brows together. "Let's clarify something right now."

I squinted and mimicked his domineering stance.

"This is for her. Not you."

"Okay." I tilted my head to the right and softened my tone. "Does this pertain to naming the calf Pearl?"

His neck tightened, and tension rose in his voice. "Might be to your advantage if you and your mother rename the calf."

"Are you going to explain why the name Pearl upsets you?" I wrinkled my nose and stepped closer. "Because I don't understand."

Wade moved back with his face twisted up in a snarl. "Let's get to work." He shifted his weight and clenched his jaw. "We have a lot to do."

~

"Let the fun begin." Maggie followed Wade into the stable. "Oh, my." She made her way over to the two horses in their stalls. "Are these two Copper and Champ?"

"You remember them?"

"Of course. But they were young the last time I saw them. Too young to ride."

"And now they're nearing retirement age." After he rubbed his hand down Copper's neck, he entered the tack room while Maggie talked to the horses in a soothing tone. When he returned to the front of the stalls, he handed her a pair of black rubber boots. "Put these on. You're going to need them."

She reached for the boots and whined. "Don't you have any in yellow?"

He dipped his head to hide his grin. Her favorite color. "Nope." He handed her a curry comb. "Start with Copper and use this first and follow with those in that order." He pointed to various brushes and a hoof pick stored on a shelf across from the stalls. "When you're finished brushing, clean their hooves." He turned to leave.

"Wait." She grabbed his arm and gave it a tight squeeze. "Aren't you going to show me what to do?"

"Show you?" He tugged his arm from her grasp. "You helped with your parents' horses, didn't you?"

"I told you last week I didn't help them on the farm."

He narrowed his eyes and scrunched his nose. "But you rode the horses."

"Only when you or another farmhand were there to help Dad, so I didn't have to groom them."

Wade shook his head and frowned. "I can't believe this. Are you that self-centered that you can't help others?"

Maggie sneered, and she backed away. "I help others—people who stay at my bed-and-breakfast."

"You help them because that's your business, and you hope they'll come back or tell others about their stay." He grimaced and snatched the curry comb from her hand. "You help others only when you have an ulterior motive that benefits you." Wade led her into Copper's stall, where he made circular motions across the horse's back to loosen the excess dirt and hair.

"That's not all." She pushed back her shoulders and took on a snotty attitude. "I bake and donate cookies and an assortment of baked goods to the children's home in town."

He chuckled and focused on her eyes. "Who are you trying to impress there?"

She placed her hands on her hips. "I do it for the

children."

Wade stopped brushing the horse and softened his tone. "And since when have you had a soft spot for children?"

"I've always loved children. And these don't have parents who can care for them right now."

He peered at her and creased his brow. Was that a tear in her eye?

She looked away and touched her throat. "I enjoy doing it for them, because I don't have any of my own or nieces and nephews."

He handed her the comb. "Do what I did. I'll check on you in a while. When you finish with Copper, do the same with Champ. Then I'll show you the next three brushes to use and how to clean their hooves."

Wade exited the stable and made his way to the far side of the barn.

Time to separate the mama cow from her calf and himself from Maggie.

~

Do all horses stink? With my left hand, I swatted at several pesky flies buzzing around my head while I combed Copper with my right. I wished I had an extra hand to shield my nose from the foul odor. I glanced around the stall. Yuck. Horse poop. I suppose I'm the one who gets to clean that up too.

I moved to the front of him and petted his face. "Hi, there, horsey." I smiled and reached back to rub his neck, but before I found it, he raised his head and hit me on my jaw. "Ouch." A sudden jolt of pain shot through my mouth. "My tongue."

I returned to his side and continued with circular motions down his back while humming a lullaby. After

I rushed through his left side, I moved around the front to his right. "You are such a handsome boy."

A loud commotion sounded outside. Groaning. Was someone about to die? I dropped the comb and zipped through the stable door to the driveway. There on the opposite side of the fence stood Pearl mooing with everything she had. Poor baby. What could be wrong? And where was Wade?

I found him with the mama cow on the far side of the barn. "What are you doing?"

He said something to the cow and made his way to me. "They can't stay together forever." Wade gestured toward the calf beyond the gate. "She's the last one to wean. I should have separated them before now."

"I wish you had." The poor calf and her mama tried to reach each other through the fence. They both wailed for one another. My chest tightened. I sprinted to the gate. Fumbled with the latch. I had to put a stop to this. I had to set the calf free.

A mama and her baby needed to be together.

~

Wade jolted to Maggie's side. What was she doing? "Stop. Now."

His warning didn't sway her. He wrapped his arms around her from behind. A surge of frustration welled up inside him. He wrenched her away from the fence with her kicking and crying.

"She needs her mama, and her mama needs her."

With the pounding of his heart echoing in his ears, he released Maggie and turned her to face him. He wanted to scold her. But he detected pain in her eyes. Grief? Regret? He pulled her closer and held her. "The calf will recover in a few days. She'll join the others after she's weaned." He closed his eyes and inhaled the sweet fragrance of Maggie's hair, longing to run his hand through her soft waves, but he held back.

She seemed to relax, and he loosened his hold on her. With his arm over her shoulder, he led her through the barn and back to the stable. He pointed to a wooden bench along the wall in front of the tack room. "Sit and tell me what happened. Why did you try to open the gate?"

Maggie sat but said nothing.

Wade took a seat next to her. "I'm here if you're ready to talk about it."

Her eyes widened, and she bowed her head. "Talk about what?"

"Something caused your outburst over the cow and her calf. What was it?" He rubbed the back of his neck.

She jumped up and bolted to the horse stalls. "Time to finish with Copper and start on Champ." She retrieved the comb from the floor of the stall.

Wade left the stable, his neck muscles tight. Was he ready to learn the truth? Without knowing for certain, he could pretend none of his suspicions were real.

He headed to the house, kicking gravel as he walked. Why had he embraced and offered comfort to someone he didn't trust?

Lord, what are you doing?

Twelve

When I arrived home from the Ruby farm, after what seemed like a long morning, I called and made an appointment for my mom to have her cough checked. Respectable men still existed, didn't they? Except for Wade. I sighed. Perhaps Doctor Stewart? A teeny bit of flirting with the man couldn't hurt. Jill didn't need him with two additional men vying for her attention.

I fixed myself a cup of coffee. This morning had been tough. Brushing Copper wasn't bad, but Champ didn't like me using the hoof pick. He almost kicked me. And I didn't have time to muck out their stalls. Wade said that was my job, and I'd start with that first thing on Wednesday. I huffed and stomped my foot. The more I was near him, the more bothersome he became.

"Where did you run off to so early this morning?" Mom slid into a kitchen chair.

I stared at my coffee cup. I wasn't ready to admit I had to work with Wade to pay off her cow. She'd interrogate me to find out if the two of us had made amends. "Errands. And I made you a doctor appointment for 1:00 this afternoon."

"Splendid." A mischievous grin spread across her

face. "I hope you plan to tell him that you're available, because if you don't, I will."

"Please don't interfere with my love life."

"Your love life?" She chuckled and removed an apple from the fruit bowl on the table. "I meant mine. I'd love to find a gorgeous young man to take care of me in my golden years."

Mom made me laugh. The playful grin on her face brightened my morning, and I kissed her cheek. "I love you, Mama." I turned toward the door to the bed-and-breakfast shared area. "After I check the rooms upstairs and verify everything is in its place, I'll take Snowbunny outside for his exercise." I dashed through the door.

After his exercise, I changed into something I hoped would catch the eye of the handsome Doctor Stewart.

~

Reed prayed a short blessing over lunch and asked Wade how his morning went with Maggie.

"I should never have agreed with this crazy idea of yours. She can't do anything. More of a burden than help."

"Give her a chance. She needs tender guidance and understandin'. Those are traits I've seen in you often. Don't let somethin' she did twenty years ago interfere with what the Lord may want to do in her now."

"What are you talking about?" His posture stiffened, and he crossed his arms. "Tender guidance and understanding?"

"From what Lou told me, Maggie's dad was hard on her. Her actions all those years ago may have been driven by him.

Wade took a bite of his sandwich, shook his head, and swallowed. "That makes little sense. Her dad was a remarkable guy. How can she think otherwise?"

Reed stood, moseyed to the opposite side of the table, and placed his hand on Wade's shoulder. "Often a tiny thing festers and grows until it becomes a big problem. Somethin' he said may have hurt her, or she might have misunderstood him. Happens all the time. And maybe between you and Maggie too?"

"Nope. She made it clear a long time ago. She wanted nothing to do with me or my proposal."

"Well, I'm sure people have misinterpreted somethin' I've said or done. So, if I've hurt you, please tell me. I want nothin' to hinder our relationship."

Wade rose and embraced his dad. "Not a thing. If I can accomplish half of what you have, I'll consider myself successful."

~

After we checked in at the doctor's office, we took our seats, and Mom updated her medical history form. Soft instrumental music filled the room, creating a calming ambiance.

"Look at this question." She shoved her clipboard at me. "Would you like the doctor to pray for you?" She checked the *Yes* box. "Done." She handed me the form and clipboard. "Will you take care of this for me?"

I carried the items to the assistant at the front desk. While I waited for her to end a phone call, a pair of gorgeous green eyes locked onto mine. With his wavy reddish-brown hair and a smile that lit up the office, I had to glance away. I didn't want him to think I found him to be the most attractive man I'd ever seen. But indeed, he was.

The assistant tapped her pen on the counter. "I'll take your form now."

I handed her the form and kept my eyes down.

"We'll call your mom back soon."

I thanked her and floated back to my seat.

"What happened to you?"

"What do you mean?"

"Your hands are shaking."

I clutched Mom's hand to steady my own. "I'm fine. But will it be okay if I wait for you in the car? I'm not feeling well, and I don't want to contaminate anyone."

Mom put her arm around my shoulder. "Maybe you should schedule an appointment for yourself."

"I need a little fresh air, and I'll be fine." I stood and darted to the door. Fresh air. Yes, that should do it. Why did seeing Doctor Stewart affect me the way it did? I don't dare flirt with him. He'd break my heart for sure.

Thirty minutes later, Mom climbed into the car. "Are you feeling better?"

I nodded. "How about you? What did the doctor say?"

"He gave me a prescription for cough medication and expressed a hint of sadness you didn't join me in the examination room." She nudged my arm. "He asked about you."

"Okay. Let's run to the drugstore and pick up your medicine." I backed out of my parking space and pulled out onto the road. "Did he pray for you?"

"Yes. Such a sweet man of faith." She touched her chest. "Aren't you curious about what he said about you?"

"If he said something nice, it only means no one has told him my blog posts cause some people trouble."

"If you realize your blog posts cause problems, why do you continue to write what you do?"

"I know some people get upset when I write about them, but others love to know what's going on."

"But at the cost of your love life?"

"I have no desire for a love life."

"But I want you happy and fulfilled as a wife and mother. What you wanted growing up."

I turned into the grocery store lot and parked so she could pick up her prescription. "Circumstances change. I've changed." I peered into Mom's eyes. "And you want grandchildren. I'm sorry I haven't provided them for you. But it won't happen." A knot tightened in my belly.

"Honey, don't you think it's time to move forward?"

"I have. I love my life the way it is."

"Then I hope you won't be mad at me."

My eyes grew wide, and I glared at her. "What did you do?"

"I invited Doctor Stewart to join us this evening for dinner."

Thirteen

Mom entered the store alone, and I stayed in the car. I crossed my arms and huffed. I'm a grown woman and she wanted to arrange my dates. And with the new doctor? No man had captured my attention like he had since I first met Wade. And that only caused pain and heartache.

I tapped my chin and glanced across the street to Ivan's Ice Cream Shop. Let's see if I can cure her of interfering with my love life. There's got to be someone who I can invite to dinner for Mom. I covered my mouth and giggled. Widower Ivan Romano may be the perfect candidate.

He'd eyed her two weeks ago when I took her to his ice cream shop. A nice-looking bald man with a gray beard and mustache. He and mom, with her full head of short, spiky, gray hair, would make a fabulous match. Time to invite him to dinner too.

I crossed Main Street and strolled into his shop. The moment I entered, the irresistible aroma of fresh-baked waffle cones floated toward me.

"Maggie dear. I'm delighted to see you." He flashed me a smile. "Where's your mama?" He stared out the window into the parking lot.

"She's shopping across the street. Fixing lasagna tonight for dinner, and she needed a few things."

He closed his eyes, gave his belly a quick rub, and opened them again. "Sounds scrumptious. I haven't had a real Italian dinner in ages."

"Please join us. She'll make plenty."

"That's kind of you, but I don't want to intrude."

"I'm sure if Mom were here with me, she'd invite you too."

"She would?" A look of pure delight lit up his face. "What time should I arrive?"

"Six o'clock will work." I turned and headed to the door.

"Wait." His voice echoed through the shop. "Don't you want ice cream?"

"Yes. Can you bring some with you for dessert?" I grinned. "Your choice."

He agreed, and I exited the store, crossed the street, and climbed into my car.

Mom was in for a treat.

An arranged date and free ice cream. What could be better?

~

With afternoon chores completed, Wade strode to his office in the stable and sat at his desk. How could Maggie think her dad was hard on her? From what Wade observed when he'd helped her dad out on their farm, Maggie held a special place in his heart. He always gazed at her with adoration. Wade shook his head. What had her dad done to hurt her?

Wade grabbed a pencil off his desk and snapped it in half. Maggie once held a special place in his heart too. Had he ever hurt her? He tossed the broken pencil into the trash. Was that why she'd lied to him?

He snagged his Bible and scolded himself for avoiding it for the past four days. His go to for hope and strength. He turned to a section titled "Listening and Doing" and read James 1:19.

He groaned. "Slow to become angry?"

Help me, Lord, to not lose my temper with Maggie. You know that's a struggle for me right now.

~

The clock on the range read 5:25 p.m. Time to tell Mom about our second dinner guest.

"How's dinner coming along? Do you need any help?"

She thanked me for my offer and pointed at the dessert cooling on the counter. "I baked a pie and got the salad ready while you tidied up the shared area, and I put the lasagna in the oven ten minutes ago."

"Is that an apple pie? The cinnamon smells heavenly."

"Yes."

"Perfect." I peeked at the stove. "Are you fixing anything else?"

"Garlic toast. Once I pop it into the toaster oven, it should be ready by 6:15. That's the earliest Doctor Stewart said he could arrive."

I twirled to model my white sundress covered in red and yellow flowers. "How do I look?"

"Beautiful as always." She stepped closer and embraced me. "I'm so glad you warmed up to the idea of having the new doctor come to dinner. You'll hit it off well with him."

I pulled out of her grasp. "We'll see." I motioned toward the hallway to her bedroom. "You should freshen up for our guests."

She took a step back and touched her neck. "Guests?"

I gave her my sweetest smile. "A surprise."

"What have you done?"

"I asked a charming gentleman who yearned for a delectable Italian meal to join us."

"Who?"

"You'll find out soon." I peered at the clock on the stove again. "He'll arrive in about twenty-five minutes."

She clutched her head and let out a piercing screech. "How could you do this to me?"

"I asked that same question after you informed me that you'd invited Doctor Stewart to dinner."

She zipped into the hallway, and I hoped next time she'd check with me before she asked someone over.

Ivan arrived on time, but Mom was nowhere to be seen. I welcomed him inside, and he handed me two containers of ice cream—vanilla bean and butter pecan.

"These will be perfect." I thanked him, led him to the living room, and asked if he'd like a sweet tea.

"Sounds good." His eyes grew large, and he patted his belly. "Did you hear the loud growl from my stomach? The aroma of a delicious Italian meal always awakens my senses."

"And Mom's homemade sauce is the best, bursting with the flavors of garlic and basil."

"Where is your mom?"

"She'll be out soon." I pointed to the sofa. "Let me get your tea and check on dinner."

I dashed to the kitchen, placed the ice cream in the freezer, and poured a glass of tea.

Mom joined me and shoved the garlic toast into the toaster oven. After she set the timer, she bolted past me, checked the lasagna, and muttered something unintelligible.

"What did you say?"

"You've taken things too far this time." With a firm grip on my arm, Mom led me to her bedroom and slammed the door behind us. "Inviting someone over. Why did you do that?"

"I did what you did to me."

"This is different." She gritted her teeth and tightened her fist.

"How? I'm an adult, like you. Is it acceptable for you to disregard what I want while expecting me to always consider your wishes?"

Mom took a deep breath and released it slowly. "Honey, your dad hasn't been gone for a year yet. Too soon for me to consider dating."

"But you said you wanted someone to take care of you in your golden years."

The front doorbell rang, and I twisted to face her bedroom door. "We'll need to discuss this later."

Mom stepped in front of me and blocked my escape. "Who did you invite?"

After I told her who and that he had arrived, she plodded to her bed, plopped down, and closed her eyes.

"One, two, three . . ."

Oh, my. Mom still counts to ten like when I was a child. Trying to stay calm with me? I don't think she was happy to learn that Ivan, the man who often flirted with her, was in our living room.

With a slight turn of the doorknob, I slipped out of her room, entered the kitchen, nabbed Ivan's tea, and hurried into the living room. The door leading to the front entrance, where we welcome our overnight guests, was open. I placed the glass of tea on an end table and made my way to the foyer.

Ivan and the town's new physician stood chatting as if they were the best of friends.

I touched Ivan's elbow. "Thank you for letting our other guest inside." I extended my hand to the gorgeous man in jeans and a well-fitted polo shirt. "Wonderful to meet you. I apologize for not welcoming you sooner."

"No problem. Ivan and I are already friends. I rent the apartment above his shop, and often go down for ice cream."

"How convenient." I led the gentlemen to our living room and handed Ivan his tea. "Would you like a glass of tea, Doctor Stewart?"

After he declined and requested a glass of water instead, he winked. "Save Doctor Stewart for when you visit my office. I'm Nick the rest of the time."

Mom ambled into the living room and greeted our two guests. "Please move the party into the kitchen. Dinner is ready."

Nick led the way, and we followed him and Mom into the kitchen. "Mrs. Stone, I haven't seen or smelled anything better since I moved to town. This is fine dining quality, but in a relaxed and intimate setting here in the kitchen. I like it."

Mom blushed and thanked him. He sat on her left while Ivan took a seat on her right, and I sat across the table from her.

Nick offered a prayer of thanksgiving at Mom's request, and she scooped a large helping of lasagna onto each of our plates.

Mom, who's usually a big talker, said little throughout dinner. When she asked or answered questions, she attempted to avoid eye contact with Ivan, focusing instead her attention on Nick. When Ivan offered to help her clean up the kitchen before dessert, I asked Nick to join me on the back porch. He jumped up without hesitation and pulled the door closed behind him.

"This fresh air and slight breeze provide a pleasant change." He walked to the swivel rocker along the left side of the porch and sat. "Was it warm and stuffy inside, or did I imagine your mom wasn't in the mood for Ivan's company?"

I sighed and took a seat on the rattan bench up against the house. We could both overlook the backyard and view the flower garden on our right and the container plants near the steps. "She wasn't too happy I invited him to dinner. I hope he accepted my invitation simply for the Italian meal and not with any intention of forming a meaningful relationship with her. She made it clear to me that she's not ready to date."

"Appears that she wanted to make it clear to him too." He crossed his ankle over his knee. "Seems like a nice guy."

"He is, but it's a tad soon. Perhaps with us out of their way, Ivan can soften her up."

He nodded with his eyes locked on mine. "So, what hobbies or interests do you pursue when you're not working around here?"

"I enjoy my garden, my dog—he's spending the evening in a spare room upstairs—and writing my blog posts."

"Your blog? I'm familiar with that." His eyes

crinkled at the corners. "You enjoy eliciting reactions from your readers, don't you?"

"Is that bad?" I narrowed my eyes and tapped my foot.

He winced and lifted his palms. "I believe it's healthy to ruffle some feathers occasionally. Keeps us alert."

"Few people around here agree with you. Some individuals can't be pleased, regardless of what I write. And I only write the truth."

"My goal is to stay on your good side." He chuckled. "So you'll write positive things about me."

I raised my eyebrows and tilted my head. "We'll wait and see if there's enough room for you on my good side."

Fourteen

After I drained my orange juice glass and placed it in the sink, I grabbed a peanut butter and dark chocolate protein bar from the pantry. Another early morning at the Ruby farm. Today had to be better than Monday. At least I got to rest yesterday. I needed it to recuperate. And who wouldn't want to start their day with mucking out stalls?

"Are you heading out early again this morning?" Mom yawned and pushed a clump of hair off her forehead. "Where do you go this early?"

I hugged her and kissed her cheek. "I want to check on your calf and make sure the Rubys are taking care of her."

"This early?" She padded to the coffeepot. "Let me take a shower and join you."

"No time to wait. I've got a lot to do this morning. My blog post goes out at 9:00 a.m., and you know how much I enjoy reading comments on Wednesdays. And I must bake cookies for the children's home." I gave her shoulder a soft squeeze. "After I drop off the cookies this afternoon, we can swing by to visit Pearl and, if you'd like, go to the strawberry farm to pick fresh, juicy berries." I didn't have the heart to tell her that Wade wanted us to change Pearl's name.

Mom pressed her lips together. "We have guests checking in after 3:00 p.m., so we won't have time for berry picking."

I thanked her for keeping track of guests and assisting me. Working with Wade three mornings a week now, I realized how much I relied on my mom's help and how grateful I was to have her living with me.

"Before I go, I want to apologize for last night." I dropped my chin to my chest and frowned. "I shouldn't have invited Ivan to dinner without talking with you first. That was childish of me."

"And I shouldn't interfere with your love life." She peeked out the kitchen window. "Don't you worry about it. All ended well."

Was that a twinkle in her eye?

"It did?" I lifted my eyebrows. "Please elaborate on that comment."

She chuckled. "Don't you have some place you need to be?"

"We'll talk about this later." I told her goodbye and drove to the Ruby farm.

I slammed on my brakes when I pulled into their driveway and tipped my head back to get a clear view through my windshield. A black, wrought-iron, arched sign loomed above me. I twisted my neck from left to right. "Ruby Ranch." The silhouette of a cow hovered between the two words. I snickered. What in the world?

No one in Pleasant Springs owned a ranch. Only farmers here. But I didn't dare write a blog post about my former boyfriend. And I knew this sign was his idea and not his dad's.

I continued down the driveway and parked near the

barn. No sign of Wade. I climbed out and wandered into the stable where my work awaited me. Two dirty horse stalls. I put on my ugly black boots and hurried behind the stable to check on the horses. They grazed in a grassy penned area near a small pond, where the high-pitched chirping of grasshoppers filled the air.

Wade approached from behind and stood next to me. "After you muck their stalls, I'll get them back inside for you to groom." He walked toward the horses and raised his voice. "Today, I want you to start with their hooves while I supervise." He stopped and turned toward me. "Questions?"

I saluted him with a full grin. "No. Sir. I can do this." I darted inside the stable. How hard could it be to shovel up poop? I found a large, heavy shovel and moved an empty wheelbarrow in front of the stall entrance. Inside, I scooped up the droppings, coughed, gagged, and coughed again. After four scoops of droppings and wood shavings, my shoulders and arms ached. There must be a better way.

Wade loomed outside the stall and eyed the wheelbarrow. "Those extra shavings you're throwing away are going to come out of your wages." He smirked, turned around, and strode over to a pitchfork along the wall. When he returned, he handed it to me. "Use this. Scoop, then shake it so the shavings fall out, leaving the manure for the wheelbarrow."

"That makes sense." I took the pitchfork, scooped up the next batch of poop along the edge of the stall, and jostled the shavings away. "Like this?"

He moved the wheelbarrow out of the doorway and joined me inside. "You're shaking it too hard and making a bigger mess by breaking up the manure." He snatched the pitchfork from my grip. "Shake it like this." He shook it with a gentler touch and closer to the ground, which saved more shavings and kept the droppings intact.

I remembered his gentleness with me, too, many years before. The way he'd tuck my hair behind my ear and place soft kisses on my neck.

With a quick jerk, I straightened to attention and hoped I hadn't shared my innermost thoughts aloud. "What?"

"I said, 'Can you handle this now?'"

"Yes." I averted my eyes. He treated me like a child. Like my dad used to talk to me. I wouldn't allow that to bother me. Or the memories. I'm a strong, independent woman now. I yanked the pitchfork from his hands. No man will take advantage of me again. Especially Wade. I'll show him what I'm capable of. He'll miss me when I get Mom's cow paid off and I'm no longer helping him on his fancy ranch.

I finished mucking Copper's stall and moved to Champ's. Not sure what came next, I strolled outside to search for Wade but found Reed instead. After we greeted each other, I said, "What do I do in the stalls after I scoop up the droppings?"

He led me back to the stable and showed me where they kept the new shavings. "You're goin' to put these down where you scraped up the wet shavin's."

I blinked several times and grimaced. "Wet shavings?"

"You don't want those horses sleepin' in their urine, do you?"

"Oh. So, they sleep on the shavings too? I guess I forgot about that."

Reed wrinkled his nose. "Didn't Wade show you what to do?"

"Not really."

Wade sauntered in and removed his cowboy hat. "Miss know-it-all said she could handle it. So, I let her. With the horses safely out of her reach, I thought she'd do okay."

I crossed my arms and scoffed. "But you knew I didn't have any experience. You should have realized I'd need some instruction."

Reed shook his head and looked from me to Wade. "You two act like you're still kids. Grow up and work together on this." He squinted and fixed his eyes on the two of us. "Do you think it pleases the Lord when you act this way?"

I spoke in a loud whisper. "You tell him, Reed."

Wade scowled and narrowed his eyes. "He's including you in his sermon. Have you checked your attitude lately?"

Reed flinched and backed away. "That's it. I'm goin' inside to pray for the both of you." He rushed out the stable door.

I sank onto the bench and stared at the stalls that still needed my attention. "Do you think he'll pray for me?"

"If he said he will, then yes. He's praying now." Wade took a seat next to me.

"I can't believe anyone would pray for me." I gazed into Wade's blue eyes.

Wade shifted on the bench. "I'm sure your mom does. And Lou. She prays for you too."

"Lou? Why would she pray for me? She's nice to me, but . . ." I lowered my head and moaned.

Most likely, she prayed I'd become a nicer person.

~

Wade stood and made his way to the stalls. He couldn't empathize with Maggie. He needed to remain disinterested in everything concerning her. Sad that she didn't think anyone cared enough about her to pray for her. Then again, if she treated others the way she'd treated him, didn't she deserve his attitude? He entered Champ's stall and ran his boot over the shavings. No, his dad was right. The Lord expected him to show kindness to everyone. And that included Maggie.

He glanced at her sitting on the bench. "Come over and let me show you what's left to do." He apologized for leaving her without guidance and showed her how to finish cleaning the stalls.

When he returned later, she had just spread the new shavings. She'd done well. But he didn't want to praise her too much. He didn't want her ego to inflate. He remembered it being a problem in the past and wasn't sure if she'd outgrown it.

"The stalls look better." He kept his expression blank. "Take the wheelbarrow out to the dump pile and unload it." He took her to the back doors of the stable and pointed to the pile.

"Why is it so far away? Can't I dump it there?" She motioned to an area closer to where they stood.

"What acts like a magnet for flies?"

"Poop?"

"Do you want more flies this close to the stable?"

She crinkled her nose and rolled out the wheelbarrow. When she returned, he had Champ in his stall, ready for his grooming.

"Can't I start with Copper? He's easier to work

with."

"Champ was the one closest to the stable and easier to round up. He'll behave."

"And how do you know that?"

"Just do."

She peered up at him and smiled. "He must have listened to your dad's sermon too."

Wade couldn't allow himself to be drawn in by her beautiful smile, but he needed to overcome his hostility toward her. Following Christ's example had been a way of life for him until he returned home and faced the woman who had scorned him. Wade scanned the stable wall across from him. He couldn't fall for her tricks again.

Fifteen

When I returned home, I showered and went to work baking two dozen chocolate chunk cookies for the kids at the children's home. While the cookies baked, I opened my computer to check comments from my blog post. This week's post would be popular among the townsfolk. They loved knowing who's dating whom.

The first comment came from someone I didn't know. "Would love to know her secret. I haven't had a date in six years."

The next one from Anonymous said, "You should be ashamed of yourself. Eddie is a magnificent example of a godly man. And why raise questions about Jill? We know she's a warm-hearted woman of God." I chuckled and raised my brows. Anonymous must be the president of Jill's fan club.

Comment three read, "I agree with your description of our new doctor. The sight of him makes my heart skip a beat."

And comment number four came from one of Dad's old friends who works at the hardware store. "You were hard on Eddie. He's quiet, but he's the best mechanic this side of the Mississippi."

True. Without fail, he could diagnose the problem

with my car just from my description. And he repaired it every time.

I'd follow up with comments after I removed my cookies from the oven.

Their enticing aroma drifted through the air as the chocolate chunks melted and oozed from the warm dough. After placing them on a cooling rack, I resisted the urge to gobble up one and went in search of my dog.

I found Mom dusting upstairs with Snowbunny at her feet. "Time for Snowbunny's walk out back before lunch." His ears perked up at the mention of his name. "Ready, boy?"

He raced me down the stairs and won. My mind lingered on other things. Will Wade learn to tolerate me again? I sometimes wonder if he ever cared for me.

I'm convinced his proposal was out of duty and not for love.

~

Things had gone better this morning. Maggie showed interest and wanted to do well. If she worked faster, Wade would have additional tasks for her. Tasks that would free him up to complete other, more enjoyable chores. But he'd felt no joy when she told him she would return this afternoon with her mom. Their visit would only put him further behind.

He led Copper to the trough of fresh water. They both raised their eyes at the sound of gravel. Wade sighed and Copper whinnied. "You mean you're not thrilled about her return either?"

Wade met them on the barn side of the driveway where Maggie had parked her car.

Mrs. Stone climbed out first. "I love your new

Ruby Ranch sign."

He thanked her and looked at Maggie. "And what do you think?"

"I would have considered Twin Hills Ranch, because you can spot two hills when you drive in."

"A decent name."

"Ruby Ranch fits this place well. The perfect name." Mrs. Stone squeezed his arm.

He smiled and thanked her again.

Her eyes scanned the property. "Where's my Pearl?"

"That must be her bawling over that way." Maggie pointed behind the barn. "But I need to tell you something."

Wade cleared his throat and ran his fingers along his chin. "We need to tell you that I separated Pearl from her mama on Monday, and I moved her behind the barn. She can still see her mama though, and they continue to cry for one another." He lifted his elbow in a gesture of politeness to Mrs. Stone. "The grass is thicker and greener there."

Mrs. Stone wrapped her elbow around his.

He glanced at Maggie. Her face lit up with a grin when he mentioned Pearl's name and expressed an interest in her mom.

They strode a short distance past the barn and stopped before the driveway gate where Pearl grazed with another young heifer. Mama cow had drifted ten or more feet away from the fence but made her way back often to check on her calf.

"She's such a beauty." Mrs. Stone released Wade's arm. "Thank you so much for allowing her to stay here."

"My pleasure." He tipped his hat.

Mrs. Stone reached her hand over the top of the fence and raised her voice as if she was talking to a dog. "Oh Pearl. Sweet Pearl. Come here, girl."

The calf looked up. She fixed her big brown eyes on the lady wearing pink capris and a white top. Pearl took a step toward the fence.

Mrs. Stone's voice filled with giddiness when she turned to Maggie. "She's coming closer. She likes me."

"Of course she does, Mom. Everyone likes you."

Wade caught Maggie's eye. "I'd like to discuss something with you." He motioned across the driveway to the stable, where they could have a conversation without her mom overhearing.

Maggie told her mom that she'd return soon and followed him inside.

"Why haven't you told your mom about our arrangement? Why the charade?"

She shrugged and shook her head. "She's always liked you. If she knows I'm working with you three days a week, she'll make me miserable with questions about how we're getting along. I want to discourage the ideas that might enter her head."

"I get it." He nodded and retreated a step. "But isn't the truth the best?"

She cringed and avoided his eyes. "Not what I've found."

Mrs. Stone entered the stable and rubbed her eyes. "I'm ready to go now." She covered her mouth to hide her yawn. "I'd like to go home and rest."

Wade walked them out to their car and whispered to Maggie. "Tell her the truth and make sure she understands we're not interested in renewing our relationship. This is a business deal."

Maggie's dark brown eyes peered into his.

Did she hope to rekindle that spark?

~

With a tingling sensation climbing up my neck, I climbed into my car. Doctor Stewart might be the most attractive man I've ever seen, but he didn't have Wade's adorable dimples. When he grinned at my mom, my heart melted. That's what drew me in when he helped Dad on our farm. That and his bright blue eyes. The gray, now peppered throughout his dark brown hair, only made him more appealing.

Mom waved goodbye while I backed the car down the driveway. We drove back through town and stopped at Creekside Children's Home.

"I'll only be a minute because you want to rest."

She thanked me, and I made my way to the front door. I rang the buzzer, and Lanie greeted me with a sneer.

"Oh goodie. Look who's back. Miss Uncaring."

"What do you mean, uncaring? I care about everyone."

"Then why don't you tell the complete story in your blog posts?"

I stepped back and waved her off. "I rewrote your story the way you asked me to."

"But you're still up to your tricks and writing half-truths." Lanie pushed the door closed a few inches. "That's uncaring, if you ask me."

I lunged forward and jammed my foot into the doorway. "But I planned to ask you if things were going well with Luke's foster son, Billy."

She scrunched up her face. "Billy is no concern of

yours."

"But I care about him and his friend. What was her name? Kylee? I think about them both often."

"Don't bother." She tried to close the door, but my foot didn't budge.

"Excuse me?" I pushed my shoulder against the door, reopening it several inches, and shoved my plate of cookies at her. "What gives you the right to treat me this way?"

"When you attack my family and friends in your blog post, I have every right." Lanie grabbed the cookies.

"I said nothing untrue."

"Ladies?" Todd interrupted our quarrel and focused on Lanie. "I'll take care of this." He took the plate of cookies from her and eyed me. "You touched on a nerve or two with your post this morning. In the future, call me before you stop by, and I'll meet you at the door."

A knot formed in the pit of my stomach. "Oh, I suppose I can do that." I took a step back and bristled at his comment. "Are you on her side or mine?"

"Side?" He gave off a stern vibe. "I can't side with either of you. Haven't read the post yet. But if what I just witnessed from Lanie and what she told her sister on the phone earlier, I'd say you upset people today."

I turned and bolted to my car. He didn't deserve a response. That may be the last batch of cookies I deliver. And forget about volunteering in the clothing closet.

After I slammed my door, I backed out of my parking space and onto the road.

"Is everything okay?"

"It seems my post has certain people upset with me."

Mom twisted to face the passenger window.

I turned south on Main Street and headed home. "What did you think of it?"

"I haven't read it."

"Why not?"

She gazed out the window. "They upset me too much."

"What? Why?" I turned east toward home and peeked at her.

She stared at me with her lip curled upward. "The information you share is often private. If I need to know, I'll learn it from those involved."

I turned into our driveway. "How long have you felt this way?"

"Since I moved in with you." She continued to stare at me. "Honey, I consider a lot of what you write to be gossip."

"Gossip?" My chest tightened, and I gaped at her. "Do you really think I'm a gossip?" A car pulled in behind me. "Appears that our guests arrived an hour early."

I climbed out to meet our guests, but Jill Drake met me instead with clenched fists.

Sixteen

I backed away and put my hands up. "Whoa. What is your problem?"

Jill stopped in front of me, glanced at Mom, and greeted her.

Mom returned a greeting and headed to the back door. "You girls can have your conversation on the back porch and hopefully you'll allow the tranquil sounds of God's chirping birds to soothe your hearts and minds. I'm going inside to take a nap."

We climbed the stairs, and I sat on the bench. Jill took a seat across from me in a matching chair.

"How could you?" Jill raised her voice. "How could you hurt Eddie like that?"

I raised my eyebrows and steepled my fingers under my chin. "I only reported the truth. He's shy."

"Shy? You think that's all you said?" She stood and paced across the porch. "You said he sounded like a caveman with his grunts and brief responses. Then you renamed him Barney after a television character and implied he's goofy."

"I reported the truth."

"Who was your eyewitness?" With a sudden spin, she faced me, her eyes locked onto mine. "You implied

I gave you the information."

"Not true. I said I had an eyewitness account. I sat in the booth behind yours and caught the whole thing."

She took a seat next to me on the bench. "Then why didn't you report what he shared from his heart about his deep love for the Lord? Or the passion in his voice as he spoke about his family and how he enjoys helping others. He loves God and people. Why did you omit those things in your post?"

"I left before he said any of that."

Jill rose and shook her head. "You slandered his name. You judged him and didn't give him a chance to prove himself." She wiped her hand across her forehead. "I doubt Nick Stewart minded you calling him a hunk or Doc Winston got upset by saying he was a respectable guy with a corny sense of humor, but Eddie? Don't you ever think of others?"

I stood and narrowed my eyes. "Of course, I think of others."

"When? Give me an example because you're the most selfish person I know." Jill glared at me.

I'd kept calm to this point, but for her to say I'm selfish cut deep. She didn't know how much I'd given up in my life to put others first. I told her about the cookies I bake for the children's home each week.

She rolled her eyes and returned to her chair. "What else?"

"I'm working on a farm to pay off a cow for my mom because she wanted one since she had to sell her and Dad's farm."

Jill touched the base of her neck. "You're doing farm work? Like what?"

"Don't tell Mom." I pushed back my shoulders and

placed my hands on my hips. "I'm mucking stalls and grooming horses."

Her deep brown eyes grew wide. "Wow. I'm impressed."

"I can go on and tell you more, but I won't bore you with any further unselfishness on my part."

Her tone turned snooty and demeaning. "Oh, please bore me with another."

"Enough."

She stood and waved her hand in dismissal. "Well, if that's all."

"I broke off a relationship with the love of my life twenty years ago because of my dad." I stared at my feet. "That and another thing were the most unselfish things I've ever done." I raised my head and saw compassion in the eyes of someone who thought I was a terrible person.

She pinched her bottom lip. "I can relate to losing someone you love. Losing my husband left me empty and shattered. Apart from your dad, I didn't realize you'd lost someone close to you too."

I crossed my arms and smirked. "How could you? You and your friends are too busy hanging out together and enjoying each other's company. Why would you care about me and my life?"

"Of course we care about you. Yes, I'm upset right now, but I do care." She frowned and pointed her index finger at me. "I know what you're doing. Take the blame off you and the way you treated Eddie and put it on me and my friends." She furrowed her brows. "Let's talk about Eddie." Jill returned to her chair and sat.

"We've already discussed Eddie."

"But we didn't finish."

I sat again on the bench. "I have work to do, so make it quick."

"Eddie won't return my calls or texts. I think he blames me for this mess." She tapped her fingers on her thigh. "I need you to make it right."

"How?"

"Retract what you said about him. Make sure he understands you didn't receive any information from me." Jill fanned herself with her hand. "Also, tell him that you didn't hear the entire conversation. And set the record straight with your readers that only my time with Eddie was a date."

"Only Eddie?"

"Doc Winston and I expected his retiring assistant to join us, along with his niece, Emily, who is his new assistant. But neither of them came. And Nick and I are friends. He showed me house plans for the home he's building."

"I doubt my readers care about that."

"But Eddie does."

"Not my problem."

"Yes, it is. You wrote a lousy story and need to fix it. Because of what you said, and with his shyness, he may never have the courage to ask anyone out again."

"Then I'd be doing y'all a favor by sparing you from a dull date."

Jill squinted and leaned forward. "He may seem like a caveman to you, but he's an incredible guy."

I sagged back on the bench and lifted my palm upward. "I'll consider it." She wasn't about to win this confrontation. I'd done nothing wrong. Reported what I heard—the truth.

"Consider?" She tilted her head. "Don't you mean,

'I'll pray about it'? You pray, don't you?"

I stood and stuck out my chin. "Yes. I pray." I pointed to her car in the driveway. "Now move your car and leave. I have guests arriving soon."

Jill stomped down the steps and climbed into her car.

What did she want me to do? Retract my post?

Not going to happen.

Seventeen

After reviewing my updated blog post on Friday morning, I scheduled it to go live at 8:00 a.m. Not only had Jill asked me to retract my post, but Mom sided with her. She'd read the original and muttered that I'd crossed the line. I didn't agree, but to keep peace, I honored my mother's wishes. Not Jill's. I didn't owe her anything.

When I arrived at Ruby Ranch and couldn't find Wade, I got right to work on my jobs. I'd studied proper horse grooming and stall mucking by watching online videos on Thursday. Even when Wade showed me which brush to use after combing, he hurried through it. Today I would do a thorough job without his help.

The two stalls stood empty, and I got to work cleaning them with a new technique I'd learned. I finished in record time. An hour. I stepped to the back door of the stable and peered through the window, to where Copper and Champ feasted on grass near the pond. Did Wade expect me to get them into the stable for their brushing?

I scanned the stable for a treat to entice them to follow me and found carrots in a small bin. With one in hand, I tugged open the back door, went outside, and held out the carrot to them while a robin perched on the fence observed my every move.

Copper hesitated before approaching me in a slow walk. I backed away, and he followed me to his stall, where he munched on his carrot. About halfway through his grooming, Champ wandered inside.

"You want a treat too?" I made my way to the treat shelf and pulled out another carrot from the bin. "Follow me to your stall."

He whinnied and moved his head up and down.

"Hurry now, or I'll give your treat to your friend." Champ approached me where I waited in front of his stall, followed me inside, and accepted the carrot. "Good boy." I slipped out, closed the half door, and returned to Copper's grooming.

Where was Wade? A few minutes later, I stopped grooming and looked out both doors. Still no sign of him. After I finished with Copper, I walked to the stable's main door. Reed's car sat in the driveway at the back of the house, but no sign of Wade's pickup. Who cares? Not my problem. I shrugged. Time to groom Champ.

I gathered the comb and brushes and moved to Champ's stall. A little while later, a truck door slammed, and Wade sauntered inside the stable.

"I need your help out back." He entered the tack room and returned with two bridles. He placed the bridles on hooks outside of each horse stall and reentered the tack room. When he came out again, he unlatched Champ's door, shoved a saddle at me, and turned. "You saddle up Copper, and I'll take Champ."

The curry comb fell from my hand, and I dropped

the heavy saddle to the floor. "But I haven't groomed Champ yet. I'm just getting started."

Wade spun to face me and thrust out his chin. "What takes you so long?"

"I mucked the stalls, got Copper and Champ into them, and brushed Copper."

"That's it?" He peeked at his watch. "You've been here for two hours and that's all you've gotten done?"

I rubbed a knot that had formed in my abdomen. I'd tried to get the job done and done right. And all he gave in return was ridicule. What had him so upset this morning?

His eyes darted between the two main stable doors. "Did you close the front door when you went out back to bring them in?"

I glared at him and huffed. "Why would I do that?"

He stepped closer to me, his posture stiff. "What would you have done if they had both escaped out the front?"

I stared at the front door. He was right. They could have run down the driveway and out onto the road. Why hadn't I thought of that? My breathing became labored, and I refocused my attention on Wade. "It won't happen again."

"Next week I need you to get both stalls spotless within thirty minutes. And finish both horses' grooming within an hour. Plenty extra chores around here, and I expect your help if you want me to keep a cow for your mom." He pointed to the saddle.

"What about blankets? Don't you use them too?"

He turned toward the tack room and mumbled. "I'll get them."

The videos I'd watched said horses needed to be

groomed before and after a ride. Champ wasn't ready to be saddled up. I grabbed the curry comb off the floor, latched the half door, and got busy.

Tension rose in Wade's voice. "What are you doing? I said we must head out back now. The storm last night caused fence damage. We can't afford to lose any cattle to the neighboring farms." He lowered the blankets to the floor.

I stopped grooming Champ and stepped closer to the door. "Is that why you're so worked up today? Your fences?"

He scowled and pointed his index finger at me. "You."

I took a step back, stumbled over the saddle I'd dropped, and caught my balance. "Me? Why me?"

Champ stomped his front left hoof twice and whinnied.

Unsure of what the horse wanted to communicate, I edged away from him.

"That blog post of yours. What's the matter with you?"

I swung open the stall's half door and slammed it shut. Did everyone hate me for my blog post? I retracted and rewrote it. What else could I do?

I glanced at my watch and lifted my head high. "The retraction and rewrite went out two minutes ago. I apologize for being such a failure." I bolted from the stable and zipped to my car.

Now I needed to deal with my mom's displeasure with me. After today, she'd no longer have a cow to call her own.

I'm sure Wade will fire me.

~

"Maggie, wait." Wade jogged to her car and softened his voice. "I'm sorry I got frustrated with you. Instead of coming at you the way I did, I should have asked you about the blog post."

She didn't respond and kept her hand glued to her car door handle.

He hunched his shoulders and dipped his head. "You did a fine job on the stalls and you're improving every day."

She let go of the door handle and shook out her hand but didn't make eye contact. "I haven't used the hoof pick on either horse yet. I wanted you to supervise me again to make sure I don't hurt them."

He placed his hand on her lower back. "Let's return to the stable and finish their grooming, and then we'll saddle up and head out back."

She released a heavy sigh and pinched her bottom lip. "Okay."

"Ready?" He turned toward the stable.

They made their way back to the horses, where he assisted in Champ's grooming and guided Maggie one more time through cleaning the horses' hooves.

"You've got this." He smiled. "Next week, you'll be an expert."

He instructed her on how to saddle Copper while he saddled Champ. "Make sure the saddle's tight." After a few minutes, they headed out. "I made some repairs in the fence earlier, but there may be other places in need. I want you to ride west to the fence line, and I'll take the east. Travel north along the fence and note anything requiring repair. Take care to check behind trees or shrubs for downed branches. We'll meet up in the middle of the back fence."

She squirmed in her saddle and blinked several times. "What if I run into trouble?"

"You shouldn't run into any trouble. Call me on my cell if you do." He made sure she had his number and noted hers on his phone.

She rose an inch and wiggled in her seat. "How long do you expect this to take?"

"Are you getting saddle sores already?"

"I haven't done this for a long time." Her eyes crinkled at the corners, adding a touch of charm to her already appealing appearance.

"Maybe an hour."

She squirmed again and repositioned herself in the saddle. "Okay. I'm ready."

Maggie headed to the western fence line, and Wade turned to the east. Most of the ranch lay to the north.

He'd already checked a large area of fencing that morning and rode to the place where he'd stopped earlier. He made his way along the northern fence line to the larger pond at the back of the property and waited while Champ enjoyed a drink.

After he'd spent fifteen minutes at the pond listening to a symphony of frogs chirping, he mounted his horse and rode in search of Maggie. She should have joined him by now. Had she gone home after all? Why was he so harsh with her? He raked his hand through his hair. Because she had a knack for irritating him. That's why.

A glimpse of movement behind a tree to his right caught his attention. He urged Champ closer and squinted in the bright sunlight.

Copper grazed on plush, green grass. His saddle

had shifted to his left side, but he didn't seem to mind. Wade's neck prickled. What happened to Maggie? He gripped the reins, leaned forward, and urged Champ into a gallop to find her. *Lord, I get upset with her and she makes me crazy, but please take care of her. Help me find her safe and unhurt. Keep your loving hands upon her.*

He drew close to a lump in the tall, dense grass.

A beautiful lump with long wavy dark hair.

Eighteen

My left side and legs ached. Thankful I hadn't landed on my head, I moaned and curled up into a ball. Would Wade bother to find me? I wasn't sure if I could make it back to the stable on my own.

I strained to sit up at the sound of a horse's hooves growing louder.

Wade flew off Champ as soon as he brought the horse to a stop. "Are you okay? Can you stand up?"

"I ache all over but haven't tried to stand yet."

He asked me to move different parts of my body and when everything checked out okay, he wrapped his arm around my shoulder and helped me up. "Lean on me."

His compassion overwhelmed me.

"Are you in much pain?" His gaze met mine, and he tucked a stray strand of hair behind my ear, his touch tingling my skin. His eyes drifted down to my mouth.

Yes, please. Oh wait. No. My heart raced, and I closed my eyes.

I shot them open when a loud yowl in a nearby bush startled us both. A black and white feral cat pounced on something in the grass.

Wade loosened his hold on me. "That lizard

doesn't stand a chance."

The cat sprinted away, with its jaws gripping the squirming reptile.

Wade nudged me toward his horse. "I'll help you mount Champ and take you to the house. After you get settled, I'll ride back out and lead Copper to the stable."

I shook my head and groaned. "No horses. I have no intention of getting back on. I'll walk back."

"You can't walk back. It's nearly a half mile to the house. You can barely stand."

"I'll make it. You get Copper." I scanned the surrounding pastureland. "Which direction is the house?" I pointed to my left and crinkled my nose. "That way?"

He turned me in the opposite direction and gave me a lecture about the morning sun in the east and how the house was south of us.

I took two steps and winced. "I'm okay. You can go now."

"Stubborn woman." He placed his hand around my waist and led me to a large rock near a pine tree. "Sit and wait here. I'll be back with the truck."

"What if there's another reptilian creature? Even creepier than a lizard'?"

He surveyed the surrounding area and assured me that I was safe. After he helped me down onto the rock, he mounted Champ, waved goodbye, and galloped off for the house.

Despite the pain wracking my body, my heart softened at his tender care and almost kiss. Had his heart softened for me too? My eyes followed the path he and his horse had taken. Perhaps it's time to tell him the truth.

I wrapped my arms around me and imagined his arms holding me close until my phone vibrated in my pocket. I answered and greeted my mom.

"Where are you? I thought you'd be home by now."

"I'll be there soon."

"Jill called. She wants to meet you for lunch at Mama Lou's at noon."

"Okay. I'll call her at work." I hung up and gawked at my cell. What now? I did what she asked. Does she want to remind me of what a failure I am? I dialed Jill and left a message on her voicemail. "Noon works for me."

I peeked at my home screen—11:05. I'll never make it to Mama Lou's in time. What's taking Wade so long? I pulled myself up and limped toward the house. My muscles and joints loosened with each step. I can do this.

I'd trudged along for a minute when Wade stopped his truck in front of me.

"Couldn't you wait?" He took my elbow and led me to his pickup. After we buckled up, he made a U-turn in the grass, flew across the pasture, hitting ruts along the way, and stopped at the gate near the stable and barn. "Let me open the gate and take you to the house so you can rest awhile before you go home."

"I have lunch plans. I'll be fine."

With a sudden motion, he jerked his head back. "You feel okay to drive?"

"One or two bruises won't stop me." I cringed when I repositioned myself in my seat.

When he climbed back into the truck, I kept my voice calm and said, "I wouldn't have fallen if you had checked the saddle before our ride."

"Me?" He opened and closed his mouth without saying a word, before raising his voice. "I told you to tighten and check it."

I matched his severe tone. "And what do I know? I haven't ridden in twenty years."

"So, this is my fault?" He smacked his hand on the steering wheel and drove me to my car. "I hope you don't need any help to climb down. Time for me to get back to work."

I gaped at him and extended my hands, palms facing upwards. "How does someone go from being kind and concerned to someone who won't help me out of his truck?"

"Because you are still the most selfish person I know. I'm saddened you've changed little over the years." He dropped his head and shut his eyes. "You write about people meanly, blame others for your mess ups, and treat people with contempt."

"Oh, so you think you know me?" I opened the door, slid out, and landed on both feet with a thud. Do I do those things? Jill and Mom think so. Now Wade. My stomach twisted and turned.

If that's who I am, there's nothing I can do to change.

~

Wade backed down the driveway, parked his pickup in front of the barn, and climbed out. He untied Champ from the fencepost near the barn and mounted his horse. They trotted to the northern fence, found Copper, and led him back to the stable.

After he groomed the horses, he led them into the field. Why wasn't he able to admit the mistake was his?

He should have checked the saddle. Maggie wasn't as familiar with horses as he was. And scolding her only made things worse.

She aggravated him but sparked his curiosity too. He shrugged and let out a deep sigh. What was he supposed to do? He wanted to befriend her enough to learn the truth, but not so much that he'd want her back in his life. He kicked a clump of grass. And to think he almost felt the warmth of her lips against his own. Could never happen again. He could forgive her for the lies and turmoil she'd caused, but could he ever trust her?

He was certain he'd set the record straight, that he wasn't interested in her when he dropped her off at her car. She'd know the almost kiss was a fluke—a major mistake. He lowered his chin to his chest. If only he could convince himself.

He checked on Pearl in the pasture near the barn. She was doing better since being weaned. Didn't cry for her mama as often. But how had the loss of her baby affected her mama?

It must be difficult for a mama to be separated from her baby.

~

After sneaking past Mom, I changed into a pair of navy capris with a navy and yellow top, gathered my hair back into a ponytail, and slipped out the door. I drove faster than usual to Mama Lou's but still arrived five minutes late and found Jill already seated at a booth on the left.

She bent forward when I took a seat across from her. "Why are you limping? Did you hurt yourself?"

"I'm fine."

"And the grass in your hair?"

I ran my hand along my ponytail. "Fell off a horse this morning." I chuckled. "All in a day's work."

Jill's voice rose in pitch, and she covered her mouth. "And I guess you didn't have time to clean up afterward?"

"I changed. Didn't have time to shower." I leaned forward and spoke in a hushed tone. "Is it that noticeable?"

"A little." She giggled and waved her hand. "Order whatever you want. My treat."

"I rarely eat much for lunch. A coffee for me." I tapped my fingers on the table. I didn't appreciate that she found amusement in my appearance.

"Have you tried Lou's grilled chicken salad? Delicious." She flattened out a crease in her shirt.

Debbie Sue arrived at our table with a pad and pencil. She peered at me without a hint of emotion. "Your usual? Coffee?"

I nodded, and Jill ordered the grilled chicken salad and a sweet tea. Debbie Sue dashed away, and I focused on Jill. "What's the reason behind your lunch invite?"

"I wanted to thank you for retracting your blog post about me and for your apology to Eddie. I hope he reads it."

"Has he talked to you yet?"

"He still won't return my calls or texts, and he didn't answer his door when I went to his house yesterday. I'm hoping that will change with your updated post."

"Have you tried him at work?"

"Luke said to give him time. He wouldn't appreciate me bothering Eddie on the job."

I'd done what she asked. Did she want me to do more? Is that why she asked me to join her?

When Debbie Sue set our drinks on the table, Jill thanked her and turned to me. "I want to apologize for getting upset with you. I treated you unfairly when I said you were selfish. That's not true. I took my hurt and frustration out on you."

I rested my hands in my lap and stared at them. Do I tell her it's no big deal? Or tell her the truth? She hurt me.

She stretched her arm across the table and rested her hand near my coffee cup. "And I'm sorry I implied you don't pray." Her chin quivered, and she pulled her hand away. "That was cruel of me. I know from seeing you at church that you love the Lord as I do, and I'm sure you pray often."

I glanced at Jill and hoped the warmth moving up my neck wasn't noticeable. Pray often? Hardly at all. "I—"

Jill's food arrived, and she bowed her head. "Father, thank you for this food and for Maggie's willingness to rewrite her post. I ask You to bless her and hold her close. Amen."

"You prayed for me?"

Jill picked up her fork and wrinkled her forehead. "Of course, I did. I've prayed many times for you over the years."

"Why?"

She placed her fork on her plate. "Because we need to pray for each other. And because I care about you."

My throat tightened, and I pressed my fingers to my lips. Jill Drake cared about me?

Jill lifted her fork and laid it back down. "I've got a

terrific idea. Becca, Lanie, and I met on Monday evening to study the Bible. Why don't you join us next Monday? I mean Tuesday, because Monday is Memorial Day." She grinned. "We're studying the book of Proverbs."

I widened my eyes, and my voice squeaked. "A Bible study? With you, our pastor's wife, and your sister?"

Nineteen

As if I hadn't been through enough in one day, after I climbed out of a warm bath scented with soothing peppermint oil, my cell rang. Doctor Stewart. I hesitated to answer. My head already spun from my fall and the invitation to a Bible study.

My pulse quickened, and I accepted the call.

He greeted me and asked how my mother felt. After I responded she had improved, he said, "I know of a highly rated steak house in Chattanooga. Would you honor me with your presence this evening?"

I closed my eyes. I should say no. This has the potential to make my life more complicated. And to ask me out at 2:30 in the afternoon for dinner that evening?

"I apologize for calling so late. I wanted to ensure I could wrap up here at the office with enough time to change and pick you up." He cleared his throat and raised the pitch of his voice. "Tomorrow evening works, if that's better for you."

My stomach growled. How can I resist a mouthwatering steak dinner? I hope I won't regret this evening forever. "Sure. Tonight sounds great." I wiped perspiration from my brow. What was I doing?

After we decided he'd pick me up at 6:00, we

disconnected the call, and I wanted to kick myself. I didn't need a man. If I did, I'd want . . . No. He'd never care about me that way again.

I took Snowbunny for a walk and enjoyed the warm, soft breeze. When we neared the trees along the fence line, a squirrel perched above greeted us with his animated chatter, provoking my sweet dog to unleash his fiercest bark.

Upon our return to the house, we settled on the back porch and relaxed awhile. At least, my dog relaxed in a sunny spot. But my mind filled with a thick cloud of anxiety. I hadn't had a date in years. How was I supposed to act?

I smacked my forehead with an open palm. Oh, my goodness. Eddie. He didn't date often either. He was not only shy but nervous like me. I'd scoffed at his unfortunate situation, unable to empathize with his struggle.

I needed to fix this. Perhaps I could show Jill, Mom, and Wade that I'm not mean or selfish. With a sudden leap from my chair, I startled my dog out of his deep slumber. I had an important errand to run, but I had to be back to the bed-and-breakfast by 6:00 for my date. Could I speak with Eddie after PS Automotive closes at 5:00 p.m. and make it back here in time?

When I told Mom about my date and my plans to catch Eddie and make things right, she squealed and hugged me. I wasn't sure if her excitement resulted in me wanting to fix things with Eddie or because I had an actual date.

But before I could steal away to my room, she asked about my limp.

I told her about my arrangement with Wade to pay

him for Pearl and her upkeep and how I'd fallen from a horse.

"Oh, honey. I put a strain on your finances and your body. You should have told me that you didn't have the money to buy a cow."

"I have the money. Wade wouldn't accept it. He suggested I work off what I owed him instead."

She put her hands over her heart. "He wanted to spend time with you."

"Not at all. That's why I haven't told you until now." I frowned and touched her shoulder. "He needed extra help and hoped I'd learned something years ago when I lived on the farm."

Mom chuckled and patted her thigh. "I'll bet that hasn't gone well. You did nothing on the farm except take an occasional ride on the horse."

"Wade figured that out and wasn't too happy about my lack of knowledge." I snickered. "But I'm improving."

"Of course you are. You'll be the best farm hand he's ever hired."

"I doubt that, but I'm going to try."

I hobbled to my room, selected a black sleeveless dress and strappy black sandals, and laid them out on my bed.

After I applied my makeup, I dressed and added a silver heart necklace and dangling earrings to my ensemble. I loved to dress up much more than wear jeans and old T-shirts. This date with Doctor Stewart is what I needed to get my mind off my past with Wade.

A past with a secret. But . . . I sighed. On Monday, I'll tell him.

But only if he's in a decent mood.

~

Wade wrapped up his late afternoon chores and jogged to the house. He expected something delicious and hoped for meat and potatoes. As soon as he stepped inside, the aroma of meatloaf hit him. "Baked potatoes too?"

Lou sagged against the kitchen counter and scowled. "What kind of greeting is that?"

"Sorry, ma'am." He lowered his eyes, lifted them again, and greeted her properly. "Smells remarkable in here, and I'm starving."

"Wash up and help me with a salad."

He hurried to the sink and did as she asked. "So, when are you getting married?" He gathered a medium-sized bowl and the fixings for a salad.

"We considered September, but we found out Lanie Meadows and Luke Gibson are plannin' for then. We don't want to take away from their ceremony. So now we're lookin' at next month."

He dropped the head of lettuce into the bowl. "That soon? June?"

Her eyes sparkled, and she nodded. "Ours will be a small weddin'. Nothin' fancy."

Reed walked into the kitchen and wrapped his arms around Lou from behind and snuggled her neck. "No need to wait."

"When in June?"

"The sixteenth."

"Three weeks from now?" Wade sneered and shook his head. "When did you plan to tell me?"

"Tonight, at dinner. We set the date after Lou got here this afternoon."

Wade picked up the head of lettuce and continued

to make the salad.

"Think about who you want to invite. Would be nice if you had a date." Reed eyed Wade while he kissed Lou's cheek.

"I don't want to invite anyone." He added grape tomatoes to the salad. "I'll check out your guest list. Maybe I can pair up with someone at the ceremony or reception afterward." He strode to the pantry and nabbed a bag of croutons. "There will be a party, won't there?"

Reed released Lou and took a seat at the table. "We'll have party snacks and a cake at the café after the ceremony." He gazed at Lou and rubbed the back of his neck. "I called our pastor, and he's not available. He's gonna take a sabbatical starting the first of June and will have others in the church bring the message each week until he returns in August."

"That's too bad." She arched her brow and smiled. "Let's try Becca's husband, Pastor Peterson. They have a lovely facility, and he's sweet to me every time he comes into Mama Lou's."

"I'll call him while you finish cookin' supper." Reed slipped out into the living room.

Lou helped Wade finish the salad, and he carried the salad bowl to the table.

Five minutes later, Reed rejoined them in the kitchen. "He said yes."

"He'll do an amazing job." Lou clasped her hands under her chin.

They sat, and Reed said a short blessing but one filled with thanksgiving.

Lou peered across the table at Wade. "I hoped you'd ask Maggie to be your date."

"What?" He narrowed his eyes and creased his brow. "Working with her is hard enough. I have no interest or intention of asking her on a date."

"Okay. Sorry." She raised her hands and avoided his eyes.

Reed stood and approached the counter. He removed something from the top of the refrigerator and brought it to the table. "Son, this here is your mama's Bible. You should have it." He handed it to Wade.

A bookmark near the back caught his attention. When he opened it, his heart plummeted. She'd highlighted Luke 6:37. "Do not judge, and you will not be judged. Do not condemn, and you will not be condemned. Forgive, and you will be forgiven."

She'd written, "I pray someday Wade and Maggie will settle their differences and become friends again."

~

Two employees exited PS Automotive, but still no sign of Eddie. Luke came out and checked the door. I clenched the steering wheel. Had Eddie left before I arrived? I checked the time—5:15. I pushed my ignition button and traveled east toward Eddie's house. He lived in the same neighborhood as Eileen from the Hair Haven. My chest tightened. Please be home.

Someone had parked a car in his driveway, and I hoped it belonged to him and not a guest. I didn't relish the idea of having an audience when I admitted my mistakes. I climbed out and knocked on his front door.

An angry, small dog ran from the side yard to the front. He snarled and barked.

"Hal. Down boy." Eddie came to an abrupt stop, glanced at me, and then the dog. "Never mind, boy. Keep barking."

The young dog wagged his tail and wiggled his body.

"What an adorable puppy."

"As you can see. He won't hurt you. We're working on the barking."

"But he snarled at me."

Eddie grinned and patted the dog's head. "Good boy." Hal ran to the backyard and Eddie stepped closer to me. "He doesn't snarl. He smiles." Eddie's expression twisted into a grimace. "What do you want?"

"To apologize and explain."

"I read your revised post. Changes nothing. You made me the laughingstock of Clancy County."

"Can't be that bad."

"Barney? That's what people call me now. That and Caveman. I suppose you meant the caveman cartoon character. Or did you mean the dinosaur? Or the deputy? None of which are flattering."

I tilted my head to the right and took two steps closer to him. "I misjudged you, and I'm sorry." My stomach twitched, and I held my hands over my midsection. "But you don't seem to have any problem communicating to me about how I insulted you." I winked and lifted my brows. "If nothing else, I've helped you to come out of your shell."

"Sure. Turn your mess into something beneficial." He spun and retreated to the backyard.

I followed and raised my voice. "Wait. What about you and Jill?"

He stopped and turned to me. "Jill?"

"She wasn't at fault with this. None of it. The other two men she met weren't dates." I reached out and touched his elbow. "She thinks you blame her because you haven't responded to her calls or texts." I pulled my hand away.

"Don't worry about it."

"But you didn't deserve my ridicule. How can I resolve this situation?"

He stared over my head. "Go out with me."

Twenty

By the time I made it home, I had three minutes to spare. I dashed inside, kissed my mom on the cheek, and ran to the bathroom to check my appearance.

Poor Eddie. When I'd realized the time, I darted to my car without answering his question about a date. But he couldn't be serious, could he?

Mom yelled from the living room. "Sounds like your date is ringing the front doorbell. I'll let him in."

I hurried to the foyer and stopped to catch my breath. Doctor Stewart had looked handsome in his white medical coat but even more dashing in his jacket and dress pants. I smiled and stared at his attractive face. Even though I'd prefer to enjoy dinner with Wade.

"Here she is now." Doctor Stewart moved closer to me and offered his arm. "Shall we go?"

I held his elbow, said goodbye to Mom, and closed the door behind me. Despite taking extra care of my appearance, he didn't seem to notice.

He opened the passenger door of his BMW sedan, and I climbed inside.

When he joined me, I said, "You clean up well."

"Not bad for a hunk?"

Heat rose on my neck, and I gasped. "You read my

post?"

"Yep. Your flattery won you a steak dinner."

"You asked me out after I wrote you're a hunk and not because of our pleasant after-dinner chat on Monday?"

"That too." He pulled out onto the road, drove south to the interstate, and headed east toward Chattanooga. "You'll love this place. The best steaks I've ever eaten. I stop when I drive through on my way to visit my parents."

His car swerved to the right, and he pulled off the road. "Losing tire pressure. I'll check it out."

Ten minutes later, he joined me in the car. "We picked up a screw. I called for road assistance. They're sending someone out soon."

"Don't you have a spare?"

"Sure. But I don't want to ruin my clothes." He leaned closer to me. "Let's use this time to talk and become better acquainted."

I tapped my fingers on my thigh. "How long did they estimate it will take for them to arrive?"

"At least an hour, so I canceled our reservation at the restaurant. We'll need to find a different place for dinner."

"An hour?" I rounded my shoulders. If I hadn't worn heels, I would have gotten out and changed the tire myself. I let my stomach persuade me to accept this date, and I wanted that promised steak dinner.

He nudged my arm and softened his voice. "Come on now. This will be fun."

He didn't have Wade's dimples, but his green eyes mesmerized me.

"Tell me about your day."

"Nothing special." I shook my head. "I rode a horse for the first time in many years. And I fell off and bruised my side."

He reached for my hand. "You should visit the office for a check-up."

I pushed away his hand and scooted closer to the passenger door. "I'm fine."

His eyes gleamed, and he chuckled. "My physician's assistant starts next week. Be her first patient."

"Her?"

"Yep." He told me about her credentials and why he needed help.

After Nick filled me in on other changes to come, he shared about his growing-up years with Becca, his time in medical school, and his love for hiking. "I've hiked sections of the Appalachian Trail and several places in the Rocky Mountains."

I covered my mouth to hide a yawn. "South Cumberland State Park has lovely hikes. Have you done any of those?"

"Not yet."

The road-assistance truck arrived and parked behind us. I waited in the car while Nick talked with the person outside. My stomach growled. I scrounged around my purse, hoping to find a granola bar or something I could gobble down before he returned to the car.

When he finished up and climbed inside, it was 8:15.

"Time got away from us. Are you okay if I pull off at the next exit and find something there?"

"The Kimball/South Pittsburg exit?"

"If it's still there, they have a nice little diner."

"A diner?" I huffed and lifted my chin. "I guess so."

During a polite chat over chicken fried steak and home fries, he asked more about my background, the bed-and-breakfast, and growing up in Pleasant Springs. But my first date in years was a major letdown and left me discouraged. Nothing happened the way I expected. He showed little genuine interest in me and no steak dinner.

After we turned into my driveway, he jumped out of the car and rushed to my door. He offered his arm when I climbed out and held my elbow while we strolled to the back porch entrance. A lone coyote's mournful howl pierced the darkness. He must feel the same way I do. Disheartened.

"I'm certain you're dissatisfied with the turn of events, but if I can get us reservations for next weekend, will you join me for that steak dinner?"

I couldn't say yes, despite his gorgeous eyes. "Perhaps you should ask someone else to join you. I'm going through a difficult situation and trying to sort things out." I lowered my head.

He grasped my hands. "May I pray for you?"

"Pray? For me?"

He nodded and bowed his head. "Father, You know Maggie much better than I do, and Your love for her is greater than anyone else's. Reveal Yourself to her so she can understand how beautiful she is both inside and out. Speak to her heart and bring her comfort and peace in whatever situations are causing her unrest. May she find complete rest in You, Lord."

I sniffled, peered up at him, and thanked him.

"That was sweet."

"If you change your mind and want that steak, call or text me." He descended the steps and climbed into his car.

I moved closer to the back door and brought my hand to my chest. People pray for me? I guess I should pray for others too. And the way he talked to God. Like he knew Him on a personal level. I sighed and caressed the charm on my necklace. When I pray, my prayers hit the wall and slide to the floor.

Would Jill's Bible study help me learn how to pray? Those ladies have a deeper understanding of the Lord than I do. They may speak to Him like Nick does.

I stepped inside, answered Mom's questions about my date, and went to my room. I opened my phone's calendar app and made an entry for the following Tuesday evening and after that, Mondays at 7:00. Bible study at Jill's.

But studying the Bible wasn't my thing.

Twenty-one

After an uneventful weekend with Mom and meeting guests, I rose early on Monday morning to head to Ruby Ranch instead of town for Memorial Day festivities. When I pulled down their driveway, I counted five young cows in the small, penned area near the barn. A piece of equipment stood just beyond the picket fence, and I remembered I'd seen one on my parents' farm, too, but I never witnessed it in action.

I parked and found Wade in the barn. "What is that contraption out there?" I pointed toward the front pasture.

"A portable squeeze chute. Today you're helping me with ear tagging and vaccinations."

"All fifty cows?"

"Those recently weaned. We rounded up the five last night." He sauntered to the back of the barn and motioned for me to follow. "We need to get this done today because I'm leaving tomorrow to help my stepson out at the ranch in Texas and to bring back a younger horse, Cisco."

"You're getting another horse?"

"Yep. He misses me."

I giggled and lifted my eyebrows. "Does that mean

I'm in charge while you're gone?"

He shook his head. "Take the rest of the week off. Tim, from a nearby farm, will tend to things with Dad's help and will take care of the cattle and horses while I'm away."

"I can take care of the horses for you." I rubbed my aching left hip.

He smirked and led me to the gate. "Are you still sore?"

"A little. But I took it easy over the weekend. I'm fine now."

"Good." He opened the gate.

"Wait. I need my boots." I darted back to the stable, slipped on my boots, and joined Wade and five young cows awaiting their turn in the chute.

"Do you want to pierce their ears, vaccinate, or castrate the two young bulls?"

"Castrate the bulls?"

"Yeah. Turn them into steers."

"I know what castrate means." I pressed my palms into my abdomen and gagged. "Not the bulls."

He chuckled and coaxed the first cow into the chute. "This calf is a young heifer. She'll need an ear tag and vaccination. Grab the tagger." He gestured to what resembled a pair of pliers, only with a pointed tip.

"This thing?"

"Yep." He took it from me and slid a yellow numbered tag into a groove and a yellow stud over the sharp point. "This is the tag applicator. Watch how I do it. You'll do the next one."

After he gave me instructions on where to place the tag, he punched a hole in the heifer's left ear with the numbered tag facing forward. She startled but handled it better than I expected. Wade secured the syringe and opened a small door on the side of the chute to access the cow's neck. "I'm pulling up on the skin just in front of her shoulder and inserting the needle."

My stomach lurched again. But I had to stay strong. I could do this.

Reed stood on the opposite side of the picket fence near the driveway. "Need any help?"

I sighed and allowed my body to relax. Reed came to rescue me.

"Nope. Maggie can do this."

I peered at Reed with wide eyes. He nodded and smiled.

Wade freed the heifer and coaxed the next calf in line into the chute. Pearl.

When her head appeared through the bars at the front of the chute, I petted her face. "Hi, sweet baby. Promise I won't hurt you."

My hands shook while I moved closer to Pearl and got the tagger into position.

"You've got the applicator where it needs to be." Wade moved closer to me and touched my elbow. "Now snap it onto her ear."

I closed my eyes. I can do this.

Warm hands enveloped mine, and I shot my eyes open. Wade held my hands steady and whispered. "You've got this. Clamp it down."

I squeezed the handles together. Pearl let out a cry and jerked her head.

"You did it. A fine job." He smiled and removed his hands from mine.

My legs turned into rubber, and my body trembled. "I lied to her. I hurt her."

"She's fine. Now the vaccination." He picked up the syringe and held it out to me.

I put my hand on the side of the chute to steady myself. A sudden bout of nausea and lightheadedness hit me. "I can't do it. No." I pushed his hand away. "Not to my baby." I bolted through the gate and barn and across the driveway to the stable to grab my shoes. After I tossed my boots against the stable wall, I zipped to my car past Reed and Wade, who stood on opposite sides of the fence.

Even over the sound of mooing calves, Wade's voice boomed and echoed in my ears.

"No, Dad. She's no help to me."

~

Reed placed his hand on Wade's shoulder. "Lower your voice. She may hear you."

"Fantastic. Maybe she'll take the hint and stay away."

"But she's tryin'. Were you aware of how she cleaned those stalls on Friday? Did you explain how to pitch the shavin's against the wall, so the manure slides down?"

"Nope." He tipped his head back and looked up at the clouds. "Didn't you?"

"Not me. So, she must have researched it or asked someone else. Tells me that she wants to do her best to help you out." Reed watched Maggie's car drive away and turned back to Wade. "And you told her that she did a fine job with the taggin'."

"Did you notice her trembling hands?" He rubbed at the prickling sensation on the back of his neck. "She's a mess. I wanted to offer her a bit of encouragement."

"I'm sure you failed with the comment, 'She's no help to me.' If that's how you spoke to Charlotte, no wonder she found herself another man."

Wade took a step back and narrowed his eyes. "I was always kind to Char."

"How is Maggie any different?"

Wade shuffled his boot across the dirt. "I still struggle with having her nearby." He clenched his jaw and focused his attention on where the driveway and road met. "She owes me the truth, doesn't she?"

"She does. But she also needs to trust you. Don't reckon you're helpin' with that now, are you?"

Wade returned to the side of the chute and administered Pearl's vaccination.

Reed joined him inside the fenced area and helped with the last three calves. "That does it. What are your plans for the horses? Need me to groom them and clean their stables?"

"Nope. I'll put them out in the west pasture before the end of the day. They'll enjoy free roaming time."

Reed agreed and moseyed toward the barn.

"Aren't you going to help me clean up this mess?" Wade pointed at the squeeze chute, the inside floor covered in mud and manure.

Reed turned, faced him, and raised his voice. "You made the mess. You can clean it up."

Wade kicked the side of the filthy chute.

He and his dad weren't talking about the same mess.

~

After I'd showered and dressed, I paced across my bedroom. "She's no help to me. NO HELP." How can I get him to realize my true value? Am I worthless to everyone? I flopped down onto my bed. What will he say when he learns the truth about what I did? If he thinks I'm useless now . . .

I needed to occupy my mind with something beneficial. With no work at the ranch, I had time to attend the Memorial Day parade. There I could enjoy a bite to eat from a food truck and catch up on what's happening in Pleasant Springs.

But did I want to navigate through a crowd of people? I moaned and covered my face with my hands. Not today.

I rushed out of my room, put Snowbunny in his crate, found his leash, and drove to Turtle Creek Park. I'd miss a major opportunity for eavesdropping, but I needed time alone.

We enjoyed a peaceful walk around the pond, took a seat on a bench overlooking the water, and watched a graceful blue heron soar overhead. The quietness of nature gave me time to think. But I didn't like the one thought that pushed out all the others. I'm a disappointment.

By now, 11:00 a.m., the parade had ended, and the festivities had moved to the courthouse area and the town gazebo. I dropped off Snowbunny at home and with Main Street clear, drove to Mama Lou's Café for a coffee, and I hoped for an encouraging word from Lou.

Once inside, I made my way past Farmer Miller and two of his farm hands seated in a booth and hurried to the counter. I ordered a latte and asked the new server if Lou had a minute to talk.

Lou bounded through the kitchen door and hugged me. "Great to have you here. I'd hoped we could spend quality time together, but by the time I get out to the farm . . ." she covered her mouth, "I mean ranch, you're long gone."

"They must be discussing Ruby's place." Farmer Miller snickered and said something about kudzu.

Lou touched my elbow and led me to a booth on the opposite side of the café. "Let's find a place where those big ears can't hear us. They've done nothing but berate Wade and Reed for the new Ruby Ranch sign since they got here."

"That's an issue?"

"I guess it is to old farmers with nothing else to talk about."

We took our seats across from one another. The server brought over my latte and a cup of coffee for Lou.

I sucked in a quick breath and focused on my cup. "I don't know how much longer I'll be at the ranch. Wade made it clear today I'm no help to him. I can't do anything right and I'm a pain."

"Did he say that to you?"

"He said I was no help."

With her elbow propped on the table, Lou leaned forward and rested her chin on her hand. "When are you going to tell him about your dad?"

I bent forward and softened my voice. "Have you said anything?"

"I promised I wouldn't, and I haven't. Although I told Reed there's more to the story than Wade knows, and your dad was involved." Her hand stretched across the table and met mine. "I hope I didn't overstep and say too much."

"You told him the truth." I stared at the counter where Risa McDonald paid her lunch tab. "Has Reed said anything to Wade?"

"I asked him not to." She pulled back her hand.

Miss Risa's eyes met mine, and she waved. Despite being in her eighties, she moved with surprising speed to our table. "Maggie, dear. So pleased to see you. I missed you at church yesterday."

I batted my eyelashes and acted cheerful. "Now, Miss Risa, I don't miss often."

"But Pastor Peterson is such a captivating speaker. You miss one Sunday, and you may miss hearing from God."

I wanted to roll my eyes, but I refrained. "I'm pondering the idea of changing churches."

"Oh, my." She peeked at Lou and back at me. "Stop by for a visit sometime. I'd love to talk and pray with you that you find the right church." With a gentle touch, she patted my hand. "Better yet, stay with us." She dashed away.

I furrowed my brow and turned back to Lou. "I expected her and everyone else to be happy if I left."

"Why would you think that?"

"Wade wishes I'd go away." I wrapped my arms around myself and rocked in my seat.

"Then why didn't he accept your payment for Pearl instead of insisting you work it off?"

"I suppose you know the answer to that question. Reed?"

"He and I have prayed about this. We're not playing matchmakers here. But we hope you can let go of the past and be cordial with each other now."

The server approached our table and spoke to Lou. "Debbie Sue called in and said her mom still isn't well enough to leave alone."

Lou thanked her and glanced at me. "I'm working late *again* tonight." She lowered her head and frowned. "I planned to stop by the nursery. The area at the side of Reed's house and around the large maple tree in the backyard could use some bright flowers or plants to add color."

I widened my eyes and wiggled in my seat. "I'd love to select and plant flowers for you. Perhaps Wade will realize I'm useful for something."

"Honey, you're good for many things." She reached across the table and gripped my hand again. "I know that you'll do a fabulous job with the flowers." She grinned. "I'll contact the nursery and tell them to expect you."

On my way out of the café, I sensed others following me. I turned to discover Farmer Miller and his two farm hands.

"Need an idea for your blog? Tell everyone to swing by the Ruby farm and check out their fancy ranch sign. Ask them for their comments." Miller and his two buddies cackled. "If a big sign turns a farm into a ranch, I'm gonna get me one." They plodded past me and opened the doors of their pickup.

I pressed my lips together. I'm glad not everyone in a small town is as petty as these guys. Why did this bother them? Buy a sign and call your property whatever you want.

On my way home, I stopped by the nursery and bought an array of red, yellow, white, and purple flowers. Tomorrow I'd create a spectacular piece of artwork on the Ruby's property. Well, I guess I should give God a little credit, too, since He created the flowers.

God? The Bible study Jill invited me to attend meets tomorrow night. I massaged my temples. More questions about why I didn't attend church. People prying into my private life. I don't want that.

But I'd like to spend time with women closer to my age. Not so much, Lanie, but I guess I can give her a chance. She hasn't been the nicest to me. She'll lecture me or complain about something.

And when was the last time I attended a Bible study?

When I arrived home, I retrieved my Bible from a drawer and plopped onto my bed. I flipped open to Proverbs. Can God put the pieces of my heart back together?

People say He can. But I haven't seen it firsthand.

Twenty-two

Along the sunny side of the house, I planted Shasta daisies, red marigolds, yellow nasturtiums, and purple phlox. I added more of my favorite colors under the maple tree—yellow primrose and red begonias.

Exhausted from kneeling and planting, I stood, massaged my left hip, and hobbled to the front yard along the edge of the road. Tomorrow I'd use Reed's grass trimmer that I'd spied in the barn and bring a grabber tool for picking up trash. I'd have the front entrance spotless soon.

I strolled over to the driveway, gazed down at the base of the Ruby Ranch sign, and squinted. Vines lay on the ground in front of the wrought-iron base—kudzu? I bristled at the thought of someone stooping so low to make their point. Farmer Miller and his buddies. Reed needed to see this. I ran to the front door of the house and knocked.

Reed answered, and his eyes opened wide. "What are you doin' here today?"

I told him about the flowers I planted for Lou and the kudzu vines near the new ranch sign.

"Impossible. We check for that weed monster often." He hurried out the door, and I followed him to the sign.

"Seems like this showed up today." He lifted the vines that rested in front of the sign on each side of the driveway. "Who would commit such an unneighborly act?"

I knew who and what to write about in this week's blog post.

Before I left for the day, I told Reed I'd bring more flowers the next morning. No use telling him about the rest of my plans. I didn't want him to tell Wade.

I returned to the nursery and paid for two wisteria vines. They wouldn't grow as fast as kudzu, but they would add beautiful purple hues to the front entrance next spring.

When I arrived home, I assembled a sliced turkey and cheese deli sandwich and sat at my computer to type up tomorrow's post entitled "Kudzu Surprise."

I didn't name Farmer Miller or his buddies, but I mentioned a farmer on the north side of town who lived near the Ruby Ranch. I expressed my disapproval of how low he or his farm hands stooped to place kudzu in front of the ranch entrance sign. And I shared how I planned to save the day by replacing the destructive weeds with stunning flowering vines to enhance the entrance to the ranch.

When Wade returns, he'll recognize my worth and appreciate me for my contributions while he was away.

~

Wade pulled off at a rest stop to stretch his legs. A thirteen-hour road trip wasn't his favorite thing to do, but at least it gave him time to think.

He strode along the sidewalk. He needed to get rid of Maggie. Three times a week was too much time together. And she was driving him crazy. The way she tried to win his approval. The way she looked at him. The way she smiled. He trudged to a picnic table. He definitely needed to break the agreement.

But when he returned home, he first had to apologize for his earlier remarks about her. Why did he allow her to get him riled?

Wade took a seat and watched the cars and trucks speeding along Interstate 20. He didn't get angry with Charlotte. Even during and after the divorce. She wanted out, found another man, and Wade kept his cool. He still treated her with respect. Because he was partly at fault. She thought he'd been unfaithful. He hadn't, but because he'd spent time with another woman to gain information and nothing else, the damage had been done and Charlotte didn't want it repaired.

Maggie frustrated him because their breakup wasn't his fault. She was the one to blame. Her and her secrets and lies. That's why he often got upset with her. He wanted nothing to do with her until she told him the truth.

He returned to his truck for the last two hours of his trip. Time to enjoy his son and forget Maggie. But was that even possible?

~

At 7:05 Tuesday evening, I turned into Jill's driveway. Do they think I'm a failure too? Why go inside if I'll only let them down? I caught movement through my rearview mirror. Becca Peterson parked behind me, climbed out of her car, and headed my way.

I snatched my Bible and notepad off the passenger seat and stepped out. Too late to back out now.

Becca embraced me in a tight hug. "I'm thrilled to

see you. Are you here for the Bible study?"

"Yes. Jill invited me."

"I'm so glad." She released me, and I followed her to the front door.

Jill joined us outside and clapped her hands. "I wasn't sure you'd make it, but I'm glad you did."

"Thanks. I almost didn't come but reconsidered at the last minute."

Becca and I followed Jill inside. She led us through the kitchen and to the dining room, where Lanie sat at a round table. Had she eaten a worm?

Lanie grimaced, and in a flat tone, she welcomed me. Her eyes returned to her opened Bible.

Jill pointed to refreshments on the counter that separated the kitchen from the dining area. "Help yourselves to coffee, tea, and our dessert tonight, chocolate delight. If you need anything else, please tell me."

The dessert appeared too delicious to pass up. I scooped a helping into a bowl and poured a hot cup of coffee.

Jill took a seat across from Becca. "I'm glad Maggie joined us this evening." Her eyes darted to Lanie and Becca.

With a glow on her face, Becca chimed right in. "Yes. This is amazing."

I took the seat across from Lanie, who continued to stare at her Bible. Her head shot up at the sound of a shoe hitting a chair leg, and she locked eyes with her sister. "I said hi."

I pushed my shoulders back and drew my eyes to the dessert on my plate. With every delectable bite, my taste buds danced in delight. The crunchy pecan crust complemented the rich layers of chocolate pudding, cream cheese, and whipped topping. "This is like heaven on a spoon."

Jill giggled and leaned forward to explain the order of the evening. Fellowship, review the Scriptures from last week, study the new chapters, and pray. "Anyone have anything exciting happen since last Monday?"

Everyone remained quiet. I supposed because I had joined them. I had a lot to say, but would it come across as boastful to mention my date with Nick? And did Jill tell me the truth when she said they were only friends?

Jill looked my way and wiped her hands on her napkin. "Do you have anything to share?"

"Me?" I bit my lip and hesitated for a moment. "Did you know Doctor Stewart is doing so well that he's expanding his staff?"

Becca's eyes grew larger than I'd ever seen. "That's confidential. Who told you?"

I could say I didn't share my sources, but that sounded lame, considering I got the information from Nick himself. He didn't ask me not to tell anyone. I glanced around the table. "Nick told me. I mean Doctor Stewart."

"When did you talk to him?" Becca creased her brow and wrinkled her nose.

"I took Mom to see him for her cough last week."

"He must have finalized everything but not told me." Becca retrieved her phone from her purse.

Jill doodled in her notebook. "When is this supposed to happen?"

I waited for Becca to answer, but when she didn't, I said, "This week."

The three of them gawked at me.

My heart raced, and I wanted to run with it. I had their attention and information they didn't have. I couldn't have kept this a secret if he'd asked me to. The thrill of being the first to know something and sharing it with others exhilarated me. "A female physician's assistant is joining his staff first. And Nick found a dentist to move into the office next to his." I wriggled in my chair and squealed. "Our first dentist in years. Right here in Pleasant Springs."

Becca pressed her palms against her cheeks. "You gained all that knowledge during your mom's first visit with him?"

"I. Uh. Not exactly." I clasped my hands in my lap. Why hadn't I kept my mouth shut? "We spent time together that evening too. Mom invited him to dinner."

Becca squirmed and placed her phone face down on the table. "Have you seen him since?"

"Isn't it time for the Bible study?" I kept a blank expression.

"I just texted Nick. He finalized the plans with his physician's assistant on Friday afternoon." She narrowed her eyes. "Who told you?"

I let out a long breath. "If you must know, we went to dinner Friday evening."

Jill gasped and touched her chest. "You had a date with Nick?"

"I didn't know you had feelings for him." I raised my hands with my palms toward Jill. "You said you were friends."

"I don't. Except friendship. I'm just surprised." Jill focused on her unopened Bible. "Let's turn to Proverbs."

Lanie peered at her sister, and another thud of a

shoe hit the table leg. "Aren't you going to review the rules?"

Jill shrugged and waved her hand. "Do we have rules?"

"Yes." Becca grinned at Jill and winked before she turned her attention to me. "We come together to show our devotion to the Lord, acceptance of each other, and we agree this is a safe space. Anything we discuss here, we keep confidential."

I flipped open my Bible to my bookmark in Proverbs. "You don't trust me. You think I'll blog about whatever is said here. Is that why no one else wanted to share about their week?"

"We trust you." Becca brushed her fingers against my elbow. "We agreed to confidentiality last week when we met. Now we're asking you to do the same."

I pressed my lips together. They can say that they trust me, but they'll need to prove it.

Becca smiled, tilted her head, and locked eyes with me. "Unless I have permission, I won't share any prayer requests or concerns with anyone, not even Ben. Jill and Lanie have agreed to keep things private too."

"Prove it."

"Prove what?" Lanie glared at me. Her cheeks turned red.

"That y'all trust me."

"I'll prove to you that I trust you by telling you something only these two ladies and Ben know."

Jill's and Lanie's eyes grew wide.

Becca rubbed her belly. "I'm pregnant." She paused, closed her eyes, and reopened them. "I suffered two miscarriages with Michael, and I don't want anyone to learn about this until I finish my first trimester."

I grasped her hand and squeezed. "Which is when?"

"In four weeks."

With a sharp intake of breath, I pulled my hand away and cradled my midsection with both hands. "A December baby?"

She nodded and furrowed her brow.

"I understand and agree to keep this private and not write about anything shared between us." I sneered at Lanie in disgust. "And I mean it. I can keep a secret." I looked down at my hands to avoid their eyes. The Lord knew I'd kept a big one over the years.

"Okay. Let's move right into our discussion." Jill opened her Bible and tapped her pen on the table. "Does anyone have a verse from last week on chapters one through six you'd like to discuss?"

Lanie pinched her lips together and shifted in her chair. "I have a question about chapter four, verse twenty-four. It reads, 'Keep your mouth free of perversity; keep corrupt talk far from your lips.' Does this include writing things you haven't fact-checked?"

Becca brought her fingers to her mouth and gaped at Lanie. "Let's dive into chapters seven through twelve."

"She's right." I lifted my chin and eyed Lanie. "Haven't we already covered this? You asked me to remove what I'd written and rewrite it with corrected information." I settled back in my chair and crossed my arms. "I did that. What else can I do for you?"

Twenty-three

Wade traveled another thirty minutes and ran into a traffic jam on the interstate. Cars, semi-trucks, buses, motorhomes, and a few motorcycles filled the road in front of him. He smacked his hand on the steering wheel. There's nothing more irritating than sitting still in traffic and waiting. He huffed. Could be worse. Maggie. Talk about irritating. Being trapped in traffic with her would be a nightmare.

He told himself to think of something positive. Logan came to mind. He had accomplished a lot over the past twelve years, and under Wade's guidance, had grown into a fine rancher. Wade grinned at the memory of a four-year-old boy who wanted to accompany the ranch hands to help round up the cattle. Now, at twenty-four, Logan had gained the respect of many local ranchers and farmers.

Wade sat up taller. He didn't think of Logan as his stepson. He was Wade's son.

And the only thing that would make spending quality time with Logan difficult on this trip would be if his mom, Charlotte, showed up. But he'd mentioned that she and her new husband were on a cruise in Europe, which pleased Wade. He wrinkled his nose and scowled. He didn't mind Charlotte, but that husband of hers?

Traffic moved once again, and relief washed over Wade. He anticipated a big hug from his son around 9:30 p.m.

~

What about forgive and forget? Would Lanie retaliate or surrender? I'd done what she asked and apologized.

With a gentle bow of her head, Lanie lifted her eyes to meet mine. "I'm sorry. Time to let it go." She sighed and raised her head. "I recently rededicated my life to the Lord, and I have a lot of growing to do."

Jill and Becca thanked Lanie and me for getting the situation out in the open and agreeing to let it die.

Lanie cleared her throat, her voice now soothing. "And to answer your question, when you dropped off cookies last week, Billy is doing well, and Kylee lives on a horse farm near Chattanooga and loves it. I hope to visit her soon."

"Fabulous. Please tell them both I said hi." I turned over to Proverbs chapter seven and scanned the notes I'd made when I'd read it over earlier. Jill asked us to take turns reading through a chapter and discussing anything that stood out to us before continuing to the next. We spent twenty minutes on chapters eight and nine. For my turn, I read chapter ten aloud.

My heart raced, and the familiar discomfort I'd experienced earlier resurfaced when I read the chapter again. I expected Lanie to point her finger at me. Or would it be Jill? If I hurried through, perhaps they'd miss it. After I completed the chapter, I kept my eyes on my Bible and waited.

Becca tapped the table near my notepad. "Did any of the verses you read speak to you?"

My temples pounded as if I'd just run three miles. "Yes. But I'm sure not the ones you hoped would challenge me."

"What do you mean?" Becca touched my left hand. "We're not here to judge you. But if there's anything we can do to help you grow in the Lord, we're here to support you."

I glanced up at her and fidgeted. "I hurt you in the past when I wrote about you and Pastor Ben getting married, Lanie when I wrote about her job loss, and Jill about her dating habits."

"All of you have a reason to point your fingers at me. To accuse me of being the fool mentioned here in Proverbs 10:18. 'Whoever conceals hatred with lying lips and spreads slander is a fool.' Jill used the word slander when she confronted me last week."

Jill took hold of my right hand. "Please believe me when I tell you that I didn't invite you here to preach to you about what you should do or not do. I invited you because I care about you and wanted you to know you have friends you can count on. We're not perfect and don't claim to be."

"Jill's right. We all have trouble holding our tongues and talking about others in ways that don't honor them or God. Anyway, I do." Lanie's eyes drooped, and she bowed her head. "I'm sorry if what I said made you uncomfortable or gave you the impression you don't belong here."

Becca patted my left hand with a gentle touch. "Okay. Let's skip that verse on slander. Which verse challenged you?"

I kept my eyes on my Bible. "Verse twelve. 'Hatred stirs up conflict, but love covers over all wrongs.'"

Becca leaned closer and softened her voice. "Are you finding it hard to forgive someone who hurt you?"

"I suppose so. But I've never hated this person. I'm just struggling with forgiving them." Hoping to calm my nerves, I placed my left hand on my Bible, where it rested on the table, and my right hand on my lap. "Can we move along to the next chapter now?"

"Yes." Jill inched her Bible closer and read chapter eleven.

Verse thirteen mentioned gossip. I wanted to bolt out the door. Why had I come? I gripped my chair seat and braced myself for another scolding from Lanie.

When Jill finished reading, her eyes sparkled. "There's a verse here I'd like to comment on."

Intense queasiness washed over me. Verse thirteen?

"Verse twenty-five." Jill picked up her Bible and reread the verse. "A generous person will prosper; whoever refreshes others will be refreshed."

Becca giggled and focused on Jill. "We've both put that into practice, haven't we?"

She agreed and caught my eye. "I concocted a plan to get closer to someone and offered my help when he needed it. In getting to know him, I decided he wasn't the person for me. But it brought a sense of refreshment to realize I performed an act of kindness for someone."

I brought my hand to my chest. "Doc Winston?"

Jill pursed her lips and nodded.

Becca's face flushed with a shade of strawberry blonde, matching her hair. "And Jill helped me with this too. She suggested I search for ways to help a certain person and be who they needed me to be and not worry about what I wanted. By following her advice, I gained a happier marriage."

"With your first husband, Michael?"

"With Ben. Our marriage got off to a shaky start."

I widened my eyes. They'd only been married for three months.

In harmony, all three ladies said, "Confidentiality."

I didn't take offense. They wore silly grins on their faces. I peeked at my watch, which read 8:30. "How late does this Bible study go?"

Jill responded they rarely finish before 9:00.

"How can I put this verse to work for me?" I told them about my work with Wade in payment for a cow for my mom. "But he hates me because of our past and doesn't think I can do anything right." I also shared that I'd overheard him tell his dad that I was useless.

Jill creased her forehead and gazed at me. "I'm sure he didn't mean that. You told me before about cleaning the stalls and grooming the horses. That must be helpful."

"Apparently not helpful enough, even though I've gotten better and faster."

"Do things he doesn't expect you to do." Becca closed her eyes and pinched the bridge of her nose. A moment later, her eyes shot open, and her face shone. "Take him a fancy breakfast in the morning."

"I arrive at six and he's already eaten."

"Arrive at 5:30 with your best smile and a meal he can't resist."

"What else ya got?"

"What about obvious tasks on the farm that have

remained undone?" Jill waggled her brows and wrote something on her notepad.

I thought for a moment and lifted my index finger. "Like painting the barn and the stable?"

"Whew." Lanie cringed and twisted her mouth. "Those are big jobs. Anything smaller?"

"I planted flowers for Lou today to spruce things up around the house."

Jill clapped her hands and brought them under her chin. "What else like that?"

"Some bushes need trimming. And along the road in front of their house, people have tossed trash out of their vehicles. I plan to clean that up tomorrow."

Lanie frowned and shook her head. "If it's overgrown with grass and weeds, be careful of rodents and other critters."

I agreed and considered other options. "They have a picket fence along the front and down one side of the driveway in need of a coat of white paint."

The three of them agreed painting the fence should impress the entire family.

"But will doing these things prove to Wade that I'm not useless?"

"They can't hurt." Becca stood and carried her dessert plate and empty iced tea glass to the kitchen sink. "But don't believe the lie that you're useless. God doesn't believe that. And neither do we." She pointed to herself, Lanie, and Jill.

On my drive home, I pondered ways to make Wade feel an abundance of gratitude for me. When he returns from his trip and sees all I've accomplished, I'm sure he'll be in an exceptional mood. Or at least, I hope he will.

~

Wade pulled into the Harper Ranch, drove up to the house, and climbed out of his truck.

Logan met him outside of the garage and welcomed him with a warm embrace. "Great to see you, Dad."

He couldn't have asked for a more responsible and loving stepson. Logan cared for the ranch as he had cared for all his possessions growing up. He loved his mom and Wade and had developed a deep love for the Lord too.

Wade yanked his suitcase from the back seat of his pickup and set it on the driveway.

Logan shifted his weight from one leg to the other. "We have a minor situation here, and I'll need you to sleep in the bunkhouse with the hired ranch hands."

"What's up?" Wade rubbed his forehead. Logan always welcomed him into the house.

"Mom arrived today with her new husband. Unless I want to make her mad, she gets to sleep in the house."

"Yep. Makes sense now." Wade nabbed his suitcase, tossed it back where he'd found it, and patted Logan on the back. "I'll head that way, and we can catch up tomorrow."

Charlotte Harper-Franklin glided down the sidewalk. "Wade? You are not going to sneak away without saying hello, are you?"

"Nice to see you, Char." Wade held her offered limp hand.

Her current husband, Alexander, joined his wife outside and used a haughty tone. "That is the name I call her. I prefer you use Charlotte." He dipped his head and smirked. "On second thought, address her as Mrs.

Franklin."

Wade peered into Charlotte's eyes. "What do you prefer?"

She blinked several times and flicked her wrist. "Charlotte is fine."

Logan nudged Wade's elbow with more force than necessary. "I'll ride out back with you and help you get settled in."

They said goodbye to the Franklins, climbed into Wade's truck, and drove the quarter mile back to the bunkhouses.

Wade jumped out of the truck and retrieved his suitcase. "Is his superiority complex a constant thing, or was it aimed at me?"

Logan made a choking noise in his throat. "He's a total bore. I think even Mom is tired of him." He opened his eyes wide and covered his mouth with his hand. "I shouldn't have said that."

"But you did." Wade draped his arm over Logan's shoulder. "Why do you think that? I thought his arrogant charm and money attracted her."

"Only the money and travel. They just got back from Europe, and he's done nothing but complain. I think she kept busy with activities that he wasn't interested in just to avoid him."

Wade lowered his arm and carried his luggage to the bunkhouse door.

"You'll find an available bunk on the far left. The cook will have breakfast ready at 5:30, and I'll return to fetch you at 6:00." Logan backed up three steps and stopped. "You had a visitor last week."

Wade's stomach knotted at the thought of trouble. "A disgruntled former ranch hand?"

"That Sophia woman."

Wade took a calming breath. "Did she say what she wanted?"

"She wanted you, and she had her daughter, Gemma, with her."

"Gemma was with her?" Wade stepped closer to Logan.

"The most beautiful girl I've ever seen." Logan stared into the clear night sky.

Wade chuckled, moved closer, and slapped Logan on the back. "Settle down there, cowboy."

Logan locked eyes with Wade. "I've got to know something. Mom thinks you and Sophia were involved in the past. And Gemma resembles you a little . . . especially her eyes and those dimples." He cleared his throat. "Is. Uh. Is she your daughter?"

Twenty-four

After a rough Wednesday spent herding cows and giving shots, Wade strode over to a picnic table near the bunkhouse, plopped down, and called Sophia.

She greeted him with warmth and kindness. "Marvelous to hear your voice."

"How's Gemma? Is she doing well?"

"She's doing fine. And she said she's ready to meet you."

"Meet me?" Wade removed his cowboy hat, set it on the table, and ruffled his hair.

"And she's ready to do a DNA test if you're willing. She wants confirmation you're her birth dad before she spends much time with you."

With a lengthy exhale, he pushed himself up and paced. "Okay. I'll pick up two kits in town tomorrow and when we meet, we can take care of this." He wiped his palm down his pant leg.

"How long will you stay at the ranch?"

"Leaving Saturday morning."

"Can we meet up on Friday afternoon?"

"Sounds fine. Text me where you want to meet." He disconnected the call and tried to steady his breathing.

One step closer to the truth.

~

What a long week at Ruby Ranch. On Wednesday, I planted two Wisteria vines in front of the ranch sign. I planned to check on them from time to time and hoped to train them to climb along the inner arch. I didn't want the vine to cover up the cow or ranch name at the top.

After I watered the Wisteria, I trimmed bushes and picked up trash along the road in front of the house. I used Reed's grass trimmer to clean up areas Wade couldn't reach with a riding lawn mower—mainly the grass under the picket fence.

Tired as I was, I couldn't forget the children waiting for me to bring them goodies. My last visit to the children's home hadn't gone well, but that wasn't the fault of the kids. I couldn't fail them. I baked two dozen snickerdoodles and delivered them to five children with beaming faces around 5:00 p.m.

Thursday, I'd painted the front and back of the fence closest to the road. I went home exhausted. I forced a smile when Mom suggested we visit Pearl. All I wanted to do was take a nap.

When we arrived at the ranch, Pearl stood near the fence and let Mom stroke her head. Mom couldn't hide her excitement on our way back home. She laughed and clapped her hands. "Did you see the way Pearl warmed up to me?"

And Friday, I returned to paint the front of the fence that lined the driveway from the road to the barn.

Reed checked on me often over the past three days. And late Friday afternoon, he joined me outside. We surveyed all I had achieved throughout the week. My back and arms ached, but I found satisfaction in a job well done.

Reed smiled and patted me on the back. "You've outdone yourself. This place looks super."

"Oh, thank you. I needed to hear that. I hope Wade feels that way too."

"If he ain't happy about this, then somethin's wrong with my boy."

I pressed my hand against my chest, grinned, and thanked him again.

Reed left soon after for town to meet Lou at the café for supper while I cleaned up my paint supplies and loaded them into my trunk.

I'd stared across the pasture near the barn a few times while I painted the fence but hadn't seen Pearl. I wanted to check again before I left for home. After two minutes of straining my neck, I gave up and strolled toward my car.

In the distance, the unmistakable sound of a horse's whinny echoed through the air. I followed the sound behind the house to the fence line on the far west side of the property, about a one-minute walk. Two horses feasted on the neighbor's grass. I squinted to get a clearer view. Confident the neighbor didn't have horses, those two had to be Copper and Champ.

"The fence!" I ran as fast as I could to the stable, found a bucket and added horse feed. After my mishap with Copper's saddle, I forgot to tell Wade about the fallen tree branches on the west fence. It needed a major repair.

The fastest route to the horses was to cut through the neighbor's property. I zipped onto the road and to their fence line. I followed the fence until I spotted the horses. Once in sight, I squatted, wiggled the bucket, and waited. My hands shook, and I tried to calm my racing heart. Soon Copper made his way to me and stuck his face in the bucket. I petted him while I stood. "Good boy, Copper." I wanted to hug him, but I still needed to get Champ. *Lord, please help me with this.*

To my surprise, Champ made his way to me. I gave him a minute with the feed bucket, removed it from his reach, and invited them both to follow me to their stable. All the while, I sensed that someone bigger than me led those two horses home.

After I fed them more feed and distributed plenty of hay in each stall, I sank down onto the bench. "You two exhaust me."

A heavy weight settled in my chest. I would have to face Wade and deliver this news. Another mark against me?

Perhaps when he sees what I've accomplished this week, his attitude about me will improve and he'll overlook the fence mishap.

The ideal moment to unload all I've kept hidden inside.

~

Wade agreed to meet Sophia and Gemma in town at a local diner. He secured a booth in the back corner to give them privacy and wiped perspiration from his brow while he waited.

What a week. He'd avoided Charlotte's husband for most of it, but Char wanted to talk. She'd admitted Alexander was a bore and she may have been mistaken about Wade and Sophia's relationship.

"There you are. We didn't expect you to be hiding in the corner." Sophia climbed into the booth opposite him.

He slid off his bench and gazed at the beautiful young woman in front of him. "You've grown into a lovely young lady."

Color rose in Gemma's cheeks, and she joined her mother on the bench.

Wade returned to his seat.

Sophia peered at her daughter. "Well, do you remember him now?"

Gemma nodded and bit her lip. "You were my favorite person at church when I was a kid. Mom said I drew you pictures and always wanted to spend time with you."

"And you gave me the best hugs around my neck."

The server placed three glasses of water on the table and took their orders. Fish and chips for Gemma and Wade and grilled chicken salad for Sophia.

Gemma glanced at Sophia and squinted. "When we left that church, I asked if we could visit Mr. Wade, and you told me no." Her eyes darted to Wade, and she lowered her head. "I thought you didn't want to see me. That I'd done something wrong."

Sophia's voice filled with tenderness. "You did nothing wrong. Your dad and I were concerned Wade might be your birth dad, and we weren't ready to deal with that yet." She reached for Gemma's hand. "We thought it might be overwhelming for you as an eight-year-old."

"I'm ready to deal with the truth now." Gemma took a sip of water. "Crazy how alike we are—same dimples, blue eyes, and both fans of fish and chips."

Twenty-five

Despite a tiring drive home from Texas on Saturday and a hard Sunday spent baling hay, Wade wasted no time getting an early start on Monday morning. He removed a box of cereal from the pantry and popped a slice of bread into the toaster. Why did Maggie put so much effort into the yard while he was in Texas? Seemed certain that she wanted to win him back. What else could it be? No matter what his dad thought, Maggie had to go.

He snatched a bowl from the cabinet and set it on the counter.

A knock at the back door startled him, and he peeked at his watch. Who would pay a visit at 5:30 a.m.? When he opened the door, Maggie waited outside with a covered picnic basket.

"Did I arrive on time for breakfast?"

He motioned for her to come inside. "Is this for Dad?"

"Sure, and for you." She put the basket on the kitchen table. "I brought Mom by yesterday afternoon to visit Pearl. Lou said you were out in the back pasture baling hay and would need to finish up today before the rain. I figured you could use a nutritious breakfast."

He couldn't see inside her basket, but the aroma of breakfast sausage made his stomach growl. A promising beginning to a long day. But first, he needed to ask for her forgiveness.

He stared down at his boots. "I want to apologize for what I said about you last week when we vaccinated the calves." He lifted his head and slid his hands into his pockets. "I became frustrated and took it out on you when I know you've worked hard to help me around here." He pointed out the back door to the stables. "You've done great with the horses."

Maggie leaned closer to him and smiled. "I accept your apology."

Telling her that he didn't need her help any longer could wait. His stomach told him there wasn't a need to rush.

~

Along with the breakfast casserole of eggs, hash browns, sausage, and cheese, I pulled out homemade blueberry muffins. At one time, these were Wade's favorite treats when he helped Dad on the farm.

"Your mom's blueberry muffins?"

Was he drooling? I chuckled and removed the plastic cover from our breakfast. "Mom's recipe, but I made them." I grinned. "And the casserole."

He glanced up at me, his eyes beaming. "Let me get Dad. He'll enjoy this too." Wade stepped out of the kitchen and headed down the hallway.

My cheeks flushed, and I gave myself a thumbs up. But I resisted the urge to do a happy dance. This would be an extraordinary day.

He returned a minute later. "Dad said to start without him, but he'll be out soon."

We set the table for three. By the time we took our seats, Reed joined us and led us in a brief prayer of thanksgiving. After he took a bite, he assured me that my breakfast was a delectable treat.

We chatted a little but focused our attention on eating. Chores awaited Wade and me.

Wade finished his last bite and stood. I followed his lead.

"Let me tidy up so you two can work in the stable." Reed rose and grabbed our dirty plates.

Wade narrowed his eyes at his dad, and Reed nodded toward me. Was Wade upset with Reed for mentioning the stable? But how did that involve me?

Wade moved near the back door and deepened his voice. "Come on, Maggie. We need to talk."

My heart filled with dread, and I peered at Reed. He turned away and faced the kitchen sink. But I'd done everything well. What did I mess up this time? I trudged behind Wade through the back door. "What do we need to talk about?"

After he led me to the maple tree, his eyes and voice brightened. "You did an outstanding job with planting, pruning, weeding, and painting." He opened his palm and swept it in the direction of the yard and fence. "I got in late Saturday, so I didn't notice what you'd accomplished until yesterday morning on my way out to bale hay."

I exhaled after holding my breath. He liked it. Everything.

"You blew me away with your attention to detail." He raised his shoulders and let them drop. "In fact, you worked yourself right out of a job."

I flinched and moved back a step. "I what?"

"You did so much while I was gone that you've paid your debt for the cow and her upkeep for the next year. You don't owe me a thing."

"But you said you needed my help through August." I opened my palms and shrugged. "This is the beginning of June."

"You're off the hook."

"Who's going to . . .?" I placed my hands on my hips. "This is because I got sick when you wanted me to give Pearl a shot, isn't it? You apologized for what you said, but you're still upset with me." I pointed my finger at his face. "I put in endless hours of hard work to prove my worth to you and your ranch. To show you what I can do." I took a step closer and waved my hand in front of his face. "And what did I gain from working all day in the scorching sun to improve this place? Fired." I huffed and fumed on my way to my car.

I kept my furious pace, even with the sound of footsteps behind me.

"Maggie, wait."

I stopped, turned to face Wade, and waited for another apology like the last time he acted this way to me.

"We need to set a schedule for your mom to visit her cow."

"Now you want a schedule?" I clenched my teeth and rubbed my jaw. I can't believe this. No apology for firing me?

"I can't have you stopping by anytime you feel like it. I need to let her out in the back pasture with the others. It will take time to round her up and get her closer to the barn."

"I'll have Mom here every weekend." Pain

throbbed in my head. What was I thinking? I massaged my temples. That we might renew our relationship? That won't happen till the cows come home. And since the cows are already here, I guess there's no chance of that.

"Not specific enough. Every other Sunday works for me."

Frustration intensified in my voice, but I resisted the urge to shove him. "Not fair. I own Pearl. I should be able to visit her anytime I want."

"Okay." He lifted his chin. "But you and your mom will need to walk out back into the east or west pastures to find her. Or I can have her in the pasture near the barn every other Sunday afternoon."

"Fine. Have it your way." I pivoted on my heels and took two steps closer to my car.

"Wait." He jogged past me, stopped, and faced me. "Before you go, I'd like you to dig up those plants you put in front of my ranch sign."

I glared at him and got in his face. "Did you read my blog post?"

He scrunched his nose and puffed out his chest. "I've been too busy baling hay in the scorching sun to read your busy-body blog."

"You're a jerk." I bolted to my car and climbed inside. What had I ever seen in that man? Oh, no. I groaned and slapped my thigh. He needs to know about the fence, so the horses and cattle stay safe. I sighed. I'll text him.

But I will never, ever tell him the truth about the past.

~

Wade didn't have enough time to mull over his

conversation with Maggie before his dad showed up in the stable.

"I can't believe you let her go."

"We discussed this. I told you that I can't have her here any longer."

"But she can be a tremendous help to you."

"In one week, I'll have the proof to confirm the woman lied to me twenty years ago and still hasn't come clean."

"Why can't you let it go? If she lied to you, don't you think she had a worthwhile reason?"

Wade raised his eyebrows and retreated a step. "Are there ever valid reasons to lie? You taught me to tell the truth." He furrowed his brow. "Have you changed your mind?"

Reed dipped his head and frowned. "Maybe she was too scared to tell ya. Maybe if you were nice to her, she might open up."

"I'm plenty nice to her."

"Then there must be two meanings for 'nice'." Reed headed to the stable door.

"Wait. I forgot to ask you why you brought the horses up."

Reed faced him. "Not me. I thought you did Saturday night when you got back with Cisco."

"You didn't give them fresh feed, hay, and water?"

"Nope."

Wade scratched his head. "Did you see anyone around here on Saturday? Tim? Maggie?"

"Too busy in my workshop to pay any attention. Besides, Tim said he couldn't help on Saturday, and Maggie pushed herself all last week. She didn't need to be payin' attention to those horses." Reed moseyed to the stable door again, paused, and turned back. He returned to Wade's side and pulled a folded piece of paper from his back pocket. After he handed it to Wade, he slipped outside.

Wade opened the paper to find Maggie's latest blog post. With a firm grip, he crumpled the paper into a tight ball and flung it across the stable. He entered his office and took a seat at his desk. There, he eyed his opened Bible and inched it to him.

Lord, I can't let her back into my heart, and I'm afraid that's what she wants. Please don't ask that of me. I must push her away. She triggers too many memories and stirs things up in me that don't honor You. Frustration, resentment, and bitterness.

He paused from his prayer and sat in quiet contemplation.

Forgive.

"But I've given her plenty of opportunities to tell me the truth."

Forgive.

He strode from his office in search of Maggie's post. When he located the crumpled mess, he sat at his desk, flattened out the crinkled paper, and read "Kudzu Surprise."

Do you know your neighbors? Would they help you in a time of crisis? Or rejoice at your string of bad luck? Offer to help you in time of need, or wait for an opportune time to wreak havoc on your property?

A farmer in town voiced disapproval of another farmer's choice to rebrand his farm as a ranch. Why is this an issue? The farm in question doesn't grow crops—they only run cattle. Seems like a ranch to me.

The farmer asked me to write a blog post to ask

your opinion.

But before you comment, let me tell you what I overheard from this same farmer's table at Mama Lou's Café. Someone used the word *kudzu*. A day later, I found two kudzu vines in front of the rancher's new wrought-iron sign in his driveway.

Coincidence? I think not.

Everyone in these parts knows kudzu grows at an astonishing rate and will smother anything and everything in its path. For those of you who don't know, the vine winds its way around wrought-iron structures and covers every inch within days. That weed then winds its way to the trees and fences further down the driveway and consumes them too.

Fortunately, I spotted the unwelcome vines before they rooted and spread. I replaced the weeds with stunning vines. Next spring, instead of nasty kudzu, the Ruby Ranch will welcome visitors with a gorgeous display of purple wisteria.

In the comments, please answer the following questions.

Are you bothered because a local farmer now calls his farm a ranch?

Was it okay for the farmer from the café or one of his farmhands to deposit kudzu on the rancher's property?

Who went too far? The man who called his farm a ranch or the man who tried to sabotage his neighbor?

Wade folded the paper and laid it inside his desk drawer. Maggie cared about the ranch. She took quick action to keep the front entrance clear of kudzu and hoped to create a warm welcome for visitors.

His phone beeped with a text from Maggie: After my fall, I forgot to tell you the west fence needed repair. The horses got out Friday. I led them back and fed them. Followed up on Saturday. Sorry.

Her text confirmed her dedication and commitment to his ranch. And what had she said earlier? She wanted to prove her worth to him and the ranch. Did that mean she wasn't trying to win him back? He slumped back in his chair and lowered his chin.

Why did that bother him?

Twenty-six

Throughout the day, I kept myself busy at the bed-and-breakfast to avoid thinking about Wade and headed to the Bible study that evening. On my drive, I rehashed my conversation with him. Although he liked my work, he wanted me gone. He'd had enough of me. I'm a nuisance and still a disappointment.

I pulled into Jill's driveway and faked a smile all the way to the front door. Lanie greeted me and welcomed me inside. Had she forgiven me for my blog post about her jobs, or was her smile as fake as mine?

She led me to the kitchen. "Help yourself to tonight's dessert. Not as mouthwatering as my mom's, but I tried." She pointed to the counter, where an inviting glass container filled with banana pudding awaited us.

Jill entered the kitchen from the hallway. "I snitched a bite. Delicious."

Becca came inside through the back door with Jill's beagle on her heels. "The hummingbird feeder is almost empty."

Jill thanked her. "I'll take care of that as soon as we finish up here. Can't have my little friends going hungry."

After I peeked outside at the red feeder, where three hummingbirds flitted about, I greeted Jill's dog and added two spoonfuls of pudding to my bowl. "Is it my turn to bring dessert next week?"

"I've got next week." Becca ambled to the counter and plopped a scoop of banana pudding into her dish. "If you'd like, you can do the one that follows."

"What would you like me to fix?"

Lanie filled her bowl and wiggled her index finger at me. "Your cinnamon rolls are to die for. Jill and Becca would love to try them."

"Sounds fabulous." I carried my pudding to the table.

We took our seats and enjoyed our first few bites in silence.

"Your mom's pudding can't be better than this. This has the potential to win a first-place ribbon at the county fair." I meant it too. Lanie's pudding tasted of creamy goodness and exploded with more flavor than any I'd made.

She blushed and thanked me.

"Who wants to go first and share about your week?" Jill took another bite of her dessert.

They fixed their wide eyes on me.

I took a deep breath and hoped to keep my voice steady. "He fired me today."

"No way." Jill's spoon slipped from her hand and caused a loud clang when it crashed into her bowl. "I drove by there yesterday and admired the painted fence and the neatness of the front yard." She picked up her spoon. "Why on earth would Wade fire you?"

"He doesn't want me around. Either I bring back memories he doesn't want to think about, or he hates me and will never forgive me for refusing his marriage proposal."

Together, Jill and Lanie said, "You did what?"

Becca knew most of the story. I'd shared it with her years ago when her first husband was the pastor of the church. But she didn't know the entire truth. I'd lied to her, my mom, and Wade. After I sagged back into my chair, I turned to Becca. "I'm going to tell them what I told you several years ago. But there's more." I closed my eyes. If Becca can forgive me for lying to her in the past, perhaps Mom and Wade will too.

I shared the untruthful story I'd told Becca before and eyed her. "But that wasn't the way it happened." Through many pauses and sniffles, I admitted my lie, told them the truth, and waited. Would Becca forgive me?

Becca brushed a strand of hair from my forehead. "I understand why you lied to Wade and your mom. And I'm not excusing your actions. But why, years later, did you lie to Michael and me? You could have told us the truth, and we would have understood."

"I not only lied to Mom and Wade, but I convinced myself it was the truth to hide my loss."

Becca did her best to console me while she held my hand. Jill stood, moved closer to my right side, and hugged my neck. Lanie wiped a tear from her eye.

I gave Becca's hand a squeeze. "I'm sorry. Can you forgive me for lying to you?"

Becca's eyes sparkled with warmth. "Of course, I forgive you. But I'm not the only person who needs to hear your confession."

"Mom won't disown me, although she'll be upset and hurt." I averted my eyes and repositioned myself in my chair before looking up again. "And on two separate occasions, I wanted to tell Wade. Before I had the opportunity the first time, he got irritated with me, and today, he fired me." I bit my thumbnail. "If he gets this upset with me without knowing, I can only imagine how he will react when I tell him."

~

Lou stopped by with three chicken pot pies, homemade rolls, and strawberry shortcake for dinner. Wade had already eaten a sandwich, but he couldn't pass up Lou's cooking. The pot pie's crust alone made his mouth water in anticipation of the deliciousness inside. And he'd be a fool to pass up homemade rolls and strawberry shortcake.

He helped her set the table while his dad cleaned up down the hall after refinishing a cedar chest in his workshop.

"Did Maggie work today?"

"Why are you asking me that? I'm sure you already know the answer."

She frowned and tilted her head. "I wouldn't have asked you if I knew the answer."

"Maggie doesn't work here anymore."

Lou straightened and crossed her arms. "She saved you a lot of trouble with painting, weeding, not to mention the kudzu fiasco. I doubt she'd do all of that and then quit." Lou arched her brow. "What happened?"

"I let her go." Wade glared at Lou and lifted his palm toward her. "And I don't need to hear your sermon or Dad's again." He returned his dinner plate to the cupboard. "I'm not hungry." He headed outside and muttered. "But maybe I am a fool." He needed a long walk. Better yet, a long ride on Cisco.

He saddled up his horse and rode to the back pasture. After he assessed the damaged west fence, he stopped near the large pond where Pearl grazed. He shook his head at Maggie's determination to keep Pearl and her mama cow together. Maggie sure got upset that day. He had to keep a firm grip on her.

She'd felt remarkable in his arms, even with her kicking and screaming.

He rode to the back fence line, where he'd found Copper without Maggie in the saddle ten days earlier. Worried about her safety, he had a moment of panic that day. And holding her close as he helped her back to the house, and their almost kiss, brought a wave of regret their relationship ended years ago. He scrubbed his hand over his face. What had he done back then that caused her not to trust him with marriage?

And this morning, he'd hurt her again. His intention was to let her down gently. To show his appreciation for her hard work. He assumed she'd be happy not to have to clean stalls and help with the cattle. What she'd wanted in the beginning. Was her motive only to seek appreciation?

If that was the case, he'd stomped all over her ego. Knowing Maggie, she had a rather high opinion of herself. But then again, her blog post showed her concern and support for Ruby Ranch.

Forgive.

"Even if she doesn't confess the truth?" Wade didn't need to wait for the answer. He'd read Ephesians 4:32 many times. "Be kind and compassionate to one another, forgiving each other, just as in Christ God forgave you."

While the evening breeze rustled the leaves, he bowed his head and confessed his sin of judgment and bitterness against Maggie. He prayed for guidance to make things right and returned to the house to apologize to his dad and Lou.

~

We opened our Bibles to Proverbs, reviewed the chapters from last week, and took turns reading chapters thirteen through eighteen. I read chapter fifteen.

"Verse one. 'A gentle answer turns away wrath, but a harsh word stirs up anger.'"

I brought my hand to my mouth, lowered it, and told them what I'd called Wade that morning.

Jill gasped. "Oh, my. How did he react to you calling him a jerk?"

"I don't know. I hurried to my car and drove off before he responded." My stomach churned, and I rested my palm on my belly. "I need to be gentler in the way I talk to him and others. Words like those only stir up anger and get me into more trouble."

Lanie nodded, and a soft chuckle escaped from her lips. "You're not alone." She glanced at Jill and Becca. "I have to improve in this area too."

When we finished chapter fifteen, Becca read chapter sixteen.

I stopped her and reread verse three. "'Commit to the LORD whatever you do, and he will establish your plans.' What does establish your plans mean?"

"Our plans will be successful." Lanie smoothed out a wrinkled page in her Bible.

"But that doesn't mean we'll become rich or famous." Jill tapped her fingernail on the table. "More like He'll bless what we've done. He'll turn it into something worthwhile."

"So, if I had talked to God about my plans before doing all that stuff at the ranch, Wade would have been proud of my accomplishments instead of firing me?"

Becca squirmed and leaned closer to me. "You just said, 'my accomplishments.' Does God get any credit for those?"

I shrugged and crinkled my nose. "Should He?"

Becca peered into my eyes. "Are you trusting in God or in yourself?"

"God made me and gave me the ability to plant flowers, make a yard look pretty, and paint fences."

She gave my hand a little tap. "But do you trust Him to lead you and help you?"

With three pairs of eyes gawking at me, I needed to leave. I peeked at my watch and groaned. "Oh, my. I promised Mom that I'd be home early tonight." I jumped up and snagged my Bible and purse. "Thanks for everything." I darted to the front door, thankful no one stopped me.

And I added another lie to my list. Mom wasn't expecting me for an hour.

Twenty-seven

Wednesday morning Wade regretted he hadn't visited Maggie sooner, but there was too much to do around the ranch. If he hadn't let her go, she would have helped him get caught up. He lowered his head, plodded to the horse trough behind the stable, and filled it with fresh water. Did he miss Maggie? Maybe a little. And he needed to get to her house soon to ask her to come back. To tell her that he needed her help and would pay her the same amount he pays any employee. And he hoped that would be enough.

He completed his early-morning chores except for grooming the horses and cleaning their stalls. If she didn't take him up on his offer today, he'd get to those chores later. He led the three horses out to the area behind the stable and checked their food supply.

"You miss her, don't you, boy?" Wade ran his hand down Copper's neck.

Copper whinnied and tossed his head.

"How can I convince Maggie to return? Lunch?" Wade continued to pet the horse. "Yeah, I'll invite her to lunch and ask if she'll come back to help me out." He grinned while he planned out his strategy. "Admit my mistake in letting her go, brag on her blog post, and tell her the flowers she planted need her."

Copper nudged Wade's shoulder.

"Yep. And I'll tell her that you miss her too."

Wade showered and changed into a fresh pair of jeans and a navy button-down shirt. He peeked in the mirror and moaned. "No. Wait. Her favorite color is yellow." He went to his closet and selected a blue, green, and yellow plaid shirt. "This will do it."

He prayed on his way to Maggie's house, pulled into her driveway, and noticed Maggie's car was gone. Had Mrs. Stone run an errand? He parked and strode to the back door with his chin held high. The screen door was open, and the delightful scent of cinnamon drifted past him. He knocked and hollered hello.

Maggie's mom appeared at the door and greeted him. "Come in." She furrowed her brow and took his elbow. "You're not here to tell us something terrible happened to Pearl, are you?"

"No. She's fine." He scanned the kitchen and returned his gaze to Mrs. Stone. "I came to talk with Maggie, but I see that she's not home."

"Oh, dear. Was she expecting you?"

"No." He tilted his head back and looked upward. "I guess I should have realized she wasn't here when I pulled in and didn't see her car, but I thought maybe you—"

"She got a call earlier from . . ." She brought her hand to her mouth. "I shouldn't say anything. That's Maggie's business. A gentleman invited her to lunch at Mama Lou's." Mrs. Stone pointed to a chair. "Would you like to wait? I baked fresh cookies for tonight's guests. You can be my taste tester."

Wade raked his hand through his hair. Maggie had

a lunch date? He'd ask Lou about that tonight. He winced and tapped his foot. "Do you expect her back soon?"

"Oh yes. The gentleman has a full schedule this afternoon. She should return in a jiffy."

"Then I'd love to be your taste tester."

~

Nick walked me out to my car. "Your blog post this morning caught me off guard."

"What do you mean?" I clicked my fob to unlock my door.

"Makeup?"

"When not much is happening in town, I write about makeup or a recipe I've tried."

"I get it. The people of Pleasant Springs had an uneventful week."

I shrugged and pressed my lips together. "Either that, or there was a deliberate effort to withhold information from me."

He chuckled and opened my car door. "Please pray about what I asked, and let me know what you think."

I thanked him, climbed into my car, and waved goodbye.

Pray about it? I should pray about a lot of things, like a date for Lou and Reed's wedding. I almost asked Nick while we were together, but it didn't feel right. Like previous weddings, I'll attend this one alone.

When I turned into my driveway, I parked in the area reserved for guests to avoid a pickup parked in my spot near the back door. I squinted. Was that Wade's truck?

My pulse quickened, and I shuffled to the back porch. What does he want now? Did he find something else I did wrong that will deepen my sense of inadequacy?

I opened the door and found him and Mom at the kitchen table, laughing, eating cookies, and drinking coffee. I stopped. "Excuse me for barging in and interrupting your visit. I'll just slip off to my room."

Wade rose with his cup of coffee and hurried to me. "I came to see you." He glanced around the kitchen. "Can we talk?"

Mom excused herself and darted upstairs to clean a room vacated that morning.

"Let's talk in the living room." We made our way into the main living area of our private residence. Wade placed his coffee cup on an end table and plopped into the chair beside it. I sat on the couch, as far away from him as I could get, and waited for him to ridicule me again.

The silence unsettled me.

I crossed my legs and, in a split second, uncrossed them. "I like your shirt. Especially the way the green and yellow complement each other. The blue is pretty too."

His mouth twitched, and he cleared his throat. "I came to apologize."

I widened my eyes. Wade apologizing? It's about time.

"I was a bit too hasty in telling you that I didn't need your help on the ranch."

"You didn't say that. You said I'd paid my debt."

"True. You're paid up." He ran his hands down his pant legs. "But I still need your help. You've done a fantastic job. Will you come back?"

"Come back?" I stood and scowled. "So you can

mock me again? Yell at me and treat me like I'm stupid?"

He jerked his head back. "Have I been that bad?"

"Worse. You always act like you're dissatisfied with me. Like I can't do anything right." I crossed my arms and huffed. "Why should I come back?"

Wade rubbed his palm over his mouth. "Simple. I need your help with the horses—they relate to you well." He leaned forward and smiled. "And I'm thinking about adding some laying hens, and I think you'd enjoy helping with those. Mom loved caring for them and collecting their eggs."

"Chickens and horses?" I sat, narrowed my eyes, and pressed back on the cushion. "Vaccinations and castrating?"

"I'll take care of those chores."

"How many hours a week and what's the pay?"

"I can use your help six days a week, every morning, whatever time you want to start for four hours a day. And with holidays off." He quoted an hourly rate.

"Much more generous than the amount you applied to the cow per hour, but only half of what someone offered me earlier today."

"Offered?" He wrinkled his forehead and massaged his right temple. "I don't understand."

"Doctor Stewart wants to hire me as his business manager. Twenty hours a week."

"You'd be working with him?"

"Yes." I glared at Wade. "Five days a week at Nick's office."

He closed his eyes and massaged both temples. "Nick, huh?"

Twenty-eight

When Wade's eyes met mine, he resembled a mournful Snowbunny tugging at my heartstrings. "I can't compete with what he's offering you. Are you interested in that kind of work?"

"Not sure. Because of running my bed-and-breakfast, in the past I had no need for another job. But now, with Mom handling most of the responsibilities here, it might be good for me to do something new."

"As his business manager? Because you run a successful bed-and-breakfast?"

"That and when we went to dinner together, I told him that I had a business management degree. I guess that got him thinking."

"About you . . . And your degree." He rubbed his hand across his mouth again.

I rose and offered to freshen his coffee.

He reached for his mug, took a sip, and stared at the cup. "What if I offer you an additional three dollars an hour and drop you to twenty hours, five days a week?" He peeked up at me and seemed to hold his breath.

Did he want me back at the ranch or to keep me from working with Nick?

"I'll think it over and get back to you. Is Monday okay?"

He stood and pressed his fingers to his temple. "Can you at least stop by the ranch today and spend time with Champ, Copper, and meet Cisco? The boys are missing you."

I held back a smile. Copper and Champ or Wade?

~

She'd dated the new doctor? Wade returned to the ranch, entered the stable, and grabbed the grooming gear. Maggie wouldn't be any help until maybe Monday, so he'd better get the job done. At the sound of spewing gravel, he dropped the comb and brushes on the floor outside of the stalls. His heart raced. Maggie?

Lou parked her car outside of the stable and rushed inside. "Don't go draggin' your feet with Maggie. She and Doctor Stewart had a lunch date today and seemed chummy. He offered her a job."

Wade sneered and waved her off. "Old news. I already talked to Maggie." He rounded his shoulders. "I made her my best offer to come back. But I can't match what he offered. I'll need to find someone else to help me."

"Is that your only concern?"

"What do you mean?"

"Did you hear me use the word chummy?"

"You want something to happen between us. But I'm not sure if I'll ever want to reconcile with her." He trudged over to Champ's stall. He didn't have Doctor Stewart's looks or smarts, and he didn't dare admit he missed Maggie.

Lou stepped closer and laid her hand on his upper arm. "I've seen your frustration and your concern for her. Don't give up."

"Do you and Dad think I want her back?"

"We've also seen the way you gaze at her." She lowered her hand. "Your dad said he remembers that look when you two dated before, but he never noticed that same sparkle in your eye when you were with Charlotte."

"I can't imagine us working this out."

"You can't." She locked eyes with him and jabbed her finger into his chest. "But God can. He'll make a way if you and Maggie are meant to be together."

"But that's another problem. Her relationship with the Lord isn't as strong as I'd expect it to be."

"But she's working on it. I've seen changes in her, and I hope when she admits the truth, she'll be free to enjoy life again. Maybe the life she shared with you."

~

After a brief visit with Mom, I sat on my bed and leaned back against my pillows. Should I take Nick's job offer or Wade's? My goal was to show Wade that I wasn't an idiot or useless, and I could bring value to his ranch. And now, with his job offer, it appeared I'd succeeded. I didn't have to go back to the ranch to prove myself to him.

I pulled my Bible off my nightstand to reread Proverbs 16:3. "Commit to the LORD whatever you do, and he will establish your plans."

What did Becca ask me? "Are you trusting in God or in yourself?"

God, I don't pray often. Do you care about that? Does it matter to You what I do? I believe You are God. But I guess I'm supposed to ask You to lead me and help me. So, I'm asking You now. Please help me.

Okay?

After my prayer, I skimmed through the rest of chapter sixteen. I didn't stay long enough in the Bible study to take part in further discussion, but I assumed they used me as a reference for at least one verse. Proverbs 16:28, ". . . a gossip separates close friends." I picked up another pillow beside me and snuggled it under my chin. Perhaps I should increase my investigation of facts before I send out a post. Jill and Lanie both said I messed up on the posts about them.

But what about Luke? Why did Lanie say I wasn't one of his favorite people? I don't remember writing a post about him. I jumped off my bed, zipped to my desk, and opened my laptop to search my blog for Pleasant Springs Automotive and the Gibson family.

The post I found wasn't about Luke or his business, but others may have thought that.

Soon after their father's passing, I wrote a post about a man's frustration with a car repair shop. Three times, he took his car in for the same repair, but they never resolved the issue. Weeks later, word got back to me that Luke's business had suffered because the locals connected my post to his family's shop. I'd failed to mention that the shop in question was in a nearby town where the man worked, not here in Pleasant Springs.

I squirmed and grimaced. Why didn't I catch that at the time?

Does that mean Eddie disliked me, too, even before I wrote about his date with Jill? I pursed my lips and shook my head. I'm not sure what's going on. Why did he ask me out? I should call him and find out. Later.

I returned to my bed, stared down at my Bible, and reread Proverbs 16:28.

But I'm not a true gossip. I just share what I learn about people. That's news.

~

With the afternoon chores completed and another hour to wait for Lou's dinner, Wade trudged into his office. A wave of sadness crashed over him. Maggie didn't plan to visit the horses today or take him up on his offer. He could use her help, but he'd waited too long to realize that. With her spending time with the new doctor, her mind would be elsewhere.

There wasn't any reason to try again or to raise his offer. Besides, Maggie still hadn't told him the truth about what happened twenty years ago. She didn't deserve any kind of offer from him.

He pulled his Bible to him and opened it to chapter two of James. Verse thirteen grabbed his attention. ". . . Mercy triumphs over judgment."

There you go again, Lord. I should show Maggie mercy. Like Dad said, there must have been a reason she didn't tell me the whole truth. But now she's taking that job with Doctor Stewart. She won't be around here except with her mom, and I won't have the opportunity to show much mercy.

Wade raised his head at the sound of Copper's whinny in his stall. "Who's there? Dad?"

"Just me." Maggie poked her head around the corner of his office door. "Came to visit my buddies and meet Cisco."

Lord, help me show her mercy while she's here now.

~

Wade led me to Cisco's stall. "What do you think?"

I patted the dark reddish-brown horse on his forehead and brushed his black mane away from his eyes. "You're a handsome boy."

"If he could talk, he'd thank you."

"His coat shimmers." I rubbed my hand down his neck. "He feels soft. Like silk."

"He likes when you pet him and wants you to groom him tomorrow."

I giggled and continued to pet Cisco. "I suppose he told you that?"

"Definitely."

I brought my hand to my side and faced Wade. "You can't find anyone else to help you around here, can you?"

He sighed, and his shoulders slumped. "Tim's busy on his dad's farm and the help wanted flyers I distributed when I returned to town haven't resulted in any help." He frowned and glanced at Copper and Champ's stalls. "And I insulted and terminated the best helper I had."

I peered into his eyes. "Me?"

He blinked and avoided mine. "Yep." He strode to the shelves containing the grooming supplies. "I messed up. You did an excellent job, but I thought you . . ."

"What?"

When he turned and faced me, his eye twitched. "I thought you wanted something to happen between us."

"I wasn't expecting that. In fact, asking you for a cow was my last resort. Four other farmers had already turned me down. I didn't know who else to contact."

"You got rejected four times before you came to see me?"

"Yes. All I wanted from you was a cow for Mom."

"That's all you wanted?"

"Nothing more."

"Can you forgive me for misjudging you?"

"Sure. But if I make you uncomfortable, I shouldn't even consider working with you."

"That's not it. You've shown me that you care about the success of the ranch and aren't interested in renewing our relationship. That's acceptable. As long as that remains true, I could use your help."

I backed away and touched my neck. "Oh."

He cocked his head to the left. "You know that's how it needs to be, don't you?"

I nodded and softened my voice. "No relationship."

"That would make things awkward between us."

"Awkward. Yes."

"Right. We agree then?"

"Yes, of course." My voice quivered, and I broke eye contact. "Like I said earlier, I'll get back to you on Monday." I darted out of the stable. A battle raged in my head. And worse. In my heart.

Could I work with Wade every day and not expect to rekindle what we had so many, many years ago?

Twenty-nine

Sunlight poured in through the kitchen window, casting a warm glow on Snowbunny where he lay curled up on his bed. His droopy eyes and lack of zeal concerned me. "When did you say he last ate?"

Mom creased her brow and tapped her chin. "Thursday morning. He hasn't touched his food since then."

"He's skipped two meals? Last night's dinner and this morning?" I stooped and rubbed his head. "Not good. I'll make an appointment today with Doc Winston."

When I called his office, his new assistant said she could squeeze me in at 12:30, which gave me three hours. I returned to the floor next to Snowbunny's bed. "Mommy's going to take care of you, my precious puppy." I laid my head next to his. *God, please help my baby boy.*

I lumbered up the stairs to check on our vacant rooms for two new guests to arrive later today. Everything appeared ready. On my way back downstairs, I spotted a dusty shelf on one of our bookcases. After I retrieved a dusting glove, I took care of the dust bunnies and checked the rest of the furniture.

"Did I miss something?" Mom appeared out of nowhere.

"A speck of dust, but that's all." I made my way to her and pecked her on the cheek. "You do a wonderful job keeping things clean."

When everything inside met my approval, I stepped outdoors to check the grounds. The lawn care service had freshly cut the grass, and my garden abounded with color. I loved early June. Not too hot and not cold. Perfect weather.

I sat in the swivel rocker on the back porch. Despite the persistent tapping of a woodpecker in the trees behind the house, I considered all I needed to accomplish. Besides taking my dog to the vet, I needed to make a major decision. Work with Nick or Wade? But I had three more days to decide. First, take care of my dog.

And there was the matter of Eddie that I needed to address. Should I call or visit him? I didn't have his cell phone number, and I'd have to talk to Luke if I called their shop. I took a deep breath, picked up my phone, and put it back down. After a few minutes, I realized I needed to make this call and face Luke's disdain.

I dialed the shop's number and waited through four rings. When Luke answered, I greeted him and told him who I was.

"Need a car repair?"

"I'd like to talk with Eddie."

Luke grunted and deepened his voice. "Why?"

"Personal reasons."

"You have personal business with my brother?"

"Yes, I do. And I'd like to keep it personal between

him and me."

"Yeah, well, he may not want to talk with you."

"Look, Luke. I understand you don't like me, and I think I figured out why."

"Oh, yeah?"

I told him about the post I'd written three years ago. "Am I right?"

"Dad had just passed, and the townsfolk were already doubtful that Eddie and I could manage the business without him. Your post confirmed everyone's fear. Only it wasn't our shop."

"I want you to know how sorry I am. I didn't think about how it looked to others until a friend of mine told me weeks later she didn't want to take her car to you. When I asked her why, she told me because of my post. I explained your shop wasn't involved. By then, it seemed like business as usual when I drove by your place, so I didn't update the post."

Papers rustled in the background, but Luke said nothing.

Something stirred deep within me. I stood and paced. I didn't enjoy this uneasy feeling. "Can you forgive me?"

"Forgive you?"

A sense of despair filled my heart, but I didn't understand why. Why did I want his forgiveness?

"We shut down for lunch at noon. If you want to talk with Eddie, best if you meet him here on his way out to lunch."

"I can do that. Thank you."

"And Maggie." He softened his voice. "I forgive you."

Before disconnecting, I thanked him again, my

hand pressed against my chest. I sat and narrowed my eyes. What compelled me to seek Luke's forgiveness?

But he wasn't the only person I'd hurt. How many others should I ask for forgiveness? I bit my bottom lip. Probably too many to count, and too many things demanded my attention to worry about them.

I peeked at my watch—11:30. I zipped inside to my room, brushed my hair, and touched up my makeup. When I headed to the back door, I told my mom that I had an errand to run, and I'd be back to take Snowbunny to the vet.

I drove to PS Automotive and waited in my car for Eddie to come outside. He seemed kind of cute with his tousled, light, wavy hair. I hurried from my car and dashed to his side. "Can we talk for a minute?"

He smirked and grasped his car door handle. "I don't have time."

"But I owe you a favor. I want to fix things with you."

He twisted to face me and widened his eyes. "I told you what you could do two weeks ago. But you vanished and haven't contacted me since. Now you want to make it right?"

"I've been busy." I cringed at my lame excuse. "You wanted to go out with me. If you still do, I'm available."

His hand went to his chin, and he grinned. "Anywhere?"

I took a step back and winced. The gleam in his eye made me uncomfortable. "Perhaps. Where do you want to go?"

He lowered his head and his voice. "I'd like to attend the Ruby-Sterling wedding, but I didn't get an invitation. Did you?"

"Reed and Lou's wedding? Why there?"

His eyes met mine. "There will be people in attendance who think I'm a caveman. But if they see me there with the one who gave me the nickname, maybe they'll realize I'm not." He smiled. "Because everyone knows Maggie Stone wouldn't date a nobody."

"I'm sorry I put you through that." Again, that strange feeling jabbed at me. "Please forgive me for my insensitivity."

"You got it."

"And yes, I received an invitation, and I would love to attend with you."

He offered to pick me up at my place.

"Okay." I opened my phone's calendar and made a note. "We have a date set for one week from tomorrow."

I rushed home to get my baby and drove to Doc Winston's vet clinic. His new assistant, Emily, who was also his niece, greeted us when we stepped inside.

"This must be Snowbunny." She glanced at the bundle in my arms. "May I pet him?"

I nodded.

She extended her hand across the counter and rubbed his head. "He's so sweet." She updated our information on the computer and said, "Have a seat. Doc will be right with you."

After a ten-minute wait, Emily escorted us into Room One. She asked questions and noted my answers in a file folder. "Doc will join you soon." She slipped out the door.

With a booming voice, Doc Winston entered the

room and greeted me. "Tell me what's going on with your puppy."

After I filled him in on Snowbunny's symptoms, Doc checked him over.

"This respectable guy with a corny sense of humor would like to keep your dog overnight for observation and to run tests."

Heat rose on my neck, and I hoped he didn't notice. "You read my blog post?"

"I read them all. Where else can I learn so much about our town?"

I shrugged and patted Snowbunny's head. "What's the matter with my baby?"

"Probably ate something that didn't agree with him. Do you have many plants inside your home?"

"A few." My mind wandered into each room of our living quarters. Christmas cactus, Schefflera, Ficus, and African violets.

"Check them for toxicity. He may have enjoyed a snack that offered him a surprise ending."

I covered my mouth and moaned. "Do you mean he could die?"

Doc shook his head and petted Snowbunny. "Corny vet humor. I didn't mean to alarm you. You mentioned diarrhea as one of his symptoms." He chuckled and reviewed Snowbunny's file. "Let me check him out, and hopefully he'll be as good as new tomorrow morning."

I rubbed my baby's back. "Bye, sweet boy. Mommy will return for you tomorrow."

Emily entered the room and picked up Snowbunny. "I'll put him in the back, and we can break for lunch. Our order just arrived. Huge helpings too."

"Terrific." Doc peered at me and smiled. "Have you had lunch yet?"

"I'm not a big lunch eater."

"Please join us. We have a covered picnic table out back." His eyes shone, and he pointed to the door that exited to the back of the clinic. "And in thirty minutes I'll return to reexamine Snowbunny and possibly take an x-ray."

"Well, I am a wee bit hungry."

Emily either winked at Doc or had something in her eye. "I need to eat at my desk and try to get caught up. You and Maggie can have the picnic table to yourselves."

Doc raised his elbow in a kind gesture. "I am privileged to have you as my lunch date today. Shall we venture outdoors?"

I took his offered elbow. Lunch date? In the past two weeks, I'd dated Nick Stewart and now Doc Winston. And in a week, I'd date Eddie Gibson. The same three men as Jill Drake.

Would these dates end better for me than they did for her?

Thirty

Mom knocked on my bedroom door. "Hurry. I don't want to be late for church."

I cracked it open and poked out my head. "Five minutes."

"What takes you so long?"

"My hair won't cooperate."

"You look beautiful. Nothing's wrong with your hair."

"Okay." I opened the door all the way. "But what's the rush?"

"If you must know, Ivan is meeting me there."

"Ivan?" I opened my eyes wider. "Oh. Now I get it." I snatched my purse from my closet. "I thought you weren't interested in him or dating?"

"We're not dating." She flicked her wrist. "Just two friends getting together."

"Sure, Mom." I stooped to pat Snowbunny on his soft, furry head. "Bye sweet puppy. Stay out of trouble."

Mom extended her hand to help me up, and her voice cracked. "I'm sorry I let him get into the garden and didn't keep a closer eye on him. I never considered he'd eat the plants."

"No problem. He's doing well now."

Mom bolted to the car, beating me by a few seconds. Her desire to see Ivan was undeniable.

When we arrived at church, we spotted him standing outside at the front entrance.

I glanced at mom. "Don't jump out of the car until I pull into a parking spot." I turned off the ignition, and she hurried to the church entrance, leaving me behind. I chuckled when I entered the foyer.

"Maggie, dear. Seeing you this morning fills my heart with joy." Miss Risa's warm glow brightened my day. "I miss your lovely face when you're not here."

I thanked her and grinned. She was a kind lady and seemed to love everyone. When she greeted another couple, I entered the sanctuary. I needed to find someone to sit with to give my mom space and not interfere with her and Ivan.

"Will you join me?" From behind, Nick's deep voice surprised me and caused a quick twitch.

I twisted my head in his direction. "Where are you sitting?"

He laid his hand on my upper back and led me to the far-left side, halfway up. "How's this?"

"Perfect." I slid into the pew next to a long-time attender of the church and exchanged greetings with her and her family before glancing at Nick, who sat on my left. "Have you attended here before today?"

"The past two weeks." He laid his Bible beside him to his left. "Is this where you attend?"

"Yes. But I've missed two Sundays." I peered down at the Bible in my lap. Why was I discontented about missing the past two weeks?

"Do you have an answer for me yet about the job

offer?"

"Not yet."

"Okay. Keep praying about it. Ask the Lord to lead you."

"Why is it so warm in here today?" I fanned my face with my hand. Or was it the realization I hadn't prayed about his or Wade's job offer?

Nick stood, and I realized the song leader and pianist had taken their places up front.

I laid my Bible next to me, jumped up, and yanked a hymnal from the back of the pew in front of me.

"You don't need one. They have the words on the screen in front."

I jerked my head back. "Since when?"

"Last week was the first time. One of Pastor Ben's recent changes."

"Are there more?"

He raised his index finger to his mouth and inched closer. "We can talk about it at lunch."

"Lunch?" I gave my head a shake. "I have plans."

~

Wade loved the old hymns and "Great is Thy Faithfulness" was one of his favorites. Grateful he'd found Jill soon after he arrived, she showed him around and introduced him to her friend Becca and a few others at the church.

While he sang, his eyes roamed the congregation. People of all ages gathered to worship and sing to the Lord. Was Maggie among them? Would she have good news for him and his horses?

He searched the crowd again and recognized her long, flowing waves. When she turned to the woman on her right, he confirmed she was indeed Maggie by her familiar smile. But he didn't recognize the man on her left whom she stood rather close to.

When the song ended, he turned to Jill. "Who's the guy with Maggie?"

Jill followed his gaze, dipped her chin, and grimaced. "Doctor Nicolas Stewart."

Wade gave her a slow nod and stifled a sneer. Fantastic. He didn't need to know that. Looked as though Doctor Stewart may gain a new employee.

For now, Wade would enjoy the service. Tomorrow, he hoped to discover the truth about Maggie.

~

After the announcements, Pastor Ben approached the pulpit and placed his Bible on top. I eyed my fingernails. And frowned. Time to redo my polish.

Did he say Ezekiel? The Old Testament? I stared at Nick's Bible, which appeared to be opened more than halfway. I opened mine and flipped through the pages until I found it. After another peek at Nick's Bible, I turned to chapter thirty-seven. I prepared myself for a boring message. I found the Old Testament dull.

Pastor Ben read the first two verses about dry bones. A valley full of them.

I related to a dried-up life. Even when surrounded by people, loneliness, emptiness, and brokenness filled me. No one understood.

He then read verses three through six.

> He asked me, "Son of man, can these
> bones live?"
> I said, "Sovereign LORD, you
> alone know."

Then he said to me, "Prophesy to these bones and say to them, 'Dry bones, hear the word of the LORD! This is what the Sovereign LORD says to these bones: I will make breath enter you, and you will come to life. I will attach tendons to you and make flesh come upon you and cover you with skin; I will put breath in you, and you will come to life. Then you will know that I am the LORD.'"

I squirmed and tried to get comfortable. Breath and life?

Pastor Ben said, "What was necessary for these bones to live?"

I perked up and zoned in on the message. They'd need a lot. They were dead, dried-up bones.

He continued to preach. "To live these bones needed to hear the Word of the Lord and receive the breath of God."

I rested back in the pew and rolled my eyes. No need to listen to this. I've grown up with God's Word.

Pastor Ben picked up his Bible and raised it high. "We need to spend quality time in God's Word and be receptive to the Holy Spirit's guidance each day. He is our breath of life."

Something I didn't do. Not every day. I lowered my head and sighed. Not even every week or month.

Pastor Ben read verses seven through ten.

So I prophesied as I was commanded.

And as I was prophesying, there was a noise, a rattling sound, and the bones came together, bone to bone. I looked, and tendons and flesh appeared on them and skin covered them, but there was no breath in them.

Then he said to me, "Prophesy to the breath; prophesy, son of man, and say to it, 'This is what the Sovereign LORD says: Come, breath, from the four winds and breathe into these slain, that they may live.'" So I prophesied as he commanded me, and breath entered them; they came to life and stood up on their feet—a vast army.

I gave Pastor Ben my full attention. Those dry bones walking around must have startled Ezekiel. They would have scared me.

Pastor Ben leaned forward and tapped his finger on the pulpit. "Life didn't come until the breath of the Holy Spirit entered them and dwelt within. The Holy Spirit moved deep within their dry bones and transformed their lives. And He desires to transform your life too."

I brought a thumbnail to my mouth. Me? My life? I wrinkled my forehead and clasped my hands in my lap. Why hadn't He already done that?

Pastor Ben flipped a few pages in his Bible. "God's Spirit is the key to those places of brokenness, fear, rejection, and loneliness. Give Him permission to take what is dead in you and bring renewed life. He wants to do in you what He said one chapter earlier in Ezekiel thirty-six, verse twenty-six."

> I will give you a new heart and put a
> new spirit in you; I will remove from
> you your heart of stone and give you
> a heart of flesh.

Pastor Ben scanned the congregation. "God wants to bring new life into the dry, lifeless places in each of us. No matter how empty we may feel—He has not left us. He offers us hope, peace, joy, and love."

Nick said a quiet, "Amen."

I glanced at him, returned my gaze to Pastor Ben, and balled my fists, digging my fingernails into my palms. But how do I give God permission?

Pastor Ben stepped away from the pulpit and moved closer to the congregation. "If your walk with the Lord appears empty, I encourage you to pray and ask the Holy Spirit to breathe life into your dry bones and refresh you. To go beyond mere survival and contentment, and instead thrive in spiritual growth, striving to resemble Christ. Spend time in God's Word and be sensitive to the Holy Spirit's leading."

I tilted my head and furrowed my brow. All it takes is a simple prayer? I massaged my temples. That's it?

While the pianist played a soft tune, Pastor Ben invited us to come forward to pray with a member of the prayer team.

I needed to go forward, but I couldn't move. What would people think of me? I gripped the edge of the pew while my heart pounded in my ears. If I stood, I'd run out the back.

"Are you okay?" Nick angled his knees closer to mine and deepened his voice. "Would you like someone to pray with you?"

He knew I needed to go forward. Was it that obvious? But I couldn't go up front.

"I'm fine." My fingernails again gained my attention. I couldn't let anyone know my life was a lie.

Thirty-one

When the service ended, Wade turned to Jill. "Pastor Peterson is an excellent speaker."

"And a nice guy."

"I'd like to meet him."

"I can do better than that." She grinned, scanned the sanctuary, and turned back to Wade. "Pastor Ben, Becca, and I are going to La Casa for lunch. Would you like to join us?"

"Sounds fantastic. Count me in."

Jill introduced Wade to people on their way out to the foyer. She turned back toward the sanctuary, touched his elbow, and motioned to Maggie and the doctor, making their way down the center aisle. "Looks like you'll get to meet Nick Stewart too."

Maggie's eyes grew wide when she spotted Wade and even wider when she realized he was with Jill. "Isn't this cozy?"

Jill greeted Maggie and Nick and introduced him to Wade. "We're going to grab some lunch. Would you like to join us?"

Maggie locked her arm around Nick's and gave him what appeared to Wade to be a fake smile. "We already have plans for lunch."

With a nod, Nick escorted Maggie out the door.

Jill nudged Wade's elbow and whispered. "Did you think that seemed odd?"

Wade shook his head and cleared his throat. "Seemed like typical Maggie to me." He pointed to the doors leading outside. "Are the four of us driving over together?"

Jill suggested the two of them leave for the restaurant to reserve a table, and she'd text Becca to let her know.

They made their way out the door, through the parking lot, and to his truck.

"I'm having trouble picturing you as a civil engineer."

She giggled and climbed into his pickup. "Is that any harder to believe than Maggie mucking stalls?"

"You know about that?" He shut her door and strode to the driver's side.

When he got seated beside her, Jill said, "She shared that with me two weeks ago."

He started the truck and leaned back in his seat. "She's been a big help to me. Done an outstanding job."

"Have you told her?"

"Yep. But I told her too late." He smacked the steering wheel a little harder than he'd intended. "I'd like her to come back to help me, but . . ." He lifted his hands, palms facing the windshield. "Whoa. I'm sorry." He turned to face Jill. "I shouldn't unload all of this on you." He put the truck into drive, drove the short distance to La Casa, parked, and turned off the ignition.

Jill touched the door handle, paused, and faced him. "I don't mind you unloading on me. Sometimes it helps to talk about the things that bother us."

"I just get so frustrated with her."

"With Maggie?"

"Yep. But I don't get that upset with anyone else."

"Did this frustration first show up when she worked with you on your ranch or before?"

He narrowed his eyes at Jill. "What do you know?"

"Nothing I can share."

"But you know about our past. Right?"

"A part of it."

"And probably the part that keeps me frustrated."

"You are about to meet a man who is eager to assist with your frustration." She opened the door and climbed down.

Wade did the same and met her behind the truck. "Before we go inside, I want to ask you something."

"Sure."

"Lou said you plan to attend her and Dad's wedding. Are you going with someone?"

"I plan to go solo."

"Would you join me at the wedding party table as my date?"

She hesitated and lowered her head.

"I didn't mean to make you uncomfortable. Forget it."

"That's not it." She touched his arm and dropped her hand to her side. "Is this an attempt to make Maggie jealous?"

He deepened the pitch of his voice. "Not at all."

"I'd like to know going into this if it's a fake date or real."

He avoided her eyes and slid his boot along the pavement. "I'll be honest with you. Today, I can't imagine Maggie and me reconciling to the point of anything lasting." He scraped his boot along the pavement again and peeked at Jill. "But God may have other plans for our future."

~

Nick turned into La Casa's parking lot and found a spot to park. "When I suggested during the service we go to lunch today, you said you had plans. What happened?"

"You didn't want my plans to change?"

"I'd rather you didn't use me to make Wade jealous."

"That's what you think?" I brought my hand to my mouth.

Nick shot me a piercing glare. "Is he here?"

"Jill didn't say where they were going, did she?"

"Check out the parking lot and tell me if you see his car."

"He drives a pickup."

Nick strained his neck to search the lot. "Is it black?"

With a huff, I crossed my arms. "If you think that's why I suggested we come here, then take me back to the church to get my car. Now."

"I asked you a simple question, and you reply with an indignant attitude? Besides, your response failed to address my question." He backed the car out of its spot.

"Texas plates. That's Wade's." I pointed to the truck. "But I didn't know he'd be here."

Nick turned north out of the restaurant lot and headed to the church.

I placed my hand on Nick's upper arm. "I told you the truth."

"But you changed your mind so you could tell him we already had lunch plans. To make him jealous."

My chest tightened, and I slouched in my seat. "I guess so. Without realizing it. That's who I am."

"You use people without realizing you're doing it?"

I stared through the windshield and pouted. "That's why I'm not well-liked. I learn something about someone and sense an obligation to share that information."

"Why do you do that?"

"Helps me to forget my mistakes and focus on the failures of others."

"And that works for you?"

"Not much. But facing the truth is tough. I have to accept that I'm a disappointment."

He softened his voice. "You don't believe that."

I cut him a look. "Yes. I do."

"Can you explain the reasons behind your feelings?" He turned into the church parking lot and parked next to my car.

"I . . ."

Nick reached for my hands. "How could someone as beautiful and successful as you be a disappointment?" He held both of my hands with his eyes locked onto mine. "You're a child of God. He loves you."

~

Wade struggled to admit God may have other plans for him and Maggie. God could do anything. But would He?

The host led them to a table for four near a small decorative fountain along the left wall.

Jill pulled out her chair and sat. "This is my favorite table. I welcome the soothing sound of the water splashing down. Fills me with a sense of calm and peace."

Wade agreed and peered at the door. "There's Pastor Ben and Becca." He remained standing to make sure they knew he and Jill already had a table.

After Ben and Becca joined them and the two men introduced themselves, Becca took a seat on Jill's right, and Wade sat on her left.

Ben took the remaining seat. "I look forward to performing your dad and Lou's wedding ceremony on Saturday."

"I'm glad you and your church were available to accommodate them for the wedding and for their reception since they outgrew Mama Lou's Café."

Ben and Becca eyed one another, and Becca said, "I guess they haven't told you. Lou canceled the church for the reception and secured the community center. The guest list keeps growing."

Wade chuckled and picked up a menu. "I wonder what my dad thinks about that?"

After they took a few minutes to review the food options, they placed their orders. The two ladies ordered taco salads, Ben ordered chicken enchiladas, and Wade ordered a steak burrito.

Ben held his menu out for the server and turned to Wade. "I understand you're a rancher. How many cattle do you own?"

"We have fifty-two, but I hope to expand in the future."

"Horses too?"

"Three."

"I haven't ridden in years. Do you allow others to ride?"

"Sure. Let me know when and we'll saddle up." Wade glanced across the table at Becca. "You're welcome to join us."

"I'll pass for now, but thank you."

He turned to Jill and raised his eyebrows. "If you ever want to ride, or learn how to muck a stall, let me know."

She laughed and took a sip of her sweet tea. "We'll see."

The food arrived, and Pastor Ben offered a prayer. They chatted through lunch about the church and its vast differences from the one that Ben left in Florida.

Wade swallowed a mouthful of delicious, well-seasoned steak. "I hope this one stays the way it is. The hymns this morning touched me."

Pastor Ben nodded and rested his hand on Becca's arm. "We have many factors to consider before making more service changes. I appreciate your input."

"And I'd value your thoughts on something I've dealt with for a long time." He bowed his head for a moment and returned his gaze to Pastor Ben. "I'm having a hard time forgiving someone who I believe has lied to me for twenty years."

A distinct but barely audible gasp spilled from Jill's lips.

When Wade twisted back to her, she and Becca shared wide eyes.

Thirty-two

Mom rinsed the supper plates and placed them in the dishwasher while I put away the leftover Chicken Alfredo. "Tell me the truth. What do you think of Doctor Stewart?"

"He's an extraordinary guy." I closed the refrigerator and stepped to the sink. "Yesterday, after church, he prayed with me. I don't understand why someone would do that after all I've done." I put the last of the flatware into the dishwasher and closed the door. "He's thoughtful and kind."

Her entire face lit up. "Do you have plans to meet?"

"I hate to let you down, but he's not the man for me." I gave my mom a brief hug. "And marriage is not in my future. I'm too set in my ways. No point in dating anyone."

She ran her finger down my cheek. "Don't give up. You have much to offer."

I strolled out of the kitchen and onto the back porch. The balmy evening felt pleasant after a stormy afternoon. I sat on the bench, gazed at the trees along the back of my property, and inhaled the refreshing earthy scent that lingered in the air.

Mom opened the back door. "Aren't you going to the Bible study tonight?"

"Not a good idea today."

She took a seat next to me. "Why not?"

"A sense of uneasiness has weighed on me all day. Like something's going to happen. I don't think I'm supposed to go."

She wrapped her fingers around my hand. "Maybe the Lord is prompting you to go, and the enemy is trying to convince you to remain at home."

I frowned and wrinkled my nose. "Does that really happen?"

She smiled and pushed a strand of my hair behind my ear. "I hope you'll go to discover why the Lord wants you there."

"But what if He doesn't want me there? What if the devil wants me to go?"

Mom brushed her finger across her lips. "Do you think he would encourage you to study God's Word?" Her eyes crinkled at the corners.

"I suppose not." I kissed Mom's cheek and thanked her. "You're the best."

~

Wade removed Cisco's saddle. He missed having Maggie's help. She hadn't called to tell him whether she'd work for him or that doctor guy. Wade assumed that was his answer. She and Doctor Stewart. They attended church as a couple, went out to lunch, and planned to work together. Great. Anyway, he tried to convince himself of that.

Should he call her to confirm she'd decided? He removed his cell from his pocket and clicked on her number.

She answered on the fourth ring and greeted him. "I'm sorry I haven't called you."

"Have you made your decision?"

"Can you give me more time? I hope to know tomorrow."

"Something special about tomorrow?"

"Not at all. I hope to have a clearer head in the morning. Today, my thoughts are a mess, and I'm on my way out."

"That's fine."

She thanked him and disconnected their call.

Wade wrestled with their conversation. Why were her thoughts a mess? And was she on her way out with Nick?

Ten minutes later, he received a call from Sophia Garrison. He answered and asked her if she'd received any news.

"Still waiting. Gemma wanted me to call to find out if you've gotten word yet."

"Nothing. I've logged in three times today to check for results without success."

"She has too."

He told her that he'd call her when he received an update, and they said goodbye.

How would he broach the subject with Maggie? He wanted her to tell him the truth before he revealed what he knew. But would she?

Lord, I need Your wisdom. Lead me to approach Maggie so she'll respond in openness and honesty. Heal our brokenness over this situation and help me talk with her without frustration or resentment. Help me to share Your love.

~

My watch read 7:10 when I arrived at Jill's house for the Bible study. I darted to the front door and rang the bell.

Becca answered and greeted me with a hug. "I was about to call to make sure you were on your way. Come on inside. We have a special treat for you."

"For me?"

I followed her to the kitchen. On the counter sat a cake with white frosting and one large candle in the middle.

Becca, Jill, and Lanie joined their voices and sang "Happy Birthday."

I took a step back and gaped at them. "How did you know my birthday is tomorrow?"

Becca glanced at Jill and Lanie on the opposite side of the counter. "Two weeks ago, I heard your mom tell Miss Risa."

"Thanks, y'all. This is sweet." I brought my hand to my chest. Other than Mom and Aunt Tilly, no one had ever made me a birthday cake.

Jill grasped plates and a knife off the counter and carried them and the cake to the table. "Red velvet with cream cheese icing."

"And you remembered my favorite cake too?"

Becca wrapped her arm around my shoulder. "Of course. What are friends for?"

We took our seats at the table. I enjoyed every bite of my moist cake and the creaminess of the rich icing. But more than that, I cherished the thought of these three ladies wanting me here, though the reason was still unclear.

"The big wedding is coming up Saturday." Lanie beamed, likely thinking about her own wedding three months away. "I stopped by the café today and talked to Lou. She's in a frenzy, making sure everything is ready."

After we talked about the wedding, Jill stood and gathered our dirty dishes.

"Let me help with those." I rose and nabbed two forks Jill missed.

"Nonsense. Your birthday. I can get this."

I joined her at the sink, where running water splashed into a glass. "Something I want to tell you privately."

She creased her forehead and placed her hand on my arm. "I have something to tell you as well."

"Go ahead." I nodded. "What?"

She turned off the faucet and hushed her voice. "I'm going to the wedding with Wade."

I widened my eyes and dipped my chin. "Wade?" I laughed and covered my mouth. "This is too funny."

She tilted her head to the right. "Why are you laughing? I thought you might be upset."

"No. But I hope you'll laugh, too, when I tell you who I'm going with."

She leaned closer to me. We both whispered, doing our best to keep our conversation private.

I peeked behind me to make sure no one had snuck up on us, turned the faucet back on, and dropped the forks in the sink. "Eddie asked me to go with him."

She jerked her head back and raised her voice. "Eddie Gibson?"

Lanie hurried over to us. "You're going with Eddie?"

"Yes. But before either of you gets upset, let me tell you why he asked me."

They both stared at me while I related his reason. Their faces softened, and they agreed his being seen with me might change the negative perception of him created by my blog post.

We returned to the table and took our seats.

"What did you think of Ben's message yesterday?" Becca's eyes shone with love for her husband.

Lanie wrote something on her notepad. "I attended Joy Fellowship, but that's all Jill talked about when we both got home."

Jill grinned and opened her Bible. "The best message he's preached so far. I'm sure God used him to awaken many stony hearts."

Becca focused her attention on me. "What did you think?"

"Me? I. Uh." My hands shook, and I clasped them in my lap.

Becca continued to stare at me.

"What do you want me to say?"

She laid her opened palm on the table. "Please give me your hand."

I peered at her and lifted my brows. "Why?"

"You seem tense and acted like you didn't want to answer my question." She wiggled her fingers. "Did you hate it but don't want to tell me?"

I placed my hand in hers. "I didn't hate it. But it made me uncomfortable."

Lanie and Jill eyed one another and bowed their heads.

Becca asked me to focus on her. "Why did you feel uncomfortable?"

I tried to pull my hand away, but she didn't let go. "His sermon was for me, okay? Are you happy now?"

"Why didn't you come forward to pray?"

I yanked my hand from hers. "And have everyone talk about me?" I lowered my head on the table. "I'm a phony."

Becca scooted her chair closer to mine and touched my upper back. "You're not a phony. You're like the rest of us. We're all trying to live our life for Christ the best we know how."

I raised my head and massaged the back of my neck. "You don't understand. I've attended church all my life, but I'm not like you. I don't pray often, or read my Bible, or listen to Christian music, or any of those things y'all do."

"What did Ben say?" Becca's soft touch on my shoulder soothed my uneasiness. "Ask the Holy Spirit to breathe life into your dry bones."

My voice trembled, and I hesitated to speak. "I want Him to remove my stony heart and give me a heart of flesh. But I don't see that happening. I'm Maggie *Stone*—I was born with a stony heart and it's here to stay."

Jill scooted her chair closer to me. "Not true."

"But even if He gives me a new, softer heart, I'll only disappoint Him."

"None of us are perfect. But He loves each of us." Jill wrapped her arm around me in a side hug. "His death brings us forgiveness and eternal life with Him. He died for you."

"But why hasn't He already breathed His life into me?"

Jill's voice sounded like a soft melody, calm and sweet. "He wants you to make a personal decision to follow Him."

"Pastor Ben said something about praying. What should I say?"

Becca patted my hand and whispered. "Pray from your heart."

"But I've done so many horrible things. Worse than gossip."

"That doesn't matter. We've all done things we're not proud of." Jill pulled me closer, and I felt the warmth of her head against mine. "God will not only hear your words of confession, but He knows the sincerity of your heart and that you want to follow Him. Just talk with Him like you talk with us."

I closed my eyes and bowed my head. "Father . . . I need Your Holy Spirit to breathe life into my dry bones." Someone shoved a tissue into my hand. "I confess my sin, a bunch of them." I sniffled and wiped my eyes. "Thank you for sending Christ to die for me and for raising Him from the dead. Jesus, I want You to be the Lord of my life. I want to follow You."

After a few minutes of silence, I dried my eyes and noticed the glowing faces of my three friends around the table. Considering all I'd written about them, I couldn't believe how much they cared for and supported me in my commitment to follow Christ. I bowed my head once more. "I should make some changes, shouldn't I?"

Becca squeezed me in a bear hug. "Allow the Lord to lead you. You'll learn as you follow Him."

"Would you mind if I leave now? I need to go home and share what's happened with Mom." I ran my hand across my cheeks. "Please pray for me. I still must tell her what I did twenty years ago." I softened my voice and slowed my words. "And I need courage to face Wade with the truth as well."

Thirty-three

Wade rinsed the shaving cream from his face and snatched a towel. Would today be the day he confirmed what he'd expected for years? With his early-morning chores complete, he returned to his bedroom, plopped down on his cozy bed, and rested back against the soft pillows with his Bible. He opened it to James, chapter four.

He reread verse twelve. "There is only one Lawgiver and Judge, the one who is able to save and destroy. But you—who are you to judge your neighbor?"

How could he judge Maggie? He didn't know what caused her to lie to him all those years ago. She may have had a legitimate reason. He massaged the back of his neck. Did God expect him to forgive her without knowing why she did what she did? He knew the answer. But could he?

He continued reading and meditated upon verse seventeen: "If anyone, then, knows the good they ought to do and doesn't do it, it is sin for them."

Even if he never learns the truth, it would be a sin for him not to forgive Maggie. He rubbed his hand across his mouth and chin. *God, help me.*

He picked up his cell and noticed the date—Tuesday, June 12. Why did that date sound familiar? He bounded off his bed. Maggie's birthday.

He called Lou and hoped she'd help him out. "Would you make a birthday cake for Maggie today?"

"I'd love to, but I don't think it's possible. We have a special order today that's going to keep us busy." She spoke to someone nearby and returned to Wade's call. "There's a cake mix in the pantry. I'm sure she'd appreciate it if you made it for her."

"Me?"

"You're a college educated manager and rancher. You can bake a cake."

"No time. I'll send her flowers instead."

Joy resonated in her voice. "Flowers? Are you sure you want to do that?"

"Why not?"

"Flowers are rather personal. She may get the wrong impression."

"I'll take my chances." He thanked her and disconnected the call.

Too personal? They're just flowers and she'll like them. He called the florist and ordered a bouquet of red and yellow flowers and asked to have them delivered to Maggie's home.

"What do you want the card to say?"

He paced across the room. "Happy birthday, Maggie. You've been an exceptional help to me. Wade."

"Will do. We'll get them to her early this afternoon."

He thanked the lady and hung up. Did he say too much? He hoped she'd help him out on the ranch. Was that his reason for sending her the bouquet?

Or had God prompted him to open his heart and let Maggie back in?

~

Mom busied herself at the kitchen sink. A beautiful chocolate cake with chocolate frosting sat on the counter. "Happy birthday, sweet girl."

I kissed her cheek and thanked her for another one of my favorite cakes while she dried the pans. "You were out late last night."

"I wasn't that late. Ivan took me to Chattanooga for dinner. We had a lovely time."

"Perhaps I dosed off before you got here. I don't remember hearing you come in."

"And where have you been all morning, birthday girl?"

"Reading my Bible. The red-letter text."

Mom raised her eyebrows and grinned. "All of Jesus' words?"

I hugged her and shared what happened in the Bible study.

"Praise God." She lifted both hands upward. "I'm so happy for you."

How can I tell her the rest? *Lord, help me.* I clenched and released my fists and wrung my hands. "Please sit down. I've got something important to tell you."

"Okay. Just let me put these cake pans away." She put the pans inside the cabinet under the flatware drawer, grabbed a dishrag, and cleaned the countertops.

I placed my hand on top of hers. "That can wait. I need to tell you something. Now."

She patted me on my cheek. "Don't get yourself all worked up, my precious Pearl. Just one more minute."

I paced across the kitchen and spun back to Mom. "This can't wait any longer. I've kept a secret and told you a lie. I need to confess."

"Oh, my." She took a seat at the table. "Go ahead. And whatever it is, I'll love you the same. You know that, don't you?"

I nodded and bit my lip. I took a seat next to her, poured out my heart, and told her the whole truth. The truth I should have shared a long time ago. I wiped my face with the back of my hands. "I'm so sorry for lying to you. Can you forgive me?"

With tears brimming in her eyes, she took my hands in hers. "I'm hurt you kept this from me until now, but I forgive you." She hugged my neck, and her tears mingled with mine.

"Have you told Wade?"

I shook my head and scowled. "I've tried. But I've dreaded telling him more than telling you." I lowered my gaze and pinched the bridge of my nose. "I'm sure he'll hate me."

"Oh, honey. He won't hate you. He may be upset, but he'll forgive you too."

I looked up. "I hope you're right."

Mom hugged me and reassured me again that everything would work out.

I returned to my room and spent ten minutes in prayer, asking God for the right words and the right time to share them with Wade. Would he get mad at me again before I could tell him?

At my desk, I opened my computer and checked the recent blog post comments from last week. I didn't expect as many with my topic of makeup, and I still didn't have a topic for tomorrow's post.

I glanced at the comments. One person said, "Refreshing to read about makeup after the heartache you've caused people in town. Maybe write something nice about someone next week."

Their comment hit me hard. The person was right. I have caused a substantial amount of trouble. I could write something positive about Nick and the expansion of his staff. Or Wade and the hard work of running a ranch. I could mention Jill, Becca, and Lanie and their dear friendship and Bible study.

Or Pastor Ben's sermon that left me confused because it challenged my beliefs. But I wasn't ready. Or brave enough to share that story yet.

Pleasant Springs buzzed with other newsworthy happenings. The upcoming wedding of our beloved owner of Mama Lou's Café. The community center with their summer programs for kids. Creekside Children's Home and the siblings they're caring for now and the county's need for foster parents.

Must be more I can do. *Seek forgiveness.*

I leaned back and stared at my opened hands. I'm doing that, aren't I? By finally telling Mom and soon Wade.

Should I apologize and ask each person I've offended in my posts to forgive me? I sensed a gentle nudge inside.

I groaned and slumped into my chair. This will take months. Three years' worth of blog posts.

I closed my eyes and focused on the Lord. I'll write apologies on my blog.

The odd feeling inside lessened but didn't leave.

I sat up taller, opened my eyes, and pressed my hands across my churning stomach. Should I call or visit people with a personal apology?

A sense of peace washed over me. I had a substantial amount of work before me. And I still needed to call Nick and Wade. Odd. Nick hadn't called me about my decision.

I clicked on his cell number and got his voicemail. "Hey. I've decided regarding your offer. Please call me."

If I ever sold my bed-and-breakfast, Nick's opportunity allowed me growth and future possibilities. And when I tell Wade the truth, he'll renege on his offer, anyway. I'd rather spend my time with him, but everything hinges on how he takes the news. I'm not sure he'll want me around.

My heart rate quickened when I dialed Wade, but he didn't answer either. "Hi. I'd like to talk to you about my decision to work on your ranch and something else too. Thanks."

After my racing heart calmed, I retrieved a notebook from my desk drawer and prepared to jot the information down that might have been offensive in my blog posts. Time flew by while I read each word I'd written. How could I have been so cruel? And how long will it take me to make things right?

"And God, You have Your work cut out for You, too, to transform me into something worthwhile."

Mom's shrieking voice interrupted my thoughts. "Hurry Maggie. Come see this."

I opened my bedroom door and bolted into the living room. A beautiful bouquet of vibrant red, pure white, and sunny yellow flowers adorned the coffee table. "Are these from you?"

She withdrew the card from the middle of the bouquet and held it out to me. "Hurry and read this."

My hands shook when I took the card from my mom and read it aloud. "Wade." I brought my hand to my chest and considered not telling him about his baby. After all, it seemed like he was warming up to me with this note and flowers. I wouldn't want to ruin that.

He is the only man who comes to mind whenever I think of love. The only man who has captured my heart. The man I wish to spend the rest of my life with.

Thirty-four

Wade finished up his early morning chores in the stable on Wednesday and entered his office. He sat and tackled his bookkeeping tasks, thankful to the Lord for keeping the ranch afloat.

Moments later, Reed hurried into the office, his breathing heavy.

"Dad, what's wrong?" Wade rushed to his side. Was Dad having a heart attack?

"Nothing, Son. I wanted to be sure you read Maggie's blog post today."

Wade removed his hat and ruffled his hair. "Her post made you run all the way to the barn to tell me?"

"Yes." He pointed upward. "I believe the Lord is changing that woman's heart." He turned and headed out of the stable.

Must be one phenomenal blog post. The cattle can wait a few minutes for fresh water. He strode to the stable, entered his office, and opened Maggie's blog. He took a seat before he read her latest email called, "A Change in Me and My Posts."

If you're here to read about small-town gossip, you're in the wrong place. I no longer will do that. After much prayer and discussion, I plan to change the tone and direction of my posts. You can find places in town where you can get the scoop, but not from me. Not anymore.

My new focus, for the near future, will be to correct my wrongs and use my weekly blog to do that.

One of my first posts three years ago told a story about an indiscretion of a gentleman on our town council. The town found him guilty of what I accused him of, but I had no right to belittle him. I'm not the judge, nor would I wish to hold that title. Like the first time, I won't state the man's name here, but I will contact him and apologize for my interference.

If you have experienced humiliation because of me and my posts, I'll get to you too. Instead of a post once a week, I may post twice a week to speed up the process. Please give me time and know I'm sorry.

Thank you for your understanding and forgiveness.

Wade shook his head and furrowed his brow. What happened to Maggie?

He clicked on her cell number and waited. He frowned when it went to voicemail. "Wade, here. Returning your call. Talk soon."

Was God at work in Maggie's heart? He stepped out of the stable and crossed over to the barn to fill the cattle's water trough. *Father, thank you. If Maggie has taken a step of faith and is a true follower of Christ, does this mean you're preparing us . . . Never mind. I'm sure that's not what You're doing. That would take a miracle.*

~

After I returned home at noon from my weekly cookie run to Creekside, I entered my living room, gazed at the flowers from Wade, and reread his card.

"You've been an exceptional help to me." Not only had he remembered my birthday, but he used my favorite colors—red and yellow. Meant something special. I'm sure of it.

Help me, Lord, not to mess this up.

I've heard people pray, "open the door" and "shut the door." My turn to give that a try.

Lord, close the door to the opportunity where You don't want me and open the door to what You want me to pursue. Nick or Wade's job offer? I think it's Nick's, but I want to spend extra time with Wade and try to deepen my relationship with him. What do you want, Lord? I'm a mess and need You to guide me.

My cell buzzed. Nick. I chuckled. This prayer thing works. I answered his call.

"Sorry I didn't get back to you yesterday. We got slammed."

"No problem. And perhaps I can help you out with that. I'd like to accept your job offer of twenty hours a week as your business manager."

He exhaled a deep sigh and responded in a business-like manner. "About that. I'm having second thoughts. I can oversee it for another month or two before bringing a manager on board."

"So, you'll check in with me within two months?" The silence that lingered between us unsettled me.

"I intend to explore other candidates too."

"Oh?" I closed my eyes and placed my fist on my chest. "You no longer think I'm the right person for the job?"

He softened his voice and responded more like a friend. "Can we get together this evening? I hate having this conversation over the phone."

I tried not to sound annoyed, but I couldn't pull it off. "No, I get it. I said too much Sunday and now you're unsure if you can trust me. You think I'll try to use you to get my own way."

"Please try to understand."

"Read my blog post." I clicked off the phone call. I didn't mean to end it without saying goodbye, but I couldn't keep my voice steady.

God, You closed the door. Didn't You? I'm trying to trust You. But this hurts.

I logged onto my computer to research older blog posts and added names, dates, and circumstances to my notes for another apology post. But I lacked focus. I stood, found Mom in the kitchen, and told her that I needed to get out of the house. I drove to Mama Lou's Café for coffee.

Lou greeted me with a hug when I entered the restaurant. "You look radiant, as always today, in your red and yellow sundress."

"Thanks, but why are you here? Don't you have errands to run to get everything ready for Saturday?"

"Short-staffed today. Our regular customers are keeping Debbie Sue occupied, but she just got a call from a tour group of sixteen senior adults asking if we could accommodate them. They'll arrive in twenty minutes for lunch."

"Is there anything I can do to help?"

"Have you waited tables before?"

"Perhaps I can help you with wedding arrangements?"

Lou's shoulders sagged, and her tired eyes drooped. "I can use help on Saturday with decorating the community center for the reception."

"I'd love to help with that."

She thanked me and glanced at a table of four. "I've got to run. They appear impatient."

I strolled to the counter to order my coffee and had that same odd feeling I'd experienced since Monday evening.

"Your usual?" Debbie Sue dashed behind the counter and snagged a cup for my coffee.

Just when I was about to say yes, I said, "I'm here to help. Where can you best use me today?"

Her jaw dropped along with the cup. "Huh?"

"Glad that's a paper cup." I wanted to laugh at her expression but grinned instead. "Lou said you could use some help. Been a long time since I waited tables except for breakfast at my place, but I'm capable of that or helping in the kitchen."

She reached under the counter and handed me an apron and a notepad. "Table six sat down five minutes ago. Please take their order." She guided me in the right direction.

I didn't recognize the two adults or their two children, so I turned on the Southern charm. "Hi, I'm Maggie. I'll be servin' y'all today. Have you decided on your order?"

The woman eyed me up and down. "You must be the owner."

I suppose she noticed my dressy attire and didn't think it fit with the café feel. "No, ma'am. Helpin' out today. Expectin' a sizeable group soon."

They placed their order, and I took it back to the kitchen. "Someone help me here. Who do I give an order to?"

"Right here." A gray-haired woman, whom I remembered working in the high school cafeteria, pointed to a clip where other orders hung.

"Done. And do I get their drink orders myself?"

She nodded while she prepped a salad. "Debbie Sue said we got another helper." The cook smirked. "You're the last person I expected."

Two days earlier, I would have taken offense, but she had every right to say that. I made a mental note to add her name to my list of people to apologize to.

I balanced a tray with four glasses, filled two with refreshing water, one with fizzy cola, and the last with sweet tea. With steady hands, I made my way through the door and to the table, without a single drop spilled.

"Here ya go. Your order should be up soon."

I turned and spotted two four-tops, two six-tops, and three booths available. With everyone busy, I moved into action and put the four empty tables together in the most efficient way. With the tables as close together as possible, I made sure each one had menus in their holders, along with napkins and flatware at each seat.

Lou captured me in an embrace. "You're the best."

When she released me, I shrugged and shook my head. "Not me. But I'm having fun."

She thanked me and darted into the kitchen.

I smiled and sensed God's pleasure. I guess there really is joy in serving others.

Thirty-five

Wade saddled Cisco and Copper for an afternoon ride. Pastor Ben had requested a tour of the property on horseback, and the weather was perfect. Partly sunny, with a high of eighty-one degrees.

Wade turned toward the sound of gravel in the driveway. He sauntered to the doorway and waved to his riding partner.

Ben climbed out of his car and stretched out his hand. "I've anticipated this moment, but I haven't ridden for a long time."

After they shook hands, Wade led Ben into the stable and introduced him to the three horses. Ben would ride Copper—the gentlest of the three, and Wade would ride Cisco.

Wade pointed to the third stall. "Champ is our problem child—strong willed and grumpy. Dad refuses to ride him." He eyed the horse and chuckled. "But Maggie's winning him over."

"Maggie? I understand she's helped around here with a few chores. Has she done well?"

"She was a big help until I sent her away."

"And why did you do that?"

Wade led the horses out of the stable and into the pasture behind the barn while Ben followed beside him. "She can be one frustrating woman."

Ben laid his hand on Wade's upper back. "Let's take a ride. You can share whatever you'd like or nothing at all."

~

When the tour group left the café, I first met with the cook and then with Debbie Sue and apologized for my past words and actions. They both accepted my apology, and a wave of gratitude washed over me.

After Debbie Sue hugged and thanked me, she confessed the bitterness she'd held against me. How many other people in town resent me or harbor ill feelings? A bunch? That's a lot to digest, but I'm relieved to know that now there's one less.

While I removed my apron, Lou cornered me in the kitchen and thanked me. "You saved us today, my dear girl." She gave me a tight hug. "Will you still be able to help with the reception setup on Saturday?"

"I'd love to. What time?"

"Does 10:00 a.m. work for you?"

"No problem." I laughed and tossed my apron into a nearby laundry basket. "Do you have any idea who my date is?"

She clasped my arm and raised her brows. "Wade?"

A sinking feeling washed over me. "I believe in miracles, but God will have to work overtime to accomplish that one."

I turned to the door that led to the dining area.

"Wait. Who's your date?"

With a quick spin, I faced her again. "A surprise. I hope we don't attract too much attention and steal the show."

"Now you have me curious."

I waved goodbye and exited the café. Eddie and I will make quite the couple.

After I climbed into my car, I took out my phone to return Wade's call but changed my mind and drove to his ranch instead. What I had to tell him needed to be said in person.

Someone had parked a dark blue Toyota Camry with Florida plates near the barn. Pastor Ben? I pulled in behind his car, climbed out of mine, and entered the stable. Only Champ remained. I darted to the back door of the stable and gazed out across the field and pasture. Two dim figures on horseback faded from my view.

I hurried back to Champ. "Wanna go for a ride, boy?" He whinnied like he was happy to see me, but he also stomped his right front hoof twice. Not sure if that meant yes or no, so I opted to back away and entered Wade's office.

There on his desk, I found a notepad and jotted him a message. "I assume you're on a ride with Pastor Ben. He's going to be a wonderful addition to my church. Talk soon? I have something I must discuss with you. Oh, and thank you for the flowers yesterday. Beautiful and unexpected."

I didn't sign it. He'd know it was me.

My heart raced on my way back to my car. Inside, I bowed my head. *Lord, please make everything okay between Wade and me. Help me confess the truth to him. I don't want him to hate me, but I'm so afraid he will.*

Jill called me an hour later and asked if I wanted to get together for dinner. I agreed to meet her at the Pizza Shack at 6:00.

At 5:50, I hugged my mom and zipped out to my car with a grin on my face. After many years of self-loathing and feeling despised by others, it thrilled me to have three new friends.

When I arrived, the savory aroma of oregano, basil, and garlic accompanied me to Jill, who sat in a booth near the windows.

I took a seat across from her, no longer interested to see who entered the restaurant for blog material. My focus was on the rumblings of my hungry stomach and quality time with my friend. I asked how her day was.

She shared a little about her day and tilted her head to the right. "And you must have had an interesting one."

I pointed to my chest. "Me?"

"Your blog post. So many comments."

"Oh, no. I haven't taken the time to review them yet. Are they hateful?"

"Most are positive."

I relaxed and breathed easier. "This afternoon, I called the number I had for the gentleman I wrote about. But someone else has that number now, and the family moved from the area. They may never read my post."

"Someone else in town might know them and forward a copy." She extended her hand across the table and tapped her fingers. "You can only do so much. And what you did took courage."

"Courage and a gentle nudge from the Lord."

Jill smiled and snatched a menu from the holder on the table. "Want to share a pizza? My treat."

"But I want to treat you."

"Let's split our tab and pay someone else's. We can share the blessing together."

"A terrific idea." I scanned the surrounding tables. "A family across from us in a booth just prayed over their meal. We can bless them."

Jill agreed. We ordered our pepperoni and pineapple pizza and asked the server to bring us that family's bill.

The server lowered his voice. "Despite going through a rough patch, they came tonight to celebrate their daughter's birthday. Your generosity will mean a lot to them."

I thanked God I had money to give.

Jill returned her menu to the holder and leaned forward. "How are you doing since the Bible study?"

"I've experienced pain and fulfillment."

"Do you want to share about either?"

"Nick offered me a job and then reneged on his offer."

"That's terrible." She pressed back in her seat and scowled. "Why would he do that?"

"My fault." I stared at the condensation on my iced tea glass. "I was being my true self on Sunday when I tried to use him to make Wade jealous. Nick called me out on it, and I tried to deny it." I peered at Jill and shrugged. "I created the situation for myself and got what I deserved."

The server placed a medium pizza in front of us and put the extra bill and ours on the edge of our table.

"I'll tell them someone paid for their dinner. Do you want me to tell them who?"

We both said, "No."

"No problem." He slipped away in a hurry.

Jill added a slice of pizza to each of our plates, and she prayed over our meal. "I'm sorry that happened between you and Nick, but it sounds like you're dealing with it well." She drank a sip of her tea. "What brought you satisfaction?"

"I helped at the café today, and I had a fabulous time serving others."

Jill's eyes widened, and her mouth dropped open. "You are incredible. You run a bed-and-breakfast, muck stalls, and wait on tables."

I covered my mouth to avoid displaying a mouthful of cheese. "Please don't praise me. I'm nothing special. I need a lot of work."

"Pray and ask the Lord what He wants to accomplish through you and allow Him to help you." She spread her hands apart and lifted her left palm upward. "Going from here," she did the same with her right, "to here in two days, is an unattainable goal."

"But I've wasted so much time. Had I committed to follow the Lord twenty years ago, things might be a lot different now."

"You can't go back. Move forward and seek the Lord." She wrinkled her forehead and averted her eyes. "Are you upset with me that I accepted Wade's invitation to the wedding? You said earlier you were trying to make him jealous at church."

I fingered my paper napkin. "I'm sure it will bother me to see the two of you together, but I'll do my best to not let it show. He can't know how much . . ."

Jill tapped her fork on her plate until I looked up. "There's nothing between the two of us, and I'll make sure it stays that way. Okay?"

"But if you like him and he likes you, who am I to stand in your way?" I closed my eyes. When I reopened them, I said, "I missed my chance."

"I don't think you have. When you tell him what you shared with us in the Bible study, he'll understand and forgive you. Only God knows what will happen next. Don't give up hope."

Thirty-six

Lou cleared the dinner table of empty plates while Wade and Reed remained seated. "Are either of you plannin' on helpin' me?"

Wade jumped up, snagged the leftover smoked sausage and potatoes, and carried them to the counter. "I've been thinking. After the wedding on Saturday, do I need to call you Mama Lou?"

She turned from the sink and pinched his dimpled cheek. "You may call me whatever you wish to call me, but Lou is fine by me."

"Are you still planning to use the community center for the reception, or is it too small now too?"

"We never planned to invite that many people, but townsfolk were gettin' upset." Reed shook his head. "We didn't want it hurtin' Lou's café business."

"Nope. Can't have that." Wade covered the leftovers with plastic wrap and placed them in the refrigerator.

After Lou added the last of the dishes, she closed the dishwasher. "Did Pastor Ben enjoy his ride today?"

"He seemed to." Wade leaned against the kitchen counter. "He's easy to talk to."

"I hope you feel better about everything now." Reed stood. "Any news from the DNA testing site?"

"Nothing. I expected the results long before now."

"Hang in there, Son. Things don't always happen on our timeline."

Wade jerked his head back and frowned. "Do you think God is delaying the results?"

"Not sure what I'm sayin' except leave it up to Him."

Wade walked to the back door. "I have to run an errand. Maggie stopped by today while Pastor Ben and I were out on a ride. I'm going to stop by her place to find out what she's decided about helping me out around here."

Lou's eyes grew so wide they looked as though they might pop out of her head. "I forgot to tell you. She helped us out at the café today. Served a table of sixteen by herself. That girl is amazing." Lou stepped closer to him. "She apologized to two of my employees for somethin' she'd done or said in the past. Those two ladies chattered about it all afternoon like a couple of happy hens."

Maggie amazed him, too, but he couldn't share that feeling with her or Lou. Maybe after Maggie confesses the truth, but not until then. And never if he has to be the one to share what he knows with her first.

Wade said goodbye to Lou and made his way to his truck. He drove to Maggie's bed-and-breakfast, arrived at 7:10, and parked in the guest area. When he strode to the back door, he realized her car wasn't in the driveway. Had her mom borrowed it?

When he knocked, Maggie's yappy dog barked and whined.

A minute later, Mrs. Stone opened the door and greeted him. "Oh my. You missed her again. She's out with a friend."

He startled and took a step back. "Another date with Nick?"

She pursed her lips. "Well now, that's something you'll need to ask her."

His stomach quivered, and he slipped his hands into his pockets. "Do you know when to expect her home?"

"May be hours. You know how she loses track of time."

Did he? He didn't remember that about her. Was Mrs. Stone teasing him?

"Tell her that I stopped by, and I'll call her tomorrow."

"Will do." She closed the door, but he couldn't help but hear her playful giggles.

She thought he was jealous. How ridiculous. Maggie can date whomever she pleases. He didn't care. Not much anyway. Well, a little. He climbed into his truck. He'd missed her this past week. In his heart, he'd already forgiven her.

But was that enough? She wrote a convincing post that she'd changed. Would he know what that change meant when he talked to her?

He hoped the Lord was involved.

~

Dinner with Jill went well. She planned to help with decorating the community center for the reception, too, on Saturday, along with Becca, Lanie, and a few others. We hoped to have everything decorated well before we needed to get ready for the wedding.

I arrived home at 7:30, grabbed Snowbunny and his grooming brush, and sat on the living room couch.

Mom ambled into the living room with a huge grin on her face. "Guess who stopped by to visit you about twenty-five minutes ago?"

"From the way you're waggling your eyebrows, I'll guess it was Nick."

"Nope. Wade."

I opened my eyes wider and gave her my full attention. "What did he say?"

She chuckled and said he'd call me the next day. "I kind of let him believe you went on a date with Nick, though."

I squinted at her. "Why did you do that?"

"Because that's who he expected you were with." She took a seat next to me on the sofa. "He cares more than you're making it seem."

I laid Snowbunny's brush next to me and moved him to the floor. "I hope you're right. But after I tell him the truth, he may never speak to me again."

"Have you prayed about it?"

I nodded and smiled, hopeful God would prepare the way. "But I'll pray again."

She patted me on the leg and dashed down the hallway.

After her bedroom door clicked shut, I knelt in front of the couch, closed my eyes, and prayed.

Lord, I need time alone with Wade to confess the truth. Can you help me? Soften our hearts and help me speak with compassion. When he learns the truth, help him to not get angry with me. I don't want to hurt him, and I'm afraid this will end all contact with him.

I don't care if he changes his mind and doesn't want me to work with him. My concern is sharing this truth might eliminate any possibility of reconciling our friendship or relationship. Please remove my fear and fill me with Your peace.

I trust you with the mess I've made.

~

Wade relaxed on his bed with his opened Bible. He flipped to the book of James to find the verse again about joy. He found it in the first chapter, verse two. "Consider it pure joy, my brothers and sisters, whenever you face trials of many kinds."

Maggie has been a trial. That's for sure. Many trials. But God had softened his heart enough for him to realize he wanted to spend time with her. She brought him joy in the midst of his turmoil.

His phone lit up with a call from Sophia. After they greeted one another, she said, "Have you checked your spam folder? Gemma received an email earlier today but just found it."

"Hang on." He opened his spam folder. "Got it. Should I log into the portal, or do you already have the details?"

"You're a match."

His heart raced, and he took a deep breath. "How did Gemma take the news?"

"She's excited and happy and asked for your cell number. She may contact you soon."

Relieved to have the truth, he thanked Sophia and ended the call.

Now, after all these years, he hoped Maggie would confess soon.

Thirty-seven

Mom told me Thursday morning, after Snowbunny's walk, that she and Ivan had dinner plans.

"You have another date?"

She narrowed her eyes and smirked. "Not a date. Two friends enjoying one another's company."

I laughed and raised my palms facing her. "Whatever." I hung the dog's leash on a hook near the back door. "Since you're going to be gone, I'm going to call Wade and invite him to have dinner here with me."

She hurried over to me and placed her hands on my cheeks. "A splendid idea."

Ivan planned to pick Mom up at 6:00 and take her to dinner in Chattanooga, an hour away, which would allow Wade and me plenty of time to talk. I pulled my phone from my pants pocket and made the call.

He answered after three rings and greeted me warmly. We made small talk for a minute or two before he said, "You wanted to talk to me?"

"Are you available to come to dinner tonight? We can talk privately here." When he didn't respond, I said, "Mom has a date. I expect her home after 9:00."

"Your mom has a date?"

"She's not calling it that, but you know me. I tell it like it is."

His voice conveyed a mixture of frustration and disappointment. "Oh. I see."

I cringed and smacked my thigh. Why did I say something that stupid? Sounds like I still put my spin on things, even if it's not the whole truth. I shook my head. "I'd like to discuss a couple of matters with you."

He perked up a little. "Does 6:30 work?"

After we agreed and disconnected our call, I scolded myself. Why are old habits hard to break?

~

Soon after lunch, Wade drove his pickup to the back of the ranch property. The neighboring farmer to the north had called him and said Wade had a cow down. Wasn't sure if it was ill or dead. After an extensive search, Wade found no sign of a cow down along the back side of the property. Maybe the neighbor was mistaken. Just in case, Wade drove to the stable and saddled up Cisco. By using his horse, he could get into the nooks and crannies to perform a thorough check of the property and count the cattle.

When he finished, satisfied he'd counted all fifty-two cows, he whispered a prayer of thanksgiving and returned to the stable to spend time with his horses.

They each needed grooming and time in the field. Hopeful to have Maggie back to help him, he looked forward to spending time with her. He picked up the brush, ran it down Cisco's back, and sighed. He wanted to spend time with Maggie?

How did that happen, Lord? Please have her tell me the truth tonight.

His phone beeped with a text, and he retrieved his cell from his pocket.

From Logan: Gemma and I plan to come to the wedding on Saturday. I want to visit Grandpa Reed, and she wants to meet him too. And see you, of course, and meet her birth mom. What do you think?

Wade dropped the brush and wandered into his office. Meet her birth mother? Two days from now? He sat at his desk and stared at the message. How would this come together? He swallowed hard. For Maggie to find out he knew their daughter, and she'd arrive on Saturday, might throw Maggie into panic mode. Springing all of this on her at once might be too overwhelming. But how could he tell his son and daughter he didn't want them to come to the wedding?

What time do you expect to arrive? Wedding at 5:30. Reception after.

Leave at 5:30 a.m. Guess we'll miss the wedding. Hope to arrive by 8:00 p.m. Don't tell Grandpa. I want to surprise him.

Okay. Can't wait to see you both.

Surprise him? And about 120 other people.

~

Ivan's eyes sparkled when he arrived twenty minutes early for his date with Mom.

I grinned and led him to the living room. "Where are you taking Mom tonight?"

"A steak house near Hamilton Place Mall. Doctor Stewart said they have the best steaks within a hundred miles of here."

My attempt to snicker turned into a snort. "I hope you don't get a flat tire on the way there."

He twisted his mouth to the left. "Why would you say that?"

"Never mind." I offered him a seat on the sofa. "I'll tell Mom you're here."

Mom surprised me from behind. "You don't have to. I'm ready to go."

They looked adorable together. Ivan complimented Mom's hair, and she raved over his colorful striped shirt. After they whispered to one another and chuckled, they left through the back door.

I finished preparing dinner, set the table, and added Wade's birthday bouquet as a fragrant centerpiece.

I peeked at the clock on the range. Wade was ten minutes late. I checked my cell for messages. None. Had he changed his mind about coming?

From the kitchen window overlooking the driveway, I glimpsed his truck. *Thank you, Lord. Please help me tonight.*

He apologized when I opened the door. "I lost track of time after working in the stable and needed to shower."

"No problem. Glad you made it." He looked extraordinary in his jeans and snug, navy-blue button-down shirt. I led him to the kitchen table and offered him a seat. "I hope you still like chicken fajitas."

"Fantastic." He sat and scooted his chair closer to the table. "The smell of those peppers and onions made me realize I'm starving."

After a brief prayer, we chatted about the ranch, horses, and cattle while we ate.

"Copper asked me to tell you that he misses you and wants you to stop by."

"He asked for me by name?"

"Of course. I can tell by his neigh." Wade's smile showed off his adorable dimples.

"I miss the ranch and want to spend time with him and Pearl."

"Does that mean you plan to take me up on my offer?"

I focused on my near-empty plate. "After our conversation tonight, I'll let you decide if you still want me to help you out." I scooted my chair back and took my plate to the sink.

Wade followed and put his dishes next to mine. "Let me load the dishwasher while you put away the leftovers. Then we can talk. I want to learn about this change in you and whatever else you want to tell me."

Ten minutes later, we strolled into the living room and took seats next to one another on the couch.

I picked at the dry skin around my thumbnail. "Do you remember Pastor Ben's message last Sunday?"

"About the dry bones?"

I shared how I'd identified with those bones and prayed Monday evening at the Bible study. "I dedicated my life to Christ."

Wade beamed, and he hugged me. "Excellent news."

"I should have done it years ago."

All too soon, he pulled away. "Can't focus on what you should have done. Do what's important now."

I stood and paced in front of him with a heavy heart, aware his hug might be the last physical connection between us. "There's something else." A knot tightened in my stomach.

He eased his way to me and reached out his hand. "Please come back and sit next to me."

My entire body felt rubbery. What if I crumple into a heap on the floor? I gazed into his eyes. "I can't do that. You're going to hate me when I tell you what I did."

He dipped his head, looked me in the eye, and motioned toward the sofa. "Take your time."

I covered my face with my hands. "Twenty years ago, I lied to you."

Wade touched my shoulder and whispered. "Tell me about it."

God, please help me. I released a whimper and struggled to steady my trembling body. "I didn't miscarry our baby."

~

Wade led Maggie back to the couch, and he sat on her right. "What happened to our baby?"

She clenched her hands in her lap and bowed her head.

"Speak to me. Please. Tell me what happened." He caressed the back of her neck.

"I . . . I put her up for adoption."

He leaned back on the couch and clasped his hands in his lap. "Why did you lie to me? I offered to marry you. I thought you loved me."

She lifted her head and ran her fingers over her cheeks. "I did. That's why I gave her up for adoption. To protect you."

His heart raced. He leaned forward. "Protect *me*?" He pointed to his chest.

Tears puddled in her eyes, and her hands shook. "I was afraid. If my dad had found out I was expecting, he would have come after you."

"But your dad liked me."

"He liked you because he thought he could trust me to make wise decisions." She twisted toward him. "But we messed up, and our baby girl had to pay the price for our mistake."

Lord, I don't want to get upset with her. Help me. Give me wisdom here. "What were you afraid your dad might do to me?"

Her eyes took on a glazed, distant expression, and she focused on a large plant in the corner. "After we'd dated twice, Dad sat on the front porch and cleaned his shotgun one afternoon while I picked wildflowers." Her voice trembled, and she hugged herself. "When I showed him my collection, he said, 'Flowers are like young women. Meant to be admired. But be careful not to let the admirer get too close, or I may need to intervene.'" Maggie squeezed her eyes shut, and her face grew pale. "Then Dad lifted the shotgun at eye level and pointed to a tree like he planned to shoot it." Her eyes popped open.

Wade flinched. His voice rose in pitch. "You think your dad would have taken a shot at me?"

"That, or physically harmed you." She jumped up and paced again. "I was almost eighteen, and you were twenty." She folded her hands and brought them to her chin. "I didn't want him to hurt you. Or worse."

Wade bent forward, rested his elbows on his knees, and covered his face with his hands.

Maggie knelt in front of him. "I loved you but couldn't marry you. That's why I lied. Told you that I'd miscarried. Because Dad would have come after you." She wrapped her hands around Wade's wrists. "I gave birth to our baby and put her up for adoption without Dad knowing. To keep you safe."

He lifted his head and touched her cheek. Her dad wouldn't have come after him. But given Maggie's brokenness, today wasn't the day for him to say more. He slid off the sofa, knelt beside her, and held her close. Tomorrow, he'd need to ask for her forgiveness.

258

Thirty-eight

With a warm glow on her face, Mom served breakfast to our guests on Friday morning. Her date must have been a success, although she refused to share any details.

After one couple finished breakfast and checked out, I climbed the stairs to collect their bedding and towels, determined to tackle the laundry. I'd rather groom horses or muck stalls to be near Wade. When he held me close last night, a flicker of hope washed over me, but his words never confirmed he'd forgiven me. I rubbed my fist over my breastbone. I'm not sure if he wants me to even visit his ranch. But the warmth of his embrace brought me comfort and transported me back to the cherished moments we'd shared long ago.

I descended the stairs with my arms filled with laundry and headed to the utility room at the back of the house. After I loaded the bedding into the washer, I found Mom in the kitchen.

"How was your evening with Wade? Did you tell him about the baby?"

I frowned and lowered my head. "And about how I was afraid to tell Dad."

She caressed my upper arm. "Your dad loved you. Your situation would have upset him, but he would have forgiven you."

"Perhaps in time. But we'll never know for sure."

~

With the morning chores completed, Wade spent time at his desk with his Bible. After he read a page, his thoughts turned to Maggie. How would it be to have her around the ranch all the time? Would he tire of her presence? He pressed his hand against his forehead. Not a chance. He missed her and wanted her with him.

Lord, I need Your help to know what You want me to do. I forgive her for lying to me. And now I understand why she did what she did. To protect me. But if she had told me what held her back instead of telling me that she didn't want to marry me, we could have saved us both from heartache.

He stared at an old metal filing cabinet in the corner of his office. "And what about me? I'm as much to blame as she is."

He stood and strode to the house, where Reed greeted him. "I'm going to grab a bite of lunch and drive over to Maggie's. I still have a lot to tell her before the wedding tomorrow."

"No time for that, Son. I need your help."

"With what?"

"Your Aunt Dottie needs a ride to town so she can attend the weddin'."

"What about Cousin Delbert? I thought he'd bring her down."

"Flu bug." Reed placed his hand on Wade's shoulder. "I told her that you'd be happy to drive up to get her."

"But what about the ranch? I've got animals to care for."

"I'll do what I can. If you leave now, you'll be back by suppertime."

"Are you crazy? A nine-hour round trip to Louisville without stopping. I won't be back until after 9:00 tonight." He rubbed the back of his neck. "And I must talk with Maggie *today*."

"She'll have to wait until tomorrow."

~

Mom and I sat at the kitchen table, eyeing the gooey melted cheese that oozed from our grilled bacon and cheese sandwiches.

"I'd like to pray." I folded my hands and bowed my head. "Father, we thank you for these delicious sandwiches You've provided for us today. Please teach us to be as generous with others as You are with us."

I lifted my head and twisted to the driveway side of the house. "Was that a car door?"

Mom jumped up and dashed to the kitchen window. "Wade's truck. He's heading to the back door."

I followed her to the back porch and greeted him. "Come on in."

He sniffed and widened his eyes. "Do I smell bacon?" He patted his stomach. "I'm starving."

"Mom's famous grilled cheese with bacon."

He scrunched his nose and winked at Mom. "Any extra?"

Mom pointed to the table. "Sit down with Maggie and eat mine. I'll fix another."

"No time to sit." He peered at me with his eyes wide. "I have more to tell you. But Dad asked me to pick up my Aunt Dottie, and I don't have time to spare." He placed his hands on my upper arms. "Will you make the trip with me? We can talk on the way there."

I sucked in a quick breath. His touch warmed me from my head to my toes. "Aunt Dottie? Isn't she the one who lives in Kentucky?" My heartbeat raced. He wanted to spend the entire day with me?

He dropped his hands and nodded. "Louisville. We'll get home late."

I glanced at Mom and back at Wade. "But I'm working on the list of people I should apologize to. And I need to get out another blog post tonight."

His eyes darted to the stove and then to the ceiling. "What I have to say is really important."

I took a step back and shrugged. "It can't wait until tomorrow?"

He sighed. "With the wedding and chores, no, it can't."

Mom rushed to the table, wrapped our sandwiches in foil, and handed them to me. "Go. Being generous isn't just about sharing food or money. About sharing your time too. Your blog post can wait another day."

"I'll get my purse and meet you outside." I held out the two wrapped sandwiches to Wade. When he latched onto them, I didn't let go. Instead, I narrowed my eyes. "Save me one."

He grinned, took them both, and shook his head. "You'd better make it quick."

~

Wade waited for Maggie near the passenger side door of his truck. How could he pull this off? He cringed. First, he had to tell her about his conversation with her dad twenty years ago, which might bring on an avalanche of emotions. And when he tells her that he knows their daughter, Maggie may unleash her anger on him. He looked toward the back steps of the house, shifted his gaze to the driver's side of his truck, and back to the house steps. Was it too late to make the trip alone? What if Maggie becomes so upset she causes a dangerous situation while he's driving? He kicked the tire closest to him. This was a stupid idea.

"Did you eat both sandwiches?"

He stiffened at the sound of her voice. "They're inside on the console."

"I assumed you kicked the tire because you were upset with your lack of willpower."

He relaxed his shoulders. "I'm fine. But time is getting away from us. Let's head out."

They climbed inside, and he noticed she held two tumblers. "Coffee?"

"Water. We can stop and get coffee on our way."

"I'll need it for this trip." He took a tumbler of water from her and put it in his cup holder. After they buckled in and got settled, he offered a quick prayer, pulled out onto the road, and turned west to reach Interstate 24.

"What did you want to tell me?"

He turned up the radio, hoping the music would distract her, and they could delay their talk and did his best to sound cheery. "Let's enjoy our meal and stop for coffee before we have that conversation."

She eyed him and raised her voice. "Are you implying we won't enjoy our meal if we discuss this while we're eating?"

He gave her a blank stare. "Let's wait until we get our coffee."

"You asked me on this trip with you to give me terrible news, didn't you?" She plopped her sandwich down on the foil wrapper. "It would have been simpler if you had called and informed me that you no longer wish to have anything to do with me after our conversation yesterday."

"Is that what you think?" He turned down the radio and chuckled.

"This isn't a laughing matter." She crossed her arms and huffed. "I hoped last night you forgave me, but it sounds like you blame me for everything."

"You read all of that into my, 'Let's wait until we get our coffee'?" He grasped her hand and stole a peek at her. "Would I ask you on a nine-hour trip if I wanted nothing to do with you?" He squeezed her hand and smiled. "I forgave you a long time ago for not wanting to marry me. And I've forgiven you for putting our daughter up for adoption. Now that I understand why you did it."

He caught her glaring at him from the corner of his eye.

"You sound like you already knew about her."

He shifted in his seat. "First things first. Let's find coffee."

Thirty-nine

This made little sense. Wade said he wanted to talk. Was he stalling? If he stalls again, I may punch him. I'm sick of it. And I want to know what he meant by *now*.

I peered over at Wade and took a sip of water. "Are we stopping for coffee in Monteagle?"

He furrowed his brow and waved his hand. "We'll have a better selection in Manchester."

"But that's another thirty minutes."

"And there's an excellent place there." He looked at me and smiled. "You'll be glad we waited."

I rolled my eyes and faced the passenger side window. "How old is your aunt?"

"I think in her seventies."

"Will she have trouble getting into your truck? Mom would."

"Not if you help her."

I glared at him and noticed a silly grin. Oh, how I love that grin.

"We'll find something for her to step up on, and with the running board, she'll be fine."

We rode in silence for twenty miles along rolling hills and pastures—a lovely June day filled with sunshine. I love this time of year. Everything is so green and refreshing.

"Manchester's close. The next exit, right?"

"Ah, yeah. But there's a better coffee spot in Murfreesboro. A food truck."

"Another thirty minutes?" I placed my hands on my hips. "Why are you stalling?"

"I'm not."

"And when we get to Murfreesboro, you'll say Nashville, and then you'll say after we join Interstate 65 and cross the state line into Kentucky." I raised my voice. "What's up with you?" I pointed my index finger at his face and narrowed my eyes. "You invited me on a nine-hour trip to talk, and now you won't tell me anything?"

He shook his head and shrugged.

"Are you trying to pick a fight with me?"

Wade took the third exit in Manchester and turned left at the end of the ramp. After driving a short distance, he said, "I think we'll stop here. Sounds like someone needs caffeine." He turned into a well-known fast-food breakfast chain.

I shrieked. "Not here. There's a real coffee place two exits back. Only a few miles. Let's go back there."

"Takes too long." He opened the driver's side door. "I'll be back in a jiffy."

I wadded up the foil from my sandwich and threw it at him before he closed his door.

He chuckled and tossed it back my way.

How dare he. He was hiding something. Well, he'd better talk soon, or the old me might resurface.

~

Wade returned to the car with their coffee. Maggie frowned but took the offered cup. He had stalled long enough. He had to tell Maggie something. But would she blame him when he told her about her dad? Time to take that chance. He pulled back out onto the road and headed toward the interstate.

Hopefully, she'd forgotten about him saying *now*. He intended to wait until they got near his aunt's house before he revealed the news about Gemma. Maggie wouldn't press him for additional information with Aunt Dottie in the truck. Best if they waited to discuss Gemma further when they were alone back home and after Maggie cooled off.

He merged onto Interstate 24. "Next stop Nashville if we want to stretch our legs."

"And now, will you tell me why you wanted me to join you on this trip?"

"Better if we parked somewhere."

"Seriously?" She curled her upper lip. "If we couldn't turn back for real coffee, we don't have time to park and talk either. Just tell me."

He rested his hand palm up on the console between them. "Please hold my hand."

She slid her fingers between his.

"Your dad wouldn't have caused me any harm."

She leaned forward and eyed him. "How can you be so confident?"

"He . . . he gave me his blessing."

Her eyes bore a hole through his heart.

Wade cleared his throat and squeezed Maggie's hand. "When I found out you were expecting—"

"Who told you?"

"Your mom."

"That's a lie." She yanked her hand away. "Mom wouldn't do that."

"Ask her."

Maggie pouted and focused straight ahead.

"A few days later, I went to talk to your dad."

When she turned toward Wade, her mouth fell open. "You didn't tell him, did you?"

Wade's throat felt parched, and he struggled to swallow. "I told him that you might be. And I wanted to marry you." Wade angled two air conditioning vents to blow directly at him. "I sensed the situation bothered him. But after a minute or two, he shook my hand. He said he couldn't have asked for a better son-in-law." Wade softened his voice. "I had his blessing, Maggie."

~

I pressed back in my seat and tried to keep my voice and hands steady. "That means we could have married and raised our daughter. Our baby girl." I covered my mouth. But a soft whimper escaped.

Wade spoke just above a whisper. "Mag, I'm sorry." Wade's hand glided over my left shoulder. "If I'd known you were afraid of your dad, I would have told you then. The thought never occurred to me."

I nodded but couldn't speak. Besides the news he just shared, he called me by the nickname he'd given me long ago. A name I allowed only him to use. His gentle voice calling me Mag soothed my shattered heart. I bent forward and hid my face with my hands. "If only I had spoken up about my fear. This is my fault."

Wade took the exit south of Murfreesboro and parked along the side of the ramp. "I don't blame you for this." He rubbed my upper back and tugged me as close as possible. "When you told me that you'd had a miscarriage, I should have been more caring and concerned about you. I still wanted to marry you, but you said no. So, selfishly, my only thought was that you didn't want to marry me."

"And I thought you only asked me out of a sense of duty."

"When I was twenty, I didn't understand the concept of duty. I asked you to marry me because I loved you."

I squeezed my eyes shut. "Oh, Lord, I made a huge mistake."

"I messed up too. Is there any way you can forgive me?"

"We both messed up." I opened my eyes, twisted in my seat, and inched closer to caress his stubbled cheek. "Of course, I forgive you."

With a smile, he tucked a strand of hair behind my ear before our foreheads met. "You're adorable, Maggie Stone." He pulled back a bit and closed his eyes. His breath tickled my nose.

I closed my eyes and parted my lips. But instead of a soft kiss, our heads collided when a loud siren flew past.

Seriously? Again?

Wade jerked forward and tightened his hands around the steering wheel. So tight, his knuckles turned white. He drove us back onto the interstate.

I stared through the windshield. I'm adorable? And another almost kiss? My heart pounded, as if it might burst from my chest.

We passed through Nashville and into Kentucky, which gave me plenty of time to calm myself and think. "Did you contact Dad after I told you that I'd miscarried?"

"Yes. But not your mom. I assumed you'd do that." He gave a quick glance my way. "Did your mom know you gave birth?"

"Not until I told her earlier this week." I gazed through the passenger window at plush, green pastureland.

"How did you keep that a secret from your parents? Didn't you come home to visit them during your pregnancy?"

I twisted back to Wade. "No. Not until Christmas—after the baby was born."

"And they never went to Texas to see you?"

"With Dad's farmwork, they couldn't get away often. And when they tried to make plans to visit, I told them that I already had travel plans with friends." I returned my focus to the window and admired the cows grazing in a pasture when I remembered the word *now*. "Don't you still have something you want to discuss with me?"

He looked at me and squinted. "What do you mean?"

"Why you said *now*."

"What if we wait until we stop to get another cup of coffee?"

I wrinkled my nose. "Really? We're going to play that game again?" I looked around for something else to throw at him but decided my tumbler might be too hard. "I don't understand how it's possible, but you knew I put our daughter up for adoption before I told you yesterday. Didn't you?"

"Just past the next exit, there's a rest stop. We'll pull off there and talk."

I plopped back and scowled. Had Aunt Tilly told him? She was the only person who knew, and I trusted her not to tell a soul.

~

This wouldn't be easy. Wade realized that when he asked her to join him on this trip. But she needed to know. Before the reception. *Lord, this may be much harder to share and for her to receive than the news about her dad's blessing. Please give me the words to say and to say them with compassion and sensitivity for her feelings.*

He exited the interstate at the rest area just past the Horse Cave ramp, parked the truck, and drummed his fingers on the steering wheel. "Would you like to walk and talk?"

She clenched her jaw, avoided his eyes, and opened the passenger side door.

They met at the front of his truck and headed down the sidewalk, away from the restrooms.

Maggie stopped and stomped her foot. "I can't believe Aunt Tilly told you. She promised."

"She didn't." He stopped, faced her, and swept his foot across the pavement. "I attended the same church as our daughter's family."

Maggie gasped and covered her mouth with her hand. "You . . . know . . . our . . . daughter?"

Forty

How could it be that Wade knew our daughter but never told me?

A couple with beaming smiles strolled hand in hand toward us, and we shifted to the side of the sidewalk. *That won't ever be us. I'm about to strangle this guy.*

While we walked, Wade told me about knowing our daughter since she was a toddler, but he didn't realize her parents weren't her birth parents until her eighth birthday. They'd had many interactions over the years, which included him helping in her Sunday School class.

"After church one Sunday in December, this young girl, Gemma, ran up to me and gave me a big hug. She told me it was her birthday, and that we both had the same name. I laughed and told her my name wasn't Gemma. Then she said her middle name was Ruby, like my last name." Wade wiped his brow with the back of his hand. "Her mom mentioned we had another similarity—large dimples when we grinned."

I pulled a tissue from my purse and sucked in a quick breath. With my anger pushed aside, I wanted to know every detail about my precious little girl. "Tell me all about her."

"Rambunctious with long, dark, wavy hair." He put his hand on my upper back and leaned closer. "A real cutie."

"More. I want to know everything."

He removed his hand and rubbed the back of his neck. "Gemma shared that her other mom gave her the name Ruby. When I looked puzzled, her mom, Sophia, said they'd adopted Gemma at birth."

I covered my mouth and moaned. "You let me hate myself for the past twenty years, when you knew her, and you never contacted me with that news?" I stopped walking and gritted my teeth. "Didn't you think I might want to know my daughter was well and happy?"

He faced me and placed his hands on my shoulders. "I didn't know she was our daughter. Her birthday was around the time you were supposed to give birth, and the name Ruby got my attention, but you said she'd died."

My legs trembled, and a wave of dizziness washed over me. "I need to sit."

He led me to a picnic table where we sat next to one another, facing outward. "Weeks later, Gemma told me how she got her first name. She said her other mom wrote her a letter when she was born and said they both had gemstone names."

"I did write her a letter." I focused on a large tree on the other side of the parking lot. "And kept a copy."

Wade laid his hand on my knee. "On that occasion, Sophia sent Gemma off to find her dad, and I asked if the birth mom signed her name. I needed to know if you'd written that letter." Wade removed his hand and shook his head. "Sophia said she'd shared too much of Gemma's story already, but I guess when she saw how anxious I was, she told me that Pearl signed the letter."

I shot him a sideways glance. "That's why you got upset when Mom named her calf Pearl."

He nodded and clasped his hands. "When I asked Sophia if I could see the letter, her emotions reached a breaking point. I'd asked too many questions. She warned me to stay away from Gemma and her family. They went as far as changing churches."

"And you haven't seen her since?"

He pulled a worn newspaper clipping from his wallet. "Two years later, I stumbled upon this article in the local paper."

My heart plummeted. Had my baby died? With shaky hands, I unfolded the article. My baby girl. Won a barrel racing contest? I calmed my breathing. And touched her picture. "Hard to see her face." I folded the paper, clutched it against my chest, and handed it back to Wade. "Nothing since then?"

"Two years ago, during her last semester of high school, Sophia contacted me. Gemma had taken a rough fall from her horse. She needed surgery on her leg." Wade stood and turned to me. "Her dad had died two years before, and Sophia needed help with the medical expenses. She asked if I could help."

"Then this Sophia lady must have believed you were Gemma's biological father." A slight breeze blew my hair across my face, and I brushed it away. "Were you convinced that Gemma was your daughter?"

"Not one hundred percent." He returned to the bench and sat next to me. "Sophia suggested we do a

DNA test to confirm, but I said it wasn't necessary. I wanted to help Gemma."

I folded my arms across my abdomen and bent forward. "How is she now? Did the surgery take care of her leg?"

"She's fine. Living in Abilene and studying animal science in college."

I sat back, tightened my fists, and relaxed them. I glared at him, and frustration seeped into my voice. "So, you've interacted with Gemma for the past two years?"

Wade stood again and paced in front of me. "Sophia and I have stayed in touch. In fact, my marriage to Charlotte ended because of her suspicions about Sophia and me. We weren't involved romantically, but Charlotte believed we were."

He stopped pacing and faced me. "Two weeks ago in Texas, I saw Gemma for the first time in twelve years. We completed DNA testing, and I received confirmation three days ago that she's our daughter."

My body felt numb. I again bent forward, rested my elbows on my knees, and folded my hands. "I've never stopped thinking about her. She's always on my mind." I pushed myself off the bench. Tried to gather my thoughts and control my feelings. I placed my hands on my hips. "Why didn't you tell me this two months ago when you first moved back to town?" I stomped my foot. "Or years ago, when you visited your dad and mom? You could have stopped by the house and told me that you'd possibly met our daughter." I leaned into his face. My nose an inch from his. "You knew, or at least suspected, and you didn't say a word to me?"

I shoved past him and spun back. "I kept the adoption a secret to protect you. Why did you hide from me the fact you knew about our daughter? Spite? Revenge? I expected better from you, Wade Ruby. Much better."

~

Wade followed Maggie. She bolted inside the rest area building and into the women's restroom. He found a bench and sat. He leaned forward and grasped the edge of the bench. No surprise he had hurt her. When all along she had tried to protect him. Why had he kept what he knew from her? He'd misjudged her. He'd thought she was selfish and didn't care about him or their child. What could he do now to support her? *Lord, what do you want me to tell her?*

He peeked at his watch. Fifteen minutes. He pumped his legs. They needed to get back on the road if they were to get to his aunt's house at a decent hour. He rose and approached a woman with cleaning supplies. "Would you check on my friend? She's inside." He pointed to the ladies' restroom. "Long, wavy dark hair. She's wearing a yellow top."

The woman narrowed her eyes and studied him. "I'll talk with her."

"Tell her that I'm concerned about her."

The cleaning woman pushed her bucket inside.

Five minutes later, the woman returned. "She said she'd be out in a minute."

The woman reentered the ladies' room.

When Maggie appeared, she hurried past him and out the door. She stopped at the passenger side door and waited for him to unlock his truck.

He opened the door for her and apologized for waiting so long to tell her.

Without a word, she climbed inside, tugged at her seatbelt, and fastened it.

Wade climbed into the driver's seat.

"We've been here for an hour. Sorry, I held you up." Maggie crossed her arms and stared straight ahead.

He outstretched his arm and touched her shoulder. "I hope you can understand—"

"Here's what I understand." She peered at him with droopy eyes. "We both messed up twenty years ago. We hurt each other. But I don't want us to spend the rest of our lives hating one another. We both made a huge mistake. I tried to cover that mistake with another one and a bunch of lies." She leaned her head back and closed her eyes. "Please don't talk to me for the rest of the trip."

~

The next thing I remembered was Wade nudging my arm to tell me we had arrived at his aunt's house. Car travel without conversation put me to sleep.

We welcomed Aunt Dottie, and Wade helped her into his pickup. I sat in the back seat behind Wade to honor his aunt and to give them time to catch up. I still didn't feel like talking. Too much to think about.

I moaned and slouched back in my seat. But Gemma must hate me. She may never want to meet me. I twisted my hands in my lap.

Aunt Dottie laughed. At least someone seemed happy.

Except for a few questions directed at me from Aunt Dottie, I said little on the trip home. Wade peeked at me through his rearview mirror a few times, but he left me alone like I asked him to. Gave me time to calm down too.

He pulled into my driveway at 11:00 p.m. "Maggie? You awake?"

I opened my door and slid out.

Wade climbed out too. "I'll walk you to your door."

I turned to Aunt Dottie, still inside the truck, and waved.

When we made it to my back porch, I faced Wade. "I've had a lot of time to think about everything that's happened today. Everything you've told me." I twirled my hair around my finger. "I have to believe that you did what you thought was best for me. Or maybe for Gemma."

I brought my fist to my mouth, held it there for a moment, and lowered it. "God has extended so much grace to me. And I want to extend some of that to you. I forgive you for not telling me about Gemma sooner. And I'm sorry for being upset with you. I hope you can forgive me too."

He took my hands in his. "Yes, I forgive you. I think we *both* did what we thought was best."

Forty-one

Saturday morning, Mom couldn't wait to hear every detail about my trip with Wade. I shared about Aunt Dottie and delved into a question of my own with Mom while we prepared breakfast.

"Wade said you were the one who told him about my pregnancy. Is that true?"

She lifted the crispy bacon from the cast-iron skillet and spoke with her back to me. "Well, you didn't plan to tell him." She spun and faced me with her fork pointed at me. "He loved you, and as the father of your child, he deserved to know."

I looked down at my bare feet. "You're right. I should have told him before I moved to Texas." I told her about Wade's conversation with Dad.

"Your dad was full of secrets. He never informed me that he knew. But then, I never told him either." Mom added scrambled eggs to the skillet.

"He kept a lot to himself. Super quiet. But his eyes spoke volumes. And that stern tone of his voice scared me often while growing up."

"But he adored you and thought the world of Wade. I'm not surprised he gave Wade his blessing."

"His blessing?" I held onto my head and stared up at the ceiling. "I've blamed Dad all these years for ending my relationship with Wade and giving up my baby girl. And it wasn't his fault. The blame is all mine."

Mom turned off the burner and bolted to my side. She wrapped me in a warm embrace and ran her hand up and down my back. "Oh, honey. Time to let go of the past and forgive your dad, as well as forgive yourself."

"I wish I could ask him to forgive me."

"He would. I know he would." She continued to hold me, swaying back and forth.

I pulled away and thanked her for her love and support. "I'm going to my room to pray for a few minutes."

Alone with God, I knelt at my bedside and bowed my head. *Lord, I blamed Dad for so much when it wasn't his fault. I caused so much heartache. And I blame myself for keeping my mouth shut and not confiding in both Mom and Dad.* I rose from the floor and stepped into my bathroom to grab a tissue. I stared into my mirror. Mom is right. Dad would have forgiven me.

I returned to my bedside and knelt. *Lord, I forgive my dad for the perceived wrongs and confess that I judged him and held bitterness against him. I'm sorry. Thank you for Your forgiveness.*

I lifted my head. But how do I forgive myself? Stupid, stupid girl. I needed help. Perhaps Jill or Becca would guide me?

I returned to the kitchen and warmed my scrambled eggs in the microwave. "There's something else I need to tell you."

Mom took a seat at the table.

I told her about Wade knowing our daughter.

She jumped up and hugged me. "He knows my granddaughter?" She released me and pranced around the kitchen, thanking the Lord. Mom stopped and widened her eyes. "When do I get to meet her?"

"Meet her?" I took my plate to the table and sat. "I haven't asked Wade yet."

"What are you waiting for?"

"I'm not sure she'll want to meet me."

~

With the third horse groomed and out of the stable, Wade cleaned the stalls and tidied the tack room. His thoughts traveled to Maggie many times throughout the morning. He'd enjoyed her company the day before more than he cared to admit. Despite her emotional outbursts, he felt a strong renewed attraction to her. Did she share his feelings? He sure provoked her on their trip.

He needed her help on the ranch, and as hard as he'd tried to build a wall between them, he'd failed. Would she accept his offer to help him full time? And maybe someday to be his wife?

Lord, are You in this? I want her here and a part of my daily life. But I'll be asking a lot of her.

He strode to his pickup, climbed inside, and headed to the back pasture to check on his cattle. Convinced they were fine, he drove to his favorite hill, parked, and climbed out. While overlooking the serene pond and enjoying the gentle breeze, his thoughts again turned to Maggie.

They had to talk again before tonight. She needed to learn Gemma and Logan planned to join them at the reception.

He climbed inside his truck and smacked the steering wheel. This wouldn't work.

Lord, I can't ask her to marry me. I couldn't ask her to give up her bed-and-breakfast. And no way can I ask her to move in with me, Dad, and Lou.

~

By noon, those of us decorating the community center for the wedding reception had all the tables up and covered with white linen tablecloths. We stopped to eat pizza someone ordered for us and returned to our table decorating.

Jill and Lanie prepared the rectangular main table where Reed and Lou would sit just to the left of the stage, along with the wedding party. They positioned three stunning flower arrangements on the table—one per couple. Lou's daughter and Wade would fulfill the roles of matron of honor and best man.

Becca and I placed the same floral arrangements on each round table. Colors of white, cream, and mauve peonies, roses, and carnations adorned each golden vase. Four mauve candles in golden holders surrounded the centerpieces on fifteen tables—each set for eight guests.

While we continued to decorate the guest tables, Jill and Lanie prepared the buffet setup along the left wall and added greenery to brighten the serving tables.

Curious about Lou's dress, I asked Becca.

"I've seen it—a light mauve. Her daughter's is similar but darker."

"Sounds lovely."

When we finished with the guest tables around 2:00, Becca scanned our decorations and said everything looked perfect. "Except I'm not sure about you. You seem quiet today. Are you okay?"

"Wade provided me with new information from twenty years ago. I've forgiven my dad. But I made a mess of things. And I need to forgive myself. I don't know how to do that."

"Let's step outside and talk about it." She grasped my hand and headed toward the back door.

"But there's still a lot to do here." I pulled back on her hold and broke free. "Do you think we can discuss it Monday night at the Bible Study?"

She agreed. We joined Jill and Lanie near the main entrance to help them with a huge white and mauve balloon arch to serve as a photo backdrop for guests. A photographer would take pictures of attendees when they arrived as a small gift for them. Lou and Reed would also receive copies to remember who attended.

Lanie sorted through the balloons and laid them out in piles according to color. "We only have one pump, so we'll let Becca use that. Hope the rest of us can keep up with her."

We got busy blowing up balloons and adding them to the arch.

While we worked, the band members set up their equipment, tuned their instruments, and adjusted the sound levels. We had to raise our voices to speak to one another.

While I tied a mauve balloon to the middle of the arch, Becca tapped me on my shoulder and gestured to the main door behind me. Wade stood near the entrance and motioned for someone to follow him outside. I eyed Jill tying a white balloon to the bottom of the arch. What if he wanted her? She didn't move, so I assumed he wanted me. With another mauve balloon in hand, I strolled his way.

"Can we talk?"

The band was loud and practicing their set. "What?" I cupped my ear, pretending I couldn't hear him.

He shouted and tugged on my arm. "Outside."

I stepped out with him and savored the warmth of the sun on my skin. "They're going to have to turn it down tonight."

"I'll take care of it." He rubbed his hand across his mouth. "Listen, I must talk with you. Can you break away for fifteen minutes?"

"Not really."

His gaze darted to a noisy car going down the road. "This can't wait."

"Well, sorry, I don't have time right now." I motioned to the door that led inside.

He took a step forward and pointed his index finger at my face. "Then don't get mad at me when you get blindsided tonight." He turned and jogged to his truck.

I raised my voice and called after him. "What are you talking about?"

Jill poked her head out the door. "We need you."

I glanced back at her. "Coming." I stared after Wade's pickup. Had he not told me everything yesterday?

How could there be more?

~

Why had he gotten upset with Maggie? After all, she'd spent her day helping with his dad and Lou's wedding. He'd have to snag her after the wedding and talk to her then.

When he arrived home, he showered, changed into his best suit and tie, and went to find his dad. Dad and Aunt Dottie sat at the kitchen table. Their laughter filled the room while they reminisced about the good old days.

Dad rose and grabbed his tie from the table. "Will you help me?"

"With just your tie? What about your vows?"

"Dottie helped me with the vows. She said her hands are too shaky to help with the tie."

Wade grinned and helped his dad. "You ready for this, old man?"

"I reckon so." He ran his hand through his thinning gray hair. "I was tellin' your aunt about our recent change in plans."

"What plans are those?" Wade wrinkled his forehead and tightened the tie.

"We'll be spendin' the night at Lou's place tonight and leave for Colorado in the mornin'."

"Makes better sense than going to a hotel tonight."

"And when we come home, I'll move into her house and leave you with this ole place."

Wade's eyes grew large, and he swiped a piece of fuzz off the shoulder of Reed's suit coat. "But I thought Lou planned to move in here."

"I'll be okay at Lou's. That way, we'll have privacy and so will you." He waggled his brows.

Wade peered at his aunt. "What am I missing here?"

Aunt Dottie stood and shuffled over to Wade. She rose to her tiptoes and gave him a quick peck on his cheek. "Your dad needs to move out because you're the one takin' care of the ranch. And what woman in her right mind wants to live with her husband's family from the get-go? You need a wife who can call this place her own."

Forty-two

Eddie and I slipped out of the church and made our way to the reception in silence. We drove a half mile south on Main Street to Tracy Avenue and turned right. A moment later, we turned right into the community center.

"Nice wedding." Eddie parked his car in front of the center.

I stared through the windshield. Throughout the ceremony, Lou's face radiated pure happiness. More than I had ever seen on a person's face. I bit my bottom lip. Would I have to wait until I was her age to find love? Another ten or more years?

I sighed, and a tiny moan escaped. The sight of Wade in his suit. He took my breath away.

"Did you hear what I said?"

I turned to Eddie. "Of course. You're hungry."

"I didn't say that."

"Oh. What did you say?"

He shook his head and frowned. "I need you to pay attention to me on our date. Okay?" He opened his car door and twisted to climb out.

"Wait." I brushed my fingertips along the sleeve of his sports jacket. "Did I mention how fine you look tonight?"

His cheeks turned bright pink. "And you too."

"How do you want me to act?"

"Huh?" He pulled the door closed and faced me.

I folded my hands in my lap. "Do you want me to act flirty or play it cool?"

He cleared his throat and paused. "Just be you."

"Will it bother you if I talk to different men?"

"Do you usually do that on dates?"

"No. But we'll both know many people at this party."

"Of course we will. I don't care who you talk to. Just make sure people know we're together on a date."

"And I encourage you to chat with lots of women." I climbed out of his car and met him at the rear bumper. "You talk to me much easier than you talked with Jill at the Pizza Shack." I nudged his elbow. "You like her, don't you?"

He dipped his chin and gave his head a slight shake. "Nah. We're not right for each other."

"Why do you say that?"

"Because it's the truth."

I linked my arm around his. "If you don't ask her to dance tonight, I'm going to make sure the two of you end up on the dance floor. Together."

His eyes grew large, and his cheeks returned to their bright pink color. "Don't embarrass me."

"I won't." I bumped my hip against his. "Anyway, not on purpose."

~

With the wedding pictures at the church finished, Wade hopped into his truck and drove to the reception where Jill awaited him. But he preferred to spend his evening with Maggie. And he needed time alone with her before Logan and Gemma arrived in less than two hours.

When he entered the community center, he noticed the band had turned down the volume like he'd asked them to. People mingled and laughed. Maggie and Eddie chatted with an unfamiliar couple near the back of the room. He nodded. The townsfolk loved a fancy party.

He wandered over to Jill, where she stood at one of the round tables talking with her sister Lanie and Lanie's fiancé, Luke. "Glad y'all made it." He scanned the area nearby. "No Billy tonight?"

"My mom is watching him." Luke wrapped his arm around Lanie's shoulder. "And I'm grateful to have some quality time with my girl."

"I'm sure you are." Wade eyed Jill and lowered his voice. "Dad and Lou should arrive soon. When they do, I'll introduce the wedding party and give instructions for the buffet." His voice became a whisper. "After dinner, I'll invite you to dance with me. Then I have a big favor to ask."

"Is this our table?" Arm in arm, Maggie and Eddie joined the group.

Jill gave Maggie a quick hug and said hello to Eddie, who stood to Maggie's left. "Yes. Ben and Becca just arrived and will also join the two of you, Luke, and Lanie. Two seats are available if you find someone you want to invite to your table."

Maggie peered at Wade. "You're quite the sight tonight." She raised her eyebrows.

He stifled a smile and shook Eddie's hand. "Fantastic to see you again. I hope you enjoy your evening."

Wade whispered in Maggie's right ear. "I must talk to you as soon as possible."

Eddie tugged on Maggie's left arm and spoke softly into her other ear, but Wade couldn't make it out.

"We'll need to put a hold on that until after dinner." Maggie touched Wade's arm. "Eddie and I have a lot to talk about too."

Wade squinted at Maggie and Eddie and made his way to the entrance to shake hands with Pastor Ben. "Excellent ceremony. Thanks for officiating on short notice."

"No problem. I enjoy weddings." Ben headed to his table with Becca by his side.

Wade's phone vibrated in his pocket. A text from Logan: Running late. Should arrive by 8:45.

Great. But let's introduce Gemma as a friend for now. We don't want to overshadow Grandpa and Lou's celebration by surprising the town. Gemma will have time to spend with Maggie after the reception.

Can I tell people you're my dad?

Sure.

With Logan running late, that gave Wade extra time to get alone with Maggie. But minutes were slipping away. He needed to speak with her soon.

~

Ben and Becca joined us near our table, where we talked about the ceremony.

"My favorite part was when Lou got choked up saying her vows, and Reed touched her chin and winked at her." Becca laced her elbow around Ben's. "I hope you still look at me that way when we're in our fifties and sixties."

He gazed into her eyes and stroked her cheek. "I wouldn't want it any other way."

Lanie placed her hand on her chest. "You two are so cute."

Eddie and Luke stepped three feet away and appeared to be deep in conversation. Luke gestured toward me and spoke in hushed tones.

My focus returned to Becca, Ben, and Lanie. "The mauve and white roses along the pews and at the front of the church added a touch of softness and beauty to the entire ceremony."

"Made me sneeze." Eddie rejoined us and sniffled.

Luke stood beside him with a smirk on his face. "You never have liked flowers."

"May be a problem when he needs to wear a boutonniere at our wedding." Lanie took hold of Luke's arm.

"I have to wear a flower?"

"What a best man does, bro." Luke gave Eddie a playful punch to his arm.

Being an only child, I envied their brotherly affection. I brushed my fingers along my neck. "Do you have a definite date?"

Lanie lowered her arm and slid her hand into Luke's. "Three months from now on September fifteenth."

"Sounds fabulous." Commotion from across the room pulled my attention to the entrance. Wade greeted Reed and Lou. "A late October outdoor wedding would be beautiful, with the trees at their peak colors."

Eddie touched my arm and mumbled. "She said September not October."

I turned to him and covered my mouth. "Oh. I didn't mean to say that out loud."

Becca grinned at me and pulled out a chair. "I think Wade's getting ready to make his introductions."

I took a seat across from her. "Did you close on your house yesterday?"

She brought her hands together. "Yes, we did. Ben worked there all morning while I helped here. Tomorrow afternoon and evening, our plan is to camp out there with a few essentials and move our belongings from storage on Monday."

"Contact me if you need any help to unpack or move boxes."

She thanked me and said she would.

Wade blew into a microphone used by the musicians. "Hello?" He introduced everyone at the main table. Mr. and Mrs. Reed Ruby, Lou's daughter, who served as matron of honor, and Lou's son-in-law. "And for those who don't know me, my name is Wade Ruby. I'm Reed's son and his best man. And my date this evening is the lovely Jill Drake." He pointed to Jill at the main table.

My neck muscles tightened, and I crossed my arms. The lovely Jill Drake? I brushed a wisp of hair off my brow. Was Wade attracted to her?

He detailed the buffet procedure, making sure everyone understood the order of table selection. After he prayed, he asked the wedding party to get in line and exited the stage.

"There's Miss Risa with her date." Lanie chuckled and waved across the room.

A minute later, Miss Risa approached us. "May we join your table?" Her cheery disposition brought a ray of sunshine to my heart. But her date blotted out that sunshine. Nick. The man who didn't want to give me a chance to prove myself.

Miss Risa took the seat next to Pastor Ben, which put Nick next to me. She glanced across the table at Lanie. "And you didn't think he'd ever ask me out again."

"I didn't say that." Lanie pressed her palms against the table and leaned in. "If you remember correctly that day at the café, I said he'd be a fool not to."

The two of them giggled. I assumed it was an inside joke I wasn't in on.

I turned my head toward Nick. "Were you at the wedding with Miss Risa?"

"We bumped into each other here, outside in the parking lot, and walked in together."

"Hmm." I fingered my dangling earring. "Then how did someone so new to the area get an invitation? Even Eddie, who's been here his whole life, didn't get invited to this wedding except by me."

Nick moved his chair closer to mine. "They asked me to be here in case of a medical emergency, since there are several older people in attendance."

I scanned the room. "You're right. I hadn't paid attention." I turned toward the buffet line and watched Wade return to his seat next to Jill. When I looked back at Nick, his focus was also on the wedding party's table. "Are you here to check up on Lou or Reed? Is that why they invited you?"

Nick's eyes followed Jill while she returned to the buffet line. He twisted back to me. "What did you say?"

"Never mind." I placed my hand over my mouth. "You already answered."

Eddie inched closer and bumped my elbow. "Our turn at the buffet."

I pushed my chair under the table and joined Eddie in the buffet line. When we returned to our table, I tried to engage him in conversation, but he seemed more interested in his brother than me. Nice date, Eddie. Thanks. I took a bite of salad.

Nick scooted closer to me. "I owe you an apology."

"About not hiring me?"

"I thought—"

I placed my fork on my plate. "You did the right thing."

"Really? You think so?"

I tilted my head back and focused on a bird flitting across the rafters. "When someone is so caught up in themselves, like I was, they need some bumps along the way to wake them up." My attention returned to Nick. "I've messed up so many times trying to manipulate people and situations. I deserved what I got."

"Wow. You have changed."

"I want the Lord to lead me." I picked up my fork and knife and cut a bite-size piece of roasted chicken. "But I continue to react as I always have."

"You're not alone. I'm guilty of that too."

"But tonight, I've already dealt with jealousy and resentment."

"And now you know to ask the Lord to help you in those areas. Because you follow Christ doesn't mean nothing bad will happen or you won't sin again." Nick placed his hand over my fist. "Don't beat yourself up. Call upon the Lord. He'll help you."

"Thanks. I feel better." I pinched my lower lip. "A little."

"Keep reading your Bible and spending time alone with God in prayer. He'll speak to you if you listen." Nick pulled his hand away, twisted to his left, and directed his attention to Miss Risa.

After a moment, his eyes darted around the table. "This woman is fascinating." Again, he turned to her. "Do you have a granddaughter like you?"

Her face lit up. "Yes, I do. And she plans to visit me next month. I'll introduce you."

I stabbed several green beans with my fork. Perhaps Nick would find his true love soon. I hoped I'd found mine.

But would Wade ever see in me what Luke sees in Lanie or Ben sees in Becca?

Forty-three

Wade couldn't take his eyes off Maggie. The sight of her in her sleeveless yellow dress left him speechless. His heart couldn't take it. Her long, wavy hair cascading over her shoulders only enhanced her natural beauty. Was she even real? Yet, her true beauty shone through in the newfound joy and genuine warmth that radiated from her.

But he realized others had also taken notice of this change in her, which resulted in attention from two men at her table. He hadn't minded her talking with Eddie, because there couldn't be any attraction there, not after what she'd written about him. But from where Wade sat, she seemed to enjoy talking with the doctor. Much more than Wade wished she would. His stomach knotted in discomfort.

From behind, Lou whispered in his ear. "Are you ready to make the toasts and open the floor for us to dance?"

Wade shot out of his chair. "Will do." He hurried up the step to the stage and grabbed the mic.

After Lou's daughter and Wade made their toasts, he asked the bride and groom to proceed to the dance floor. The band played, "It Had to be You," a song requested by the couple. Before the song ended, Lou's daughter and husband, along with Jill and Wade, made their way to the dance floor. By the time the next song started, twelve other couples joined them.

Wade peeked at his watch.

Jill broke their embrace and stepped back. "You seem jittery this evening. Is everything okay?"

"I need to talk to Maggie." He clenched his teeth. "But between Eddie and Nick, I'm not sure I'll get the chance."

"You sound jealous."

He frowned and gave her a heartfelt apology. "Someone is about to arrive. Could affect Maggie's life. I've got to warn her."

Jill flinched and stared at him. "Sounds serious." She turned back to Maggie's table. "Is there anything I can do?"

"Support Maggie as a friend in case things go awry."

"Of course."

When he eyed the table, Maggie wasn't there. Eddie and Nick were both missing too. Wade scanned the dance floor and found Maggie in Nick's arms. What's she doing with him? He's not even her date.

Jill released Wade's hand and backed away. "Go cut in. I'll be fine."

He thanked her, made his way through the crowd, and approached Nick. "Excuse me, may I cut in?"

"Sorry, Wade. My turn." Eddie took control, escorted Maggie three steps away, and tugged her into his arms.

Scowling, Wade locked eyes with Nick. "Where did he come from?"

"He'd gone outside with Miss Risa. She said her car made a funny sound yesterday, and he offered to check it over."

Nick watched Eddie and Maggie sway to the slow melody. "He seems protective of her. That's why I secured my dance when I could." After giving Wade a playful jab on his upper arm, Nick strode to his table and whispered in Miss Risa's ear. She laughed and motioned for him to sit down.

Wade's attention shifted back to Maggie on the dance floor. He sighed. He had to share his feelings. Tonight.

~

Eddie's slow dance skills and fast dance moves impressed me, especially on a crowded dance floor.

"You've done this often, haven't you?"

"Dance?" He shook his head. "I took some lessons a year ago."

"You have hidden talents."

After the song ended, he thanked her. "One more. Then if you want to dance with Nick or Wade, be my guest."

A minute into the song, Wade approached and tapped Eddie on the shoulder. "Excuse me. My turn."

I smiled at Wade and fingered his tie. "After this song."

"After this song, Dad and Lou will cut the cake." He pursed his lips. "I must talk with you now."

Eddie narrowed his eyes at Wade. "Then she'll be available after the cake cutting."

Wade checked his watch and tapped it. "But it's 8:15." Wade glared at me and huffed. "I'll be back soon."

After the song, Eddie and I took our seats just in time to see Lou and Reed cut their cake and smash it into each other's faces. They seemed happy and in love. What would it be like to smash a piece of cake into Wade's face at our wedding? A dream I shouldn't dwell on.

Wade announced the bride and groom would leave within the next thirty minutes. If anyone wanted to greet them before they left, they needed to hurry.

When the band played a country tune, Eddie scooted his chair closer to me. "Wade looks too busy to ask you to dance. How about one more? I'll show you my cowboy boogie moves."

"Ooh." I batted my eyelashes. "Can't wait." I kicked off my heels and followed Eddie to the dance floor.

Soon after, Wade and Jill made their way toward us. He grasped my hand and pulled me out of the line, and Jill slid into my place. I twisted back to Eddie. His mouth opened and closed, and he shrugged.

With a squeal, I tried to retract my hand. "But I was having fun."

Wade whispered through gritted teeth. "There's no time for fun." He led me to the far side of the room and glanced back at the main entrance doors. "Now. Out the back."

My heart rate shot up while we rushed to the door and slipped outside to the melodious sound of chirping crickets. The moon cast a soft, enchanting glow around us, and fireflies illuminated the night sky with their twinkling lights.

"What was that about?" I'd never seen him so persistent.

"I hoped to have five more minutes, but I got a text that told me otherwise."

"What text? And how does that concern me?"

He brought my hand to his chest and held it there, where I could feel the steady rhythm of his heartbeat. "We've got to talk. Like an hour ago. You need to know some things. Even before I explain the text."

~

Wade gazed into Maggie's eyes and couldn't contain himself any longer. He had to gather the courage to express his true feelings for her before he told her about Gemma's arrival.

"I've been hard on you these past four weeks."

She patted his tie. "We've already dealt with this. I've forgiven you."

"But do you like me?"

She widened her eyes. "Do I like you?"

He inched closer and held her other hand. "Do you like being with me?" He brought her hand to his mouth and kissed her fingers.

Maggie's chin quivered, and her voice squeaked out a yes.

He grinned, knowing it would gain him an advantage because she loved his dimples. "I don't want you to work for me part time any longer. I want you at the ranch full time."

She tilted her head to the left and scrunched her eyebrows. "Full time? We've never discussed that."

"Right. But would you want to be with me all the time?"

She took a half-step back and kept her hands in his. "I don't understand what you're asking."

"I love you, Mag."

~

"You love me?" I couldn't breathe. My pulse quickened. I felt I might collapse. "I love you too."

He drew me into his arms and brushed my lips with his.

I returned his kiss. Was this a dream? He loved me, even after the secrets I'd kept from him?

He leaned his head back and continued to hold me close. "Full time?"

I stepped back. The moment died with his awkward question. What? Did he mean full-time help on the ranch? Was his "I love you" manipulation, or was this something else? "Full time what?"

"Before I answer that question, there's something else I must tell you. About the text." He scrubbed his hand over his face. "Logan is here. He wanted to surprise his grandpa and meet his new grandmother."

"I get to meet Logan? Wonderful." I clapped and twirled in place. I snatched Wade's hand and tugged him closer to the door. "Let's go." I stopped. Put a hand on my hip. "Wait. Was that a diversion to make me forget full time what?"

He pulled me back to him, our noses just inches apart. "First, I need to tell you this." He wrapped me in his arms again. "Gemma traveled with Logan."

"Gemma?" I gaped at Wade. "She's here? Now?" I wriggled from his embrace.

He raised his brows. His eyes sparkled. "Our daughter wants to meet you." He searched my face, his eyes pleading. "Are you ready to meet her?"

I curled my lip and whined. "And you're just telling me this now?"

He placed his hands on my upper arms. "How many times today have I tried to get you to talk with me?"

"I need time to prepare." I broke free from his hold, pivoted to my left, spun back to the right, and faced Wade. "What do I say to her?" I brought my folded hands to my mouth and bit my thumbnail.

"Start with, hello."

I moved my palms to my cheeks. "My makeup. How do I look?"

"Beautiful."

"Oh, dear." I shook out my hands. Turned toward the door. Twisted back to Wade. "And you'll be with me the whole time?"

"I wouldn't want to be anywhere else." He tapped his finger on the tip of my nose. "Or be with anyone else."

I wiped my cheek and reached for his hands. Sensing both warmth and strength. My breathing calmed. "I think I can do this now." I squeezed my eyes shut and reopened them. "But first. Full time what?"

He leaned in for another kiss. His tenderness soothed me. "Let's save the rest of our conversation for another time. Soon." After one more kiss, he took me by the hand and led me to the door. "Are you sure you're ready to meet our daughter?"

I took a deep breath and slowly released it. "Yes. I know the Lord is with me, and He'll give me the strength I need."

I moved my hand up to Wade's elbow. "What they say is true, isn't it?"

"What's that?" He paused and gave me his full attention.

"God makes all things possible."

Dear Reader,

Thank you for reading *All Things Possible*. If you enjoyed Maggie and Wade's story, please leave a review to help other readers discover it. Thanks so much!

Would you like a gift? When you sign up for my newsletter and monthly blog posts, you'll receive a free novelette—the prequel for my Love in Pleasant Springs series. Sign up here: www.luannkedwards.com.

Where to follow me and connect.
Amazon
BookBub
Goodreads
Facebook

Other books by LuAnn K. Edwards.

Love Comes Again
Only A Glimpse
Let Him Go
Charm And Perfection

An Undeserved Gift (a novella)

Love in Pleasant Springs
An Odd Request

<u>Our Faithful Love</u>
<u>All Things Possible</u>

I hope you enjoy the first chapter of Lanie and Luke's story from Book Two, *Our Faithful Love.*

One

Mid-April
Pleasant Springs, Tennessee

I smacked my palm against the steering wheel. My first day in a new position, and I didn't want to be here. I blamed my sister, Jill Drake. She talked me into this. I loved my work helping children and families in Chattanooga, but not here in Pleasant Springs. I couldn't stand this place. And I'd vowed to never return.

My heart longed for Nashville, ninety miles northwest of this small, dull town. My hometown only offered memories. Ones I didn't care to think about.

Late Monday morning, I prepared for my first visit at Creekside Children's Home. After I parked, I took three deep breaths, plastered a smile on my face, and climbed the stairs to the front porch. Before I had a chance to ring the buzzer, a man greeted me and introduced himself as the director of the home, Todd Butler.

We chatted in the foyer, and he filled me in on Billy, an eight-year-old boy removed from his home the evening before.

"He's still upset and frightened. His mom was out of control when he called 911. He knew he needed help, but now he's scared about what will happen to him and his mom." Todd led me through his office into a medium-sized room. After he explained they often used this space for supervised family visits, he left through the kitchen to fetch Billy.

The room housed shelves filled with puzzles, books, and board games, along with craft paper and supplies. Four wooden chairs surrounded a square table in the center of the light orange painted room. I waited near the table for Billy.

Five minutes later, Todd returned with an adorable, red-eyed little boy clutching a stuffed elephant. I introduced myself as Miss Mel and assured Billy that I was there to help. Todd whispered something in Billy's ear and left him alone with me.

I took a seat on the opposite side of the table from where he stood. A terrified young boy. I wanted to give him a big hug. His large brown eyes and short, dark brown hair reminded me of an old friend when we were young. One I hoped to never see again. "Would you like to sit down?"

Billy clutched his elephant in a death grip.

"It's okay to be afraid." I made a pouty look to match his.

Poor little guy. He sounded upset. "I'm not afraid. But my mom is." Tears trickled down his cheeks. He said he thought the cops took her to jail.

"I'm sorry, Billy. Adults don't always make the right choices as grown-ups. We make mistakes. There are people helping your mom now, and I'm here to help you." I rose from my chair and pulled a book about fire trucks off the shelf. "Would you like to read a book together?"

Billy nodded and moved to the chair on my left.

I sat and slid the book toward him.

"I like fire trucks." Billy pointed at the bright red engine on the cover.

"Have you ever been inside one?"

Billy opened his eyes wide. "No. Do you have one?"

"No." I grinned. "But we might visit the fire station where you can get an up-close look at one."

"That would be awesome." Billy's smile turned upside down. "I lied to you. I am scared."

"That's okay. Sometimes I get scared too."

"But you're big. Why are you afraid?"

What could I share with an eight-year-old? "I returned to Pleasant Springs two days ago, after being gone for a long time. I don't want to see someone who hurt me many years ago."

He drew his eyebrows together. "Did they hit you?"

"They hurt me in here." I touched my chest.

"We're both afraid." Billy patted my hand. "We can help each other."

I spent an hour with Billy and promised to return the following day. Before I left, I offered to be Billy's transportation to and from his school in Shady View, eight miles north of Pleasant Springs. Todd thanked me but said they could manage his afternoon transportation.

When I returned to my car, I read a text from my sister. Miss Risa wants you to visit. Jill included the address. Risa McDonald was a sweet woman in her eighties who I'd known all my life from church. But our visit would need to wait. I had lunch plans with my parents and drove to their home.

"How's my beautiful daughter?" Dad opened his arms wide and hugged me.

We talked for a few minutes before Mom and I sat next to each other at the round kitchen table to enjoy homemade chicken noodle soup.

Dad sat across from me and bowed his head. "Father, I thank You for bringing us back to Pleasant Springs a few months ago and for the agency cutbacks that brought our baby girl home too. Bless and guide her, Lord. Amen."

I smirked and leaned forward. "You forgot to thank Him for the food."

He laughed, bowed his head again, and thanked God.

"You know I'm not staying here, right? I plan to move to Nashville."

Mom touched my hand. "We're praying the Lord changes your mind."

"Whatever." I rolled my eyes.

She passed a box of crackers to me. "How was your first morning at your new job?"

"Good. I guess." I dipped my spoon into the soup and told them about the little boy.

"Anyone we know?"

"Sorry, Dad. That's confidential." I took another bite of soup and complimented my mom. "This is so good."

She thanked me. "Have you seen anyone else since you've been back?"

"Jill texted and said Miss Risa wants to see me. I'll try to run by for a visit later today."

"I'm sure she'd appreciate someone to read to her." Dad wiped his mouth on a napkin. "Older people like that, especially if their eyesight has deteriorated."

"That's a good idea." After we chatted about Miss

Risa for a few minutes, I stood and put my empty bowl in the dishwasher.

Mom joined me and placed her hand on my back. "Dad and I want to invite a couple of people for Sunday dinner this weekend, and we'd like you to join us." She had a glint in her eye. The look that said, "You need a man."

"And what about Jill? Did you invite her?"

She chuckled. "We see her often. But you haven't visited us since we moved back to Pleasant Springs. We wanted you to move in with us instead of Jill, so we'd get to see more of you."

I apologized for my absence during the past few months and for picking Jill over them. But I knew my mom. She had her matchmaking twinkle in her eye.

"No matchmaking. But I'm sure Luke would love to see you."

"Luke?" I cringed and in a harsh tone said, "No. I told you when I stayed in Chattanooga after college graduation, I didn't want to hear about anyone in Pleasant Springs except for Jill."

Mom pressed her fist to her mouth. "Because of Luke? What did he do?"

"I must go. Great to see you both." I hurried out of the kitchen, grabbed my jacket from the couch, and kissed my parents, who followed me to the front door with raised eyebrows.

How could I spend time in the same room with Luke, his wife, and his children? I had to get a job in Nashville before my parents invited him and his family for dinner.

Thank you for reading, and God bless!

LuAnn

Acknowledgements

Above all, I want to give thanks to the Lord for Maggie and Wade's story and for His guidance in bringing it to life. Without Him, none of this would be possible.

All Things Possible includes two events from my personal life. My husband's parents had two horses named Copper and Champ. I, like Maggie, fell off one of them when the saddle slipped to the horse's side. Another similarity was the message that changed my life. Thank you, Pastor Tony Scott, for preaching from Ezekiel, chapter thirty-seven, about those dry bones. God used that message to draw me into a relationship with Him back in 1974.

A big thank you goes out to Cynthia Hickey and Winged Publications—Forget Me Not Romances—for believing in my work and giving me the opportunity to publish this novel and series.

Thank you, Larry J. Leech II, for your thorough critique and guidance. Your insights and vast expertise are a true blessing.

A heartfelt thank you to my beta readers, Judi, Julie, Kim, Kiran, Leah, and Moss, for investing your time and providing valuable feedback and suggestions. Y'all are the best.

To my husband and family, thank you for your unwavering love, support, and encouragement in my writing journey. I love and appreciate each one of you. And a big hug to my youngest daughter, who gave me the idea for Maggie's character—a blogger who realizes she's living a lie.

About the Author

LuAnn writes heartwarming Christian contemporary romance filled with faith, hope, and a touch of humor. A 2021 Selah Award finalist for *Let Him Go*, she has lived her own love story and happily ever after since marrying her sweetheart in 1975. She is Mom to three children and Nana to three grandchildren. Besides the Lord and her family, she loves hiking, traveling, pizza, and anything chocolate. When she is not writing, you'll often find her making eyes at her husband, in the kitchen baking bread, or taking photos of birds at their backyard feeders. Visit her at www.luannkedwards.com.

www.ingramcontent.com/pod-product-compliance
Lightning Source LLC
Chambersburg PA
CBHW070410310726
48977CB00003B/629